DEAD WOMAN WALKING

BOOKS BY CAROLYN ARNOLD

Detective Amanda Steele series
The Little Grave
Stolen Daughters
The Silent Witness
Black Orchid Girls
Her Frozen Cry
Last Seen Alive
Her Final Breath
Taken Girls
Her Last Words
Missing Before Daylight
The Wildfire Girl
Her Deadly Rose
Hidden Angels
Three Girls Gone

Sandra Vos series
Save Her Life
Every Last One

Brandon Fisher FBI series
Eleven
Silent Graves
The Defenseless

Blue Baby

Violated

Remnants

On the Count of Three

Past Deeds

One More Kill

DETECTIVE MADISON KNIGHT SERIES

Ties That Bind

Justified

Sacrifice

Found Innocent

Just Cause

Deadly Impulse

In the Line of Duty

Power Struggle

Shades of Justice

What We Bury

Girl on the Run

Her Dark Grave

Murder at the Lake

Her Buried Past

SARA AND SEAN COZY MYSTERY SERIES

Bowled Over Americano

Wedding Bells Brew Murder

MATTHEW CONNOR ADVENTURE SERIES

City of Gold

The Secret of the Lost Pharaoh
The Legend of Gasparilla and His Treasure

STANDALONE

Assassination of a Dignitary
Midlife Psychic

CAROLYN ARNOLD

DEAD WOMAN WALKING

bookouture

Published by Bookouture in 2026

An imprint of Storyfire Ltd.
Carmelite House
50 Victoria Embankment
London EC4Y 0DZ

www.bookouture.com

The authorised representative in the EEA is Hachette Ireland
8 Castlecourt Centre
Dublin 15 D15 XTP3
Ireland
(email: info@hbgi.ie)

Copyright © Carolyn Arnold, 2026

Carolyn Arnold has asserted her right to be identified
as the author of this work.

All rights reserved. No part of this publication may be reproduced, stored in any
retrieval system, or transmitted, in any form or by any means, electronic,
mechanical, photocopying, recording or otherwise, without the prior written
permission of the publishers.

ISBN: 978-1-83618-073-9
eBook ISBN: 978-1-83618-072-2

This book is a work of fiction. Names, characters, businesses, organizations,
places and events other than those clearly in the public domain, are either the
product of the author's imagination or are used fictitiously. Any resemblance to
actual persons, living or dead, events or locales is entirely coincidental.

PROLOGUE

Woodbridge, Virginia

There were better ways to spend a Friday night than a late-night showing, but selling the house would make up for any inconvenience. It was a luxury listing on Charmed Court with a sticker price north of a million. The sale would earn her the title of top real estate agent of the year with her firm, and the commission would pad her bank account.

She let herself into the house after grabbing the key from the lockbox. The entry lights were set up with a motion sensor, and a glow welcomed her into the home. She disarmed the security system but turned around and flipped the dead bolt. It was an affluent neighborhood, but it was always best to take precautions.

Her phone rang, and her daughter's name came on the screen. She answered before the second ring. "Hey, sweetie. Everything okay? I thought you would have called hours ago."

"We're here, Mom. You worry too much. I've been having some fun. You remember what that is?"

Vaguely... "No need to be smart." But she'd always worry

about her daughter. It didn't matter if Riley was five or nineteen. Let alone driving to a cottage rental that was six hours away with her friends.

"Listen, Mom, I've gotta go. We're gonna go for a dip in the lake."

Before she could respond, her daughter was gone. She stuck her phone in her purse and shoved it into the main closet before setting out through the house. She turned on the lights as she went along. Every single one. The brighter the space, the more attractive it was for buyers. Unfortunately, they would miss how sunlight drenched the home with natural light, unless they requested a second showing during the day.

The house was pristine, and everything was gleaming. The hint of vanilla from a candle or cleaning spritz made the house feel warm and homey.

She entered the primary suite and soaked in the tray ceilings and sparkling chandelier that hung over the California king bed. A sitting area overlooked the backyard with its woods and natural pond, and there was an en suite that rivaled high-end spas with its jet tub and walk-in shower with eight nozzles. The walk-in closet was the size of her first apartment. It contained enough jewels, watches, and shoes to value into the high six figures, if not higher.

Her watch told her it was ten o'clock, giving her a half hour to pass before her clients arrived. She'd go downstairs to wait and spend the time visualizing an offer.

Turning to leave the bedroom, she stopped. Frozen.

A person stood in the doorway.

The skin tightened on the back of her neck, and goosebumps rose on her arms. "You need to leave. You're trespassing." It was a challenge to find her voice, and she realized how foolish her request sounded. This person had gotten past a locked door. They weren't here for any noble purpose.

They didn't move and continued to block her escape. The

person's eyes were menacing and dark, piercing right through her.

"Please, leave." A sick foreboding tossed her stomach. She went against protocol and didn't tell anyone she was here tonight.

The person raised their right arm. She had just enough time to register the gun before there was a burst of light.

A loud wet *smack* ignited a fire in her chest.

She looked down and touched the wound. Her hand came away soaked in blood. Slowly and not comprehending, she faced the shooter. "You—"

Another flash. A second hole in her chest.

The pain was unfathomable. "Why are you—?"

The person pulled the trigger again.

She never felt the last bullet hit.

ONE

Present Day
Woodbridge, Virginia

This week was set up to be an anomaly. The heat advisories were off the charts, and Amanda's nine-year-old daughter, Zoe, was staying with her grandparents. It wasn't often she and Zoe were apart, but the arrangement freed up some time for spending with friends or Carter Paulsen, who she'd been seeing for the last couple months. She certainly had no intentions to sit around by herself, but her social plans were something she could decide after her shift ended.

Amanda sipped on the Hannah's Diner coffee she picked up on the way to work. The place served the best brew she'd ever tasted. The downside was since more people had discovered the place, it took longer to get in and out in the morning.

Most of the paperwork from her last case with her partner, Trent Stenson, was tidied up, making today, and this week, a fresh slate. Not that she'd admit as much out loud. She wasn't superstitious, but in her experience just as soon as she declared work slow, all hell broke loose. For her, working Homicide with person's eyes were menacing and dark, piercing right through her.

"Please, leave." A sick foreboding tossed her stomach. She went against protocol and didn't tell anyone she was here tonight.

The person raised their right arm. She had just enough time to register the gun before there was a burst of light.

A loud wet *smack* ignited a fire in her chest.

She looked down and touched the wound. Her hand came away soaked in blood. Slowly and not comprehending, she faced the shooter. "You—"

Another flash. A second hole in her chest.

The pain was unfathomable. "Why are you—?"

The person pulled the trigger again.

She never felt the last bullet hit.

ONE

Present Day
Woodbridge, Virginia

This week was set up to be an anomaly. The heat advisories were off the charts, and Amanda's nine-year-old daughter, Zoe, was staying with her grandparents. It wasn't often she and Zoe were apart, but the arrangement freed up some time for spending with friends or Carter Paulsen, who she'd been seeing for the last couple months. She certainly had no intentions to sit around by herself, but her social plans were something she could decide after her shift ended.

Amanda sipped on the Hannah's Diner coffee she picked up on the way to work. The place served the best brew she'd ever tasted. The downside was since more people had discovered the place, it took longer to get in and out in the morning.

Most of the paperwork from her last case with her partner, Trent Stenson, was tidied up, making today, and this week, a fresh slate. Not that she'd admit as much out loud. She wasn't superstitious, but in her experience just as soon as she declared work slow, all hell broke loose. For her, working Homicide with the Prince William County Police Department, that meant bodies started piling up. She wouldn't wish that on anyone.

Trent walked in at eight twenty-five, cutting it close to the start of their shift, which was eight thirty. "Good morning."

"Yes, it is." She was grinning, unable to push down the memories from the weekend of rolling in the sheets with Carter.

"I'm not even going to ask." Trent headed for his cubicle. It faced hers, and the partition was just high enough to afford a modicum of privacy. They could see from the bridge of each other's nose up.

"Well, I'm going to ask why you're cutting it close." *Why did I do that?* She was bound to get some story about his girlfriend, Kelsey, pulling him back to bed. Things were comfortable between Amanda and Trent, so why was she trying to upset that balance? A part of her thought the more open they were about their relationships, the easier it would be to ignore their underlying attraction toward each other.

"You're not the only one in a… healthy coupling."

Amanda laughed. Sex was clearly screwing with his brain because he never spoke like that. "Uh-huh." Her cell phone rang, saving her from feeding this awkward conversation. She caught the caller's identity just as she picked up. "Spencer?" He was her half-brother, the product of an affair her father had twenty-nine years ago. His mother, as it turned out in the small world of Prince William County, was Emma Blair, a crime scene investigator Amanda often worked with.

"Amanda, I need your help."

She didn't know him well, but the tone of his voice alerted her that something was wrong. She sat up straighter. "What's going on?"

"I can't reach my girlfriend, and it's not like her to ghost me. Please help me out here." Spencer's words ran together.

"Just slow down a bit. When did you see her or speak with her last?"

"I saw her on Wednesday."

"Of last week?" It seemed straightforward, but details were crucial.

"Yeah."

"And you had plans she missed or...?" Amanda was trying to figure out what alerted Spencer to a problem.

"We didn't have any plans since Wednesday, and I was on call this weekend. I still tried calling and texting her, but no response. When I called her just now, her phone went straight to voicemail like it was off. It's never off. Amanda, her phone is her job. She's a real estate agent."

Spencer was a firefighter for the Triangle Volunteer Fire Department, as one of its paid employees. He should be skilled at keeping calm under stress, so what about this had him so worked up? "All right, well, maybe her phone ran out of charge? It can happen." She grabbed onto an innocent explanation to calm him down.

"I told you. Her phone is her livelihood. Unless it's the middle of the night, that thing is on. Heck, it wouldn't surprise me if the ringer was on even then. And this morning, I went to her house. She wasn't home."

"She could be at work already. Maybe she had an early showing. It is Monday morning." Amanda struggled to see his side.

"She doesn't go in on Monday mornings. I'd call her daughter to see if she has heard from Christine, but the kid's not my biggest fan. It would be a shame to worry her if this turns out to be nothing."

"It probably is nothing."

"I thought you'd take me seriously."

There was a prolonged silence, which Amanda struggled to fill. She wasn't trying to be difficult. "You said Christine has a daughter. How old is she?"

"Nineteen."

Spencer was only twenty-eight himself, so Amanda could understand why the daughter might resist the relationship. "She's not exactly a kid, but if her mother up and disappeared, I'd think she'd be concerned. Wouldn't she call you in that case? Or file a missing person report." For that matter, one could be in the system already, and Spencer didn't know about it.

"Knowing Riley, she went off with friends for the weekend. Home is just a base point during the summer. The rest of the year, she's in DC, where she goes to school."

Amanda remembered what it was like to be that age. Her biggest responsibility was getting to class, so during breaks from school, she was footloose. Riley sounded like she lived her life much the same way. If she had gone away for a few days, she wouldn't necessarily be concerned about reaching her mother. And there was the possibility Christine was avoiding Spencer. "I don't know what you expect me to do."

"Amanda, can't you track her down? Make sure she's all right? I tried calling Christine's boss this morning, but he's not disclosing anything to me."

Amanda could understand that he wouldn't want to part with employee information. She could just tell Spencer to file a missing person report and leave it at that, but she felt a touch of obligation toward him. After all, he was her blood, if only by half. "I can call him and see if he'll talk to me."

"That would be great, Amanda. Thank you."

"No promises. I'll just see what I can do." It was a slow morning so far, but that was subject to change. "What's her full name?"

"Christine Lane. She's forty-one, and don't get into the age difference between us because I don't want to hear it."

She expected Christine to be older as soon as she heard Riley's age. But she wasn't in any position to give him her opinion. "While I look into this, you should get in here and file a missing person report." Even as she gave this advice, she knew it was rare for adult disappearances to be investigated without obvious signs of foul play.

"Okay, I'll do that."

Before ending the call, Amanda got Christine's number, home address, place of work, and her boss's name. She brought up Christine Lane's driver's license photo. It showed a brunette with curly shoulder-length hair. She next checked to see if anyone had reported her missing. No one had.

Trent was standing in the opening of her cubicle. He flicked a finger toward Amanda's phone, which she'd set on her desk. "What was that about? Everyone all right?"

"Too soon to say." Amanda shared the information from the call.

"And that's her?" Trent pointed at the photo on her monitor, and Amanda nodded. "It's quiet around here. I'm sure Malone would be all right with us stepping out and looking into this."

She appreciated his eagerness to help but wanted to try something first. "I'm going to try her phone myself." She did that and landed right in voicemail. "Huh. All right, one more place to try. I'll see if I can get anywhere with her workplace." She sounded far more confident than she felt. Even with her badge to back her up, she didn't expect better luck than Spencer had in talking with Christine's employer.

"Makes sense." Trent walked back to his cubicle while she found the number for the real estate company and put in the call.

"Good morning. Best Homes Realty. How can I help you today?" The woman who answered sounded young.

"I'd like to speak with Christine Lane, please." Amanda figured it best to try this route first despite what Spencer had told her.

"Ms. Lane isn't in the office this morning. I could take a message for her."

"Then you are expecting her in later today?"

"At one. Can I tell her who called?"

"This is Detective Steele with the Prince William County PD. When did you last speak to Ms. Lane?"

"Let me get Mr. Beasley for you."

"And who is that?"

"The owner."

Amanda wasn't given the chance to respond before she was put on hold and soft rock started spilling into her ear.

"Yes?" a man said upon coming on the line.

"Detective Steele, sir. Is this—?"

"Art Beasley. I'm the owner of Best Homes."

"You're the perfect person to talk to then." She paused, expecting to be interrupted again. When Art said nothing, she continued. "We have a report that Christine Lane hasn't been heard from for several days, and her phone seems to be off. When did you last hear from her?"

"Her phone is off?" Concern coated his voice.

It's her livelihood... Spencer's words ricocheted in her head. It was interesting, of all Amanda said, the phone was his first concern. Not the fact she was unreachable for days. "It is. If you could please answer my question."

"Friday afternoon when she came into the office to proof an offer she had her assistant draft on behalf of a client."

Since he saw her just before the weekend, that explained why he wasn't worried about her *several days* comment. That time period had been from Spencer's perspective. What if all of this was nothing more than Christine ghosting Spencer? *But he said she would never...* And that didn't explain why Amanda's call went straight to voicemail. "How was Christine on Friday?"

"Just her normal self. Uh, what's going on here? Why are the police interested in Christine? Her boyfriend called here earlier asking about her too."

"We're just trying to locate her, sir. Did you expect to hear from her after that?"

"No. You telling me her phone is off is the first I'm hearing of it, and it's so unlike her. You must realize agents are commissioned. If they don't answer their phone, they don't sell houses, and I have better things to do than manage their schedules."

For the first time since Spencer's call, Amanda got a true sinking feeling. "Is it common to go the weekend without talking to her?" She was thinking the realty business didn't sleep.

"Of course."

"If you end up hearing from her, call me immediately." Amanda left her number with him.

"Will do."

Amanda hung up with a sour pit in her stomach. "Trent, I'm going to talk with Malone."

TWO

It didn't take much for Amanda to convince Malone to let her and Trent conduct a welfare check for Christine Lane. But the moment she stepped outside, she was wishing for the comfort of her desk inside Central Station with its air-conditioning.

"Some days it feels like Earth is located right next to the sun," Trent said as he started the department car.

"That it does." Summer had taken its sweet time arriving this year, but now it had, a bit of a cold front would be a welcome reprieve.

Trent pulled in front of the home belonging to Christine Lane. The ten-minute drive barely allowed enough time for the car to cool down.

Christine lived in a beige vinyl-sided two-story house, about twenty years old, in a cookie-cutter neighborhood. The one redeeming quality of the area was the mature trees that lined the streets. There weren't any cars in the driveway, but there was a garage.

Amanda stepped out of the car, and the air hit her like an all-encompassing wall of heat. It seemed the car's A/C hadn't done that badly, after all. She was wearing a suit jacket over a short-sleeved shirt, both of which were lightweight, but not breathable enough for this weather.

"Let's hope Christine's car is in the garage and she's home." It was possible Christine had stepped out during the time Spencer had been here. Amanda led the way up the paved path to the front door, appreciating the flowering perennials in the garden. Little pink petals, others periwinkle.

Trent beat Amanda to the doorbell. A standard *ding-dong* reached the front step, but otherwise nothing but silence.

They rang it a second time and met with the same result.

"I think it's safe to say no one's home," Trent said, and they started walking back to the car.

Was Christine in trouble? Or was Amanda letting Spencer's concern, paranoia, affect her? They had one other place they could check before needing to make any further decisions.

An older woman, wearing a fuchsia visor, was at the property line watering her flowers. She kept lowering her sunglasses and peeking over at them when she didn't think they were looking.

Amanda walked toward her, thinking they might benefit from this woman's inherent curiosity. "Excuse me."

"Who are you?" She stopped spraying and let the hose fall against her thigh.

"Police detectives, ma'am," Trent said, holding up his badge while he stepped up next to Amanda.

"Well, aren't you a courteous fella. Are you looking for Christine?"

"We are," Trent said. "When did you last see her?"

Amanda was fine to stand back and let Trent do the talking. The older woman clearly had a soft spot for him.

"Hmm, I'd say last Friday morning. I was out here watering before eight AM. It's too late now, but I feel for my plants having to endure this wretched heat."

"You should be careful yourself." Amanda felt compelled to say something to nudge this woman inside. The weather network's heat advisories, suggesting the elderly or those with respiratory problems were to remain indoors, hadn't seemed to make an impact.

"Yes, dear. Just going to finish here and pop back inside to the air-conditioning and settle under a ceiling fan."

"Have you seen Christine's daughter today?" Amanda switched the subject, not comfortable with lecturing a woman almost twice her age.

"I last saw her on Friday too. She took a couple large bags with her, and she and her friends were dressed like they were going to the cottage for a few days. Or the week? I don't know." The woman offered a kind smile, but it faded quickly. She rubbed her brow. It seemed the heat was getting to her.

"If you see or hear from either Christine or her daughter, would you have them call me?" Amanda handed the woman her card.

"All right."

"You should get inside now, ma'am. I'm sure the flowers can wait until tonight." Trent used gentle persuasion.

"I think I will." She set the nozzle on the cut-in edge of the garden, but the hose itself was on her lawn. If it was left there too long, there would be a thread of dead grass.

"Let me roll up your hose," Amanda offered.

"That is so kind of you, dear." She looked at the card. "Amanda."

"My pleasure."

THREE

Amanda was hotter than she thought possible by the time she loaded into the car. She adjusted the fins on the vents, making sure they were facing her. Blessedly the air blowing out was a touch cool.

"I'd say someone deserves brownie points," Trent said.

"I just did what anyone with human compassion would have."

"Nah. It was more than that."

She was sure it was something Trent would have done if she hadn't offered. *Maybe I should have given it a few seconds...* She shoved the selfish thought aside. It was over and done now, and that lady had a chance of surviving the day.

"Where to now? Spencer give you anything else to go on?"

"Not a lot, but I'm wondering if I'll get further going to Best Homes Realty in person."

"Well, if something happened to Christine, someone there might help us fill in her last movements."

"Yes, short of getting Christine's daughter involved. I just don't want to worry her if all this turns out to be nothing." She realized Spencer had said the same thing.

"I get that."

Trent got them on the road and not long after, they were walking up to the door for Best Homes Realty. It was a small boutique firm with a white storefront and a wood sign hanging from the point of the roof. It was designed like a *For Sale* sign with a red *Sold* sticker angled in the top corner.

Bells chimed when Amanda and Trent entered, and a young woman with blond hair and a phone to her ear smiled at them from the reception desk.

Amanda took in the wall behind her that showcased three framed photographs captioned *Agent of the Year*. Christine Lane was the top earner for the first two years until she lost the title last year to a redhead named Marcy Maxwell.

The receptionist set the receiver back on its cradle. "Thank you for your patience. How can I help you?"

Amanda flashed her badge. "Detective Steele. This is my partner, Detective Stenson."

"Oh, you're who I talked to on the phone, right?"

"I am. I never got your name."

"Sierra Jacobson. We haven't been able to reach Christine ourselves, and now I'm worried. Clients have started calling in, saying they left voicemails over the weekend for her, which she hasn't returned."

"And that isn't like her?" Trent asked.

"Not at all. Christine practically worships her clients, whether it's people she's worked with before or new ones." Sierra's face pinched. "Do you think she's hurt or something?"

"We can't say, but that's why we're trying to find her." Trent's calm tone seemed to have a soothing effect on Sierra's nerves. She relaxed her shoulders.

"Could you tell us her schedule from Friday afternoon until now?" Amanda based the starting point on when the manager had last seen her in the office.

"Sure. I remember she was in the office for a bit. Let me

check her calendar though. I have access to it because I help manage it for her. Sometimes she adds things, and other times I do." She tapped on the keyboard. "Okay, so she had a showing booked for Friday at seven PM, nothing over the weekend, and her next appointment is this afternoon."

Amanda fixated on her last showing. Since no one had seen or heard from her since Friday, had something gone wrong there? "We'll need to know where her seven o'clock appointment was on Friday and if she made it. Could you call the homeowner or the client to see if she turned up?"

"I have the cell phone number for the homeowner. One minute." Sierra fielded an incoming call, and then moved on to verifying the appointment. She hung up less than a minute later. "Yes, Christine was there for about thirty minutes."

They could find out the location of that listing, go over there, and see if they could determine anything from the area. But Amanda's mental wavelength took her somewhere else. "A moment ago you said sometimes Christine adds appointments or viewings to the calendar. Do you know if she ever showed a house without doing this?" Amanda imagined Christine would be eager to reclaim her title as agent of the year. In a rush to meet a client's schedule, maybe she failed to record a last-minute appointment.

"It is protocol to call in all viewing appointments or add them to the calendar. It's a safety measure." Sierra leaned forward and spoke at a lower volume. "But Christine has missed that step once or twice."

Amanda pointed at the framed photographs on the wall. "I'm sure Christine was eager to get her title back. Is there a specific property that might help her do that?" She was thinking if her disappearance was at all connected to a listing, having this knowledge might help.

Sierra sat back and nodded. "It's a luxury listing for over a mil, and Christine has been focused on moving it. This is the largest listing held by Best Homes at the moment. And Christine would have done anything to sell the place to prove herself to Mr. Beasley. She showed it more than any other listings last week."

One word Sierra used stuck like a burr. *Anything...* It wasn't a stretch to think Christine went ahead and booked a showing without following procedure. Possibly one last minute. "Could you contact the homeowner and find out if Christine showed the home over the weekend?"

Sierra got on the phone and hung up a few seconds later shaking her head. "There's no answer. Should I call back and leave a voicemail?"

"No, that's fine." They would go over there. "Where is this listing?"

"Charmed Court." Sierra gave them the house number just as a stout man sauntered up to the desk.

"What's going on here?" His beady brown eyes ran over them.

"Detectives Steele and Stenson." She held out her hand to him but drew it back when he never shook it.

"Art Beasley. We spoke on the phone. We still haven't been able to reach Christine. I'm starting to worry that..." His words petered out as his gaze traveled to Sierra.

The young woman's cheeks were a bright red, and her eyes were full of tears.

Amanda respected the man was trying to shield his employee by letting his sentence dangle. Not that it was difficult to guess what he was about to say. "We're doing our best to find her, Mr. Beasley. Until we know more, there's no reason you should stress yourself."

"Too late for that."

Amanda could understand his side. She had her own grave suspicions. "We might need more information from you as we continue to look for Christine. If you and your employees would continue to be cooperative, that would go a long way."

"Yes, of course."

"To start, if we could find out the homeowner's name and number for the Charmed Court listing," she said.

Art motioned toward Sierra. "Give them the listing sheet, and the owner's phone number."

Sierra handed a piece of paper to Amanda. She scanned down to see it covered all the details of the house, including the name of the current owner. Dominique Sharp.

Sierra's pecking on her keyboard was short-lived before she rattled off a phone number, which Trent scribbled in his notepad.

"Thank you," Amanda told her. "And as I said on the phone, Mr. Beasley, please call me if Christine calls or shows up here." She handed him her business card to stress the point. He already had her number from earlier.

Art nodded. "We will."

Amanda gave Sierra one more look before leaving the firm.

Back in the car, Trent glanced at her. "You ready?"

"As I'll ever be." She assumed she was reading his mind correctly, and their next stop was Christine's luxury listing. Was he also thinking the same as her? That there might not be a happy ending waiting for them on Charmed Court?

FOUR

The Agee subdivision was well-established, attractive to families, and catered to people with a high income. All the houses and properties in this area were quite large and meticulously maintained. From reading the listing sheet for the house, Amanda learned the place was only twenty-two years old, but it possessed characteristics of the colonial style with its redbrick facade and black shutters. "This place has five bedrooms, four bathrooms, and a three-car attached garage. That's a lot of house for one person." Amanda lowered the piece of paper as Trent parked on the street out front. She stiffened at the sight of the red Lexus RX 350 in the driveway. They had pulled a simple background on Dominique Sharp, and she had a Cadillac Vistiq registered in her name. "Don't tell me that's..."

Trent entered the plate into the onboard computer. "It belongs to Christine Lane."

After being so hot a moment prior, a cold sweat now pooled at the base of Amanda's back. "Well, let's see if she answers the door." Amanda got out of the car, her steps leaden. Every bit of her instinct was screaming at her. Something was definitely wrong here.

Amanda pressed the doorbell, and a beautiful rendition of some classical song chimed inside the home. After repeating the process two more times with no luck, Amanda tried the handle and found it locked.

She shook her head at Trent. "I've got a bad feeling about this."

"You're not alone. How about we go around back and take a look?"

"Let's do it."

They walked along the side of the house under the shade of some trees. But it did little to diffuse the heat of the day's sun. The backyard was fenced, and there was a gate, which was unlocked.

Trent pulled the lever and pried it open.

"What are you doing?" a neighbor from next door called out, stopping their steps.

"Police, ma'am. It's just a welfare check," Trent told her, not clarifying it wasn't on the homeowner.

The woman's brow tightened. "Far as I know, Ms. Sharp is away on business. Ain't nothing wrong with her."

Intel was where a small community with nosy neighbors could be an advantage. People paid attention to those around them. "Thank you," Amanda told her.

Trent carried on through the gate with Amanda following.

The backyard was more spacious than Amanda expected from the front. Majestic white oak trees lined the back edge of the property along with a fence, and a large pond added serenity.

The house itself was less luxurious from back here though. No red brick, rather white siding in desperate need of power washing, and the charm of the shutters in the front didn't follow through either. But there was a Trex composite deck with a large awning. She headed toward there and a set of sliding patio doors. Once there, she realized one panel was cracked open about two inches.

Trent gloved up and slid it back the rest of the way, and they both put booties over their shoes.

Amanda pulled her gun and entered the home. "Prince William County PD! Christine Lane? Call out if you're in here."

The door fed into the kitchen, but the main level was open concept. From this vantage point, it looked like every light in the house was on. Still, nothing greeted them but silence. This made the large house feel larger still, as did the lack of any visible personal touches. Even the counters were mostly bare.

Trent came in behind Amanda, and they walked through the kitchen toward the stairs. Upon catching a faint chemical smell, she turned around to face her partner. "We need to call this in before we go any further."

FIVE

Amanda explained the situation to Malone, and he was sending backup ASAP but cleared them to proceed. Maybe the chemical smell was nothing more than the home being deep cleaned for the showing. She wished she could believe that, but every nerve ending in her body was saying they were too late.

Several pieces of abstract artwork lined the wall along the staircase going up to the second level. "There's not one distinctive touch. It's like no one is even living here."

"Staging. It's about eliminating clutter and personal mementos, including photographs. It's supposed to help potential buyers see themselves in the home."

She could understand the logic. "Someone's in the know. And how did you come to possess this knowledge? You selling your house?"

"Nope. Kelsey loves watching those home shows. The makeovers, the flips, the buy 'em and sell 'em. Or I should say, she's *obsessed* with them."

"I see." She rarely had five minutes to watch TV, and whenever she dropped onto the couch, she was quickly nodding off.

Sitting still didn't happen often. Maybe this week, she didn't need to cram every minute with something.

They went up the stairs, and the chemical smell became stronger. But there was a strange sound that Amanda couldn't place. She looked at Trent, who must have heard it too.

"Prince William County PD," Trent called out.

No response.

Amanda hurried her steps as she followed the direction of the sound.

She entered the primary bedroom, a magnificent setting for rest and rejuvenation from the trayed ceilings to the soothing paint colors on the walls, the furniture, and the bedding. There was a sitting area next to a window overlooking the yard. One door led to an en suite bathroom, and Amanda glanced in on her way by. A jacuzzi tub and marble everywhere.

The noise became more defined and pinpointed.

"It's coming from under the bed," she said.

Trent bent over and looked under but was quick to straighten back up. His face was pale as he took out his flashlight without saying a word and shined the beam under the bed.

Amanda got down on her knees.

A robot vacuum was stuck on a blue polyethylene tarp. Something was inside it.

That's one way of storing something...

But as Amanda visibly traced the shape of its contents, another smell hit Amanda's nose. Faint but unmistakable. Decomp.

Now there was no question in her mind about what she was seeing. "There's a body in there."

SIX

Amanda called for a medical examiner and crime scene investigators to come to the house. She made a special request when it came to the latter. Her preferred investigators were Emma Blair and Isabelle Donnelly, but Emma was Spencer's mother. Since his girlfriend was most likely the victim inside that tarp, there was potential for conflict of interest. In that vein, Amanda should probably step back from the case too, though she could make an argument for herself. She just hoped that CSIs Vanessa Stuart and Ruth Keller wouldn't be assigned. They came as a package deal, and Stuart wasn't easy to work with.

Amanda called Malone again too, and he said he'd be right over. His initial response was likely to repeat in her head for a long time. *Nothing creepy about that...*

Trent had tried Dominique Sharp again with no luck, but left another voicemail, stressing that it was urgent she return his call.

That's if she can... But a quick look in the garage showed three empty bays. It would seem the neighbor was right in saying Dominique was out of town.

Amanda and Trent baked in the midday sun on the front step. All to prevent compromising the scene any further. "This is crazy. Why don't we wait in the car and blast the A/C?"

"And why the hell didn't we think of that sooner?" Trent turned to walk away when she caught sight of new arrivals.

"Hold that thought." She nudged her head toward the Crime Scene van making its way up the driveway. She couldn't see the driver or passenger for sun glare cutting across the windshield. *Come on, luck, favor me...*

Trent returned to Amanda's side, and they watched the investigators unloading from their vehicle.

So much for luck having my back...

CSIs Stuart and Keller walked toward them with collection kits in hand. Stuart also had a camera strapped around her neck. Neither of them looked affected by the heat, but they had just left a cool vehicle. Give them a few seconds in the scorching sun.

"Catch us up. We go through there and...?" Stuart pointed a finger toward the doorway behind them.

"Good afternoon." Trent pulled off what appeared to be a sincere smile.

"Afternoon," Keller responded to Trent, not looking at Amanda.

Stuart stood there, mouth pursed, impatient. Amanda expected to see her foot tapping.

"You'll need to go around back." Amanda couldn't care less that the CSI skipped the pleasantries. This wasn't a social event. "The rear sliding patio door was cracked open when we arrived, alerting us to potential danger inside the home."

Stuart's brows rose above her dark sunglasses.

"We used gloves to open the door, but it should be processed for prints and swabbed for touch DNA." Amanda regretted saying this when Stuart lifted her glasses to her head.

"Yes, we know how to do our jobs," Stuart said.

"Good to know about the unlocked door, though." Keller followed up her colleague, showing a softer side.

"Where's the body?" Stuart shifted her stance, but she wasn't even breaking a sweat. Literally. Not one bead on her forehead.

"Go through to the front of the home and up the staircase. It's in the primary suite at the end of the hall, under the bed," Amanda laid out.

"Under the bed?" Stuart's reply came loaded with skepticism.

"Uh-huh." Let her find out for herself that it was in a tarp.

"Strange, but all right." Stuart turned to walk around the side of the house with Keller in tow.

Observing Keller's rounded shoulders, Amanda felt empathy for the woman paired with Stuart. She couldn't imagine being saddled with her for an entire shift, let alone day after day.

Once they were out of sight, Amanda turned to find Malone huffing up the driveway. He must have parked on the road like Trent.

"There might soon be another victim." Malone stopped a few feet in front of them and swiped his forehead with a handkerchief. His receding hairline exposed more flesh than he'd had in his youth. And his cheeks were bright red.

"Let's go around back and talk." Amanda touched Malone's elbow, a move she was comfortable making. Malone was family, having been a friend of her father's before she was born.

"Please, don't touch me in this heat. Just tell me there's some shade around back."

"That's why I suggested it." Amanda led the way to the backyard.

"Oh, thank the heavens." Malone beelined for the awning. Stepping under it, he wiped his brow again and stuffed his handkerchief into his pocket.

Malone caught his breath while Amanda dreamed of a tiny lick of a breeze. He popped her out of the fantasy bubble when he spoke.

"Do we know if the victim is Christine Lane?"

"It seems most likely." That was the most accurate way of answering. They hadn't seen the face, but circumstantial evidence strongly suggested it was Christine.

"How can you not know?"

She had told him a body was under the bed but had left out one pertinent detail. She filled him in now.

"Enclosed in a tarp." Malone tapped out those words as if he was trying to understand them.

"'Nothing creepy about that.'" She repeated his initial reaction.

"Even more so now I know more. What do you think we're looking at here?"

"I'd say it's not a home robbery," Trent piped up.

Malone angled his head. "I think that's safe to assume. Even if they turn sideways, we rarely find victims wrapped up like mummies. That Lexus in the driveway…?"

"It belongs to Christine Lane." Amanda stiffened.

"That's why you said it's most likely Christine?"

Amanda nodded.

"Christine, who is also your brother's girlfriend." Malone talked slowly, stressing the association.

"Half-brother, yes." There was a distinction in her mind. She had a full brother, Kyle, and they were thick as thieves. She'd grown up with him around. Spencer was a recent surprise.

"Well, I think as long as there's the chance the victim is Lane, you shouldn't be anywhere near this mess. It was one thing to look into her welfare, but it's another to investigate her murder."

Amanda couldn't argue the latter part, but there was no way

she was being benched from this like Emma Blair. "I really don't see the issue with my working this case. I hardly know Spencer. Heck, I didn't even know he had a girlfriend until today. I didn't know about *him* until three years ago. We've only had coffee a few times." With her work as a detective and his as a firefighter, there weren't many free hours to get together. He didn't even attend family dinners held at her parents' house on Sundays. Though that could make for some awkwardness.

"Yet it's still a connection, Amanda. One he pulled on by calling you."

"Right. To look into the whereabouts of his girlfriend. What are you suggesting?" She could feel herself becoming defensive about Spencer and questioned where the loyalty originated.

"His call could have been rooted in genuine concern or to cover his butt." He pressed his lips.

"Are you seriously suggesting my half-brother murdered his girlfriend?" She couldn't believe what she was hearing.

"We need to consider the possibility." He leveled his gaze at her, and it was a look with which she was familiar. He was baiting her to break the silence. If she didn't, they'd remain locked in eye contact forever.

"You know I can remain objective." That's all she said. All she was going to say. Her record should speak for itself. Chad Palmer, the drunk driver who took out her husband, six-year-old daughter, and unborn child, and made her barren, was murdered four and a half years ago. She was allowed to work his case and had followed it all the way through to its heartbreaking conclusion.

Malone bobbed his head. "Fine, you can stay for now. But we may revisit this conversation." He gave it a few beats before adding, "Let's get inside before I melt to the deck."

SEVEN

The air-conditioning was a welcome relief but chilled the sweat on Amanda's neck and arms where she'd rolled up the sleeves on her jacket. She fell behind Malone and Trent when her phone rang, and she stopped to check it. They continued upstairs while she stared at Spencer's name on the screen.

There was no way she was answering this now. He'd be looking for an update, and she had none to give him. It seemed likely Christine was in the tarp, but she preferred to share facts not speculation. And even though she wasn't close to Spencer, she wasn't a skilled actor. Unless he was completely obtuse, he'd hear anxiousness in her voice. She rejected his call and sent him to voicemail.

She pocketed her phone again and caught up with Trent and Malone in the doorway of the primary suite. Her phone beeped, notifying her of a new voicemail. Trent looked at her, and she read the curiosity in his eyes. She shook her head and turned her attention to the CSIs, not about to say that Spencer had called. Especially not in front of Malone. He might twist it as Spencer trying to stay involved in a murder investigation of his own making.

As the CSIs photographed the room, Amanda caught the smaller details that matched the rest of the house. There were no personal effects, knickknacks, or photographs here either. It looked more like a hotel room than someone's bedroom. Amanda stepped into the walk-in closet. It was bigger than Amanda's bedroom, with a racking system around the perimeter and an island of drawers. On top of it was a watch-winding case and a glass cabinet displaying some jewels. Diamonds, emeralds, and rubies winked in the light.

"As we thought before, we can rule out robbery," Trent said, joining her in the closet.

"I'd say."

"Those Rolexes alone... Whoa." Trent angled his head, studying the timepieces.

Amanda wasn't as impressed by material things as he seemed to be. To her, they represented excess but to each their own. If a person had the cash, all the power to them. Life was too short not to do or acquire what brought joy.

She moved on from the island to look at the clothing. She wasn't a fashionista, but she could tell by the sheen to the dresses and pantsuits hanging on racks, they would have been expensive. Without touching them, she saw the label on one was Gucci. A rotating rack showcased the shoes: Jimmy Choo, Louboutin, and Louis Vuitton. Behind one section of glass doors, another rotating rack housed designer purses, including more Gucci and Louis Vuitton, Brunello Cucinelli, and Bottega Veneta.

When they returned to the main part of the bedroom, CSI Keller was lifting shoeprints from the floor with electro-charged Mylar. She looked at the result and shook her head.

"You didn't find any footwear prints?" Amanda asked, unable to hold back her curiosity.

"Not one." Keller played the beam of her flashlight across

the wood floors and stopped when it reached Amanda's and Trent's covered shoes. She turned it off.

The killer must have cleaned up after themselves, including erasing all trace evidence for whoever was in the tarp.

"We'll be taking a closer look throughout the home, of course," Stuart piped up.

Amanda knew all about Stuart's meticulous attention to detail. She took hours processing a scene that would have taken a fraction of that time if worked by CSIs Blair and Donnelly. Her downfall, in Amanda's opinion, was her fussiness over what to collect and what to process. Stuart's viewpoint was that countless lab tests cost time and money. Amanda couldn't argue with that, but she'd still appreciate it if Stuart were a bit more flexible in that regard.

"If I could get some help over here, that would be great." Stuart stood next to the bed and flicked a finger toward it. She had a way of asking for help that bordered on a petulant whine. "I'm thinking it would be far easier to get to the body if we removed the bed from over her," Stuart explained. "We'll take it apart piece by piece."

"Of course." Amanda stepped forward, willing to do anything that would get them closer to the victim's ID.

Trent and Malone moved in to help too while Keller took up position beside Stuart.

The five of them lifted the mattress on Malone's count of three. They walked it to the side of the room and leaned it against the wall.

Malone puffed out a deep breath afterward, but he waved Amanda off when she shot him a look of concern. He wasn't out of shape for his age, but he wasn't exactly a gym rat either. The point was *for his age*. He was in his late fifties, a time when the body starts becoming less cooperative. Something she knew from her parents.

"Well, the box springs should be easier, since each piece is half the size," Trent said.

"If you're having a hard time, young man, leave the rest to us," Malone told him.

"Very funny, old—"

Amanda shook her head at Trent. It was one thing for Malone to jest about age, but a volley back wouldn't be a smart move. "I'm ready when the rest of you are," she rushed out, trying to deflect Malone's attention from Trent.

Not long later, the two box springs were resting against the mattress.

All that remained of the bed was the frame and that ominous blue tarp and overeager robot vac determined to suck it up. Her eyes watered from the smell of decomposition, which was stronger with the box springs and mattress gone.

No one spoke while they all got their first good look at the scene. The tarp was wrapped tightly, following the curves of the corpse inside, and bundled with rope.

Amanda studied the size and shape of the victim. It was a woman. Most likely Christine. "The killer probably rolled or pushed the body under the bed." The obvious observation slipped from her lips. After all, it was doubtful the killer had removed the box springs and mattress.

"I'd say so," Trent said.

CSI Stuart, who had set her camera down to move the bed, retrieved it from the floor next to her collection kit. Keller grabbed a large evidence bag, and Amanda guessed the vacuum was her target.

Malone winced, and Amanda turned to face him. His hands were on his lower back and hips. She walked over to him.

"You all right?" Malone wasn't one for having a fuss made over him when he had a cancerous brain tumor almost four years ago. She doubted he'd want any made over a hurt back.

"It's nothing. Please don't..." Malone's eyes darted toward the others in the room. At his age, he was still concerned about other people's opinions. It must be an affliction that lasts a lifetime to varying degrees.

Trent, who had glanced over, quickly put his gaze back on the tarp.

"You should get your back looked at. You do have a chiropractor?" Not a jab at his age. She had one.

"*Pfft.*" Malone waved a hand, hissed, and placed it back on his hip. "I'm going to head out. Call me if you need anything."

"Will do."

Malone hobbled out of the room, despite trying to redeem his gait. She just hoped he didn't fall down the stairs.

"His back?" Trent said when she returned to his side.

"Yep, and the stubborn mule refuses help."

"Not surprised."

Stuart let her camera dangle from the neck strap, stood back, and looked over the area. After snapping a few more photos, she set the camera back on the floor next to her collection kit.

Keller hit a button on the top of the robot vacuum. It stopped, but Amanda swore she could still hear its whir. Keller lifted the vacuum overhead to look at the underside. "There are some long brown hairs wrapped around the spinner brush. There may be more in the rubber brushes." She took care as she sealed it in the bag.

"You'll want to find the vacuum's station too," Trent said. "Just in case it dumped into the bin before getting stuck on the tarp."

"I will do." Keller smiled at Trent.

She had a more graceful way of accepting input without taking everything as an insult. Maybe Keller knew as little about robot vacuums as Amanda. She still hauled out her parents' old

FilterQueen, a hand-me-down from them when she married Kevin. It might be time to retire the machine, but this wasn't about her or her random memories.

Amanda looked again at the blue tarp. Surely, it was Christine Lane inside, but what if it wasn't? Then they'd have a whole other set of problems.

EIGHT

Amanda forwarded the contact card for her chiropractor to Malone with a note.

She's great.

His reply came fast.

I took an Aleve. I'll live. Focus on the victim, who wasn't so lucky.

Before putting her phone away, her eye caught the little tape icon in the top left corner. She stepped into the hall to listen to her voicemail.

"Amanda, I just wanted to let you know I filed the missing person report. I'm back home now. My mind's too scattered to be any good at work. If you find out anything, please, please call me right away."

At the end of the playback, she hit delete. It was worse than she thought. Was Spencer that distressed about Christine he couldn't think of anything else until he knew she was safe? Or was there more to this? *Is he making himself appear to be the concerned doting boyfriend when all along he had...* She shook the thought, not able to let herself continue down that path. Not able to consider this was a ruse on his part to cover his back. Putting away her phone, she also shoved aside the disloyal thinking and returned to the primary suite. She came in to hear Stuart updating Trent.

"The body is ready for the ME, though I suspect he or she will prefer to take it back to the morgue before unwrapping it to preserve any potential evidence," Stuart was saying. "CSI Keller and I will process the tarp and rope back at the lab for touch DNA and fingerprints."

It was the outcome Amanda had expected, even if she hated the delay for identification.

Trent turned toward Amanda. "We need to strongly consider it's Lane because it most likely is."

"I know." The likelihood it was someone else was slim. The homeowner was gone, and Christine's Lexus was in the driveway. "We need to track down the clients who requested the showing. It had to be what brought her here."

"And since she didn't notify the office, we'll need our hands on her phone."

"If we can. Her call history from her service provider, at worst. But let's see what a search of the house turns up. She might have tucked her phone away in her purse somewhere."

The front door opened downstairs, and she overheard Hans Rideout, the medical examiner, talking to his assistant, Liam Baker. Soon, they were padding up the stairs and down the hall. Liam entered the room carrying a special wheeled cart designed to navigate stairs, and Rideout followed with his bag in hand.

"The scene is ready for you," Stuart told them.

Rideout set his bag down and walked toward the tarp, stepping as if he were toeing across glass. "This is a first. A body in a tarp. On Charmed Court, no less. Nothing much charming about murder."

Amanda caught Stuart giving the comment an eye roll. Keller smirked.

"Well, Amanda and Trent, you won't want to hear this..." Rideout lifted his gaze from the body. "But Liam and I will just be loading 'er up and taking it back to the morgue. We wouldn't want to chance losing forensic evidence. That means no ID, TOD, or COD until later."

"I'll text or call you the moment we know any of this," Liam wedged in.

Amanda unpacked each acronym with ease. ID, identity. TOD, time of death. And COD, cause of death. "We suspected as much, but we have reason to believe the victim is Christine Lane."

"The homeowner?" Rideout asked.

"The real estate agent," Amanda said. "It's her Lexus in the driveway."

"Huh. This case just got even more interesting."

"Do you have any idea when you'll get to the body?" Amanda directed the question to Liam because he kept Rideout's schedule. He'd either consult the electronic calendar on his tablet or know off the top of his head.

"The autopsy is unlikely to be today, but we'll get the decedent unwrapped, and hopefully ID'd when we get back to Manassas."

Amanda nodded. "Thank you."

"Sure. Don't mention it." Liam stepped inside the edge of the bedframe with Rideout, who was tilting his head as he observed the body. Whatever he saw, he wasn't sharing.

"Liam, help me remove the frame," Rideout said to his assistant.

While they worked on that, Amanda turned to Trent. "Let's

go see if we can find Christine's phone." She led the way downstairs and headed toward the front door and turned around.

If I were Christine, what would I do with my purse? Assuming I came with one...

Amanda ran it through in her mind. She'd wipe her shoes before making her way deeper into the house. She took the steps, passed the entry closet, and circled back. Pulling on a pair of gloves again, she tugged on the door.

It was sparse aside from a few coats, but dangling on a hanger was a compact Coach crossbody purse. A beautiful high-end brand, but having toured the walk-in closet upstairs, she'd say this didn't belong to Dominique Sharp.

"You found something?" Trent hovered over her shoulder.

"What gave it away?" She shared her thoughts, opened the flap, and peeked inside. "There's a wallet, a phone, and a portable charger with a small cable."

"That bag is deceptively big."

Amanda removed the wallet and fished out a driver's license. "Christine's." She held the card for Trent to see while fighting off nausea. The body upstairs had to be her half-brother's girlfriend. She returned the wallet to the purse and grabbed the phone. "No juice."

"Guess we know why it went directly to voicemail. But how long has it been in the closet? We figured she went missing sometime after her seven o'clock showing on Friday night. Most phones hold a charge for seventy-two hours."

"Since Christine lived on her phone, the charge could have already been depleted when she got here."

"Either way, it's safe to say it died anytime between Friday night and this morning."

"Yep. We need to get this plugged in and see if we can find out who brought her here."

"To do that, we'll need the PIN or pattern to unlock the

device. Do you think Spencer or Christine's daughter might know it?"

It would take time for Digital Crimes to hack in. Getting Christine's phone records would take even longer. "Her name's Riley... the daughter." She wasn't sure if she told Trent that much before now. "And all we can do is ask them." Not that she looked forward to talking to either one of them without seeing Christine's body for herself. They'd have questions she couldn't answer. "Come on, let's get it over with."

NINE

Before leaving Charmed Court, Amanda plugged Christine's phone into the portable charger and tucked both back into her purse. She also slipped upstairs to notify the CSIs they found Christine's purse in the entry closet. They gave little reaction to the news, but at least Amanda shared the update.

Amanda called Riley's number on the way to Spencer's and got her voicemail, where she left a message. It was two thirty by the time they were pulling into Spencer's driveway.

"The whole thing is just unsettling," Trent said as they trudged up the sidewalk to the house. "The tarp, the placement of the body. It's like..."

"Don't say 'serial killer.'"

"Well... Ordinary people killing with *ordinary* motives don't usually put their victim's body in a tarp."

She couldn't deny that logic, but she didn't want to leap to this being the work of a serial killer either. It was far too soon to go down that path. "We'll follow where the evidence takes us." Upon saying that, a wave of doubt rolled over her. *Could Spencer have done this?*

The front door was flung open before they reached it, and Spencer was standing there. "Is she...?"

Amanda stiffened. "It's best we talk inside."

"Ah, sure." Spencer retreated into the house.

"You remember Trent?" she said as they followed. They had met during another investigation, where Spencer's crew had been called to fight a fire in the woods and stumbled on a shallow grave.

"Yeah." Spencer closed the door behind them.

The three of them sat in the living room, and the silence swelled for several seconds.

"Please, guys, just tell me what's going on. Did you find her?"

She forced herself to meet her half-brother's eyes, fearing she'd get sucked in by a strong emotional response. Her weakness was feeling too much for what others were going through. "We found her Lexus, purse, and phone at a client's house in Woodbridge, in the Agee subdivision."

Spencer inched forward on the couch cushion. "She had a listing there. On Charmed Court."

Amanda nodded. "That's where all her things were."

"And Christine?" Spencer swallowed, his Adam's apple kicking out.

Trent glanced at Amanda, and she nodded for him to put it into words.

"A body was also found at the house," Trent said. "It seems likely it's Christine, though we can't confirm this yet."

"How can you not know if it's her?" Spencer's forehead scrunched up while pain and confusion clouded his eyes.

Amanda licked her lips, trying to summon her voice. She couldn't tell him about the tarp without crossing a line. "We can't disclose that, Spencer."

He blanked over and tears fell.

An ache burrowed in Amanda's chest. "I'm sorry we can't say any more."

"You're sorry?" Spencer shot to his feet and paced the living room. He stopped a few moments later, facing her. "When will you know... if it's her?"

"It shouldn't be too long from now. A handful of hours. Less?" She ballooned the timeframe. Liam made it sound like unwrapping the tarp would be their priority upon returning to the morgue. "We hoped you might help us with something."

"Name it." Spencer dropped back onto the couch.

"It could help the investigation if we could log into her phone," she told him.

"The investigation," he parroted, his voice cracking.

The clinical phrasing helped her with objectivity, but coming back to her, she heard how insensitive it sounded. "We were wondering if you know her PIN or pattern to unlock her phone."

"And possibly the code for her voicemail?" Trent wedged in.

"Her phone is a pattern." He traced it in the air, and Trent recorded a diagram on his notepad. "The code is thirty-six twenty-three."

"Thank you, Spencer." For him to know this, they must have been close, which made Amanda feel more empathy for him. "Have you and Christine been seeing each other for a long time?"

He bobbed his head. "About a year."

"Pretty serious then," Trent commented.

"I'd like to think so."

Amanda bristled. "Christine didn't feel the same?"

"I believe she did. She was just hesitant about giving her heart away. She'd been burned before, married for ten years before it blew up."

"When did it blow up?" Trent asked.

"Five years ago. Though they have a decent relationship now. I hoped that one day I'd convince her to take a chance on me."

Amanda's heart constricted. This wasn't just a casual affair for her half-brother. "You were thinking of proposing?"

Spencer pressed his lips and nodded. "At some point."

Again, another spike of empathy shot through her chest. If she wasn't careful, her emotions would derail her. "Do you know of anyone who might have reason to kill her?" *And wrap her in a tarp?* The thought flashed through her mind and, like a drive-by shooting, inflicted damage.

"No, everyone loved her." Spencer's voice cracked, but he pushed out, "Riley might know of someone. Dear Lord, Riley. Should I call her?"

"Please leave that to me, okay? I've already left her a voicemail."

Tears rolled down Spencer's cheeks as she locked eyes with her half-sibling. If she were standing, her legs may have given out on her. Her empathy, her human compassion, was both a strength and a curse.

TEN

Amanda slammed the car door shut, rocking the vehicle. Life had its glorious moments, but this one blew. There was no such thing as fairness. It was a concept, a scale of measuring things by some perceived standards, which made most things appear to fall short. The key may be expecting less.

"You okay?" Trent asked, slipping behind the wheel.

"Nope. But I'm going to find out what happened to Christine Lane. For her, her daughter, and Spencer."

"We will. Together. You've always got me, Amanda."

She dared to look over at him, but his gaze was on the road as he merged into traffic. "Yes, of course, I know that."

"Good." He glanced at her, before turning down a street that would take them in the direction of Charmed Court. The unspoken plan was to return there to access Christine's phone.

Amanda's phone rang, and Officer Cochran's name flashed on the screen. "Traci?" Amanda answered using the officer's first name.

"Hi, Amanda. So I'm here at the house on Charmed Court, and this woman has shown up claiming she's the homeowner. She's making quite a scene and—"

A woman was yelling in the background, "Let me in my house!"

"Tell Dominique Sharp that Detective Stenson and I will be there in a matter of minutes."

At the mention of Dominique, it felt like Trent pressed the gas harder.

"Will do," Traci said and hung up.

Before the line cut out, Dominique was still ranting.

"Brace yourself," Amanda said. "Dominique sounds like a handful."

It was only a few more minutes before Trent was pulling up to the cordon line on Charmed Court. A crowd had formed while Amanda and Trent had been gone, and people were lined up against the tape. It didn't matter how advanced society became, at the core people were nosy and predictable. Somehow witnessing other people's suffering made many feel better about their own lives.

A red Cadillac Vistiq was parked at a haphazard angle with its nose almost touching the tape. People were gathered all around the vehicle.

Arms were flailing in front of the hood, and Amanda could guess who they belonged to from here. She got out of the car and walked with Trent through the crowd, their badges held up to part the sea of people.

"Excuse me." She almost tripped over the foot of a woman who was slow to move out of the way. "Step aside, ma'am. Thank you."

They reached Officer Cochran, and she and Officer Brandt were struggling to hold a woman back. The crepe suit she wore flowed over her body, a tailored fit. Expensive. The clothing and her protective stance next to the luxury vehicle confirmed her identity.

"If you don't stay put, I'll have no choice but to arrest you, ma'am," Brandt threatened the woman.

"Dominique Sharp?" Amanda cut in.

The woman turned around, seeking the person who had called her name, her eyes scanning the crowds. Amanda nudged closer to her.

Traci Cochran saw Amanda then and relief flooded her expression. "That's Detective Steele, and her partner, Detective Stenson, that I told you about."

"You might recognize my name," Trent said. "I left you a couple of messages."

"Yes, I remember. What is going on here? This is my house, and they won't let me inside, let alone past this line." She shot an evil look at a woman who came within two feet of the Caddy.

"It's all right now, ma'am. You can come with us." Amanda lifted the tape, and Dominique bent under it.

"Finally. Someone's going to give me answers." Dominique looked over her shoulder. "My Cadillac, though? I'd rather put it in my garage than leave it out there on the street."

"That's not an option right now. It will be fine where it is." Amanda butted her head at Traci Cochran, who nodded.

"It better be, or I'll be suing the Prince William County PD. I'm a lawyer." She plucked a silver case from her pocket, pulled a business card from it, and extended it to Amanda between two long, slender fingers. Her nails were long and pointed, manicured and polished in a hot red.

Amanda extracted the card, careful not to get cut by Dominique's talons. The embossed logo read *Sharp & Associates*. She held the card so that Trent could see it.

"It's my company, and I didn't get to where I am by letting people tell me what I should and shouldn't do. And that includes cops."

"Well, as you might have gleaned, there's a situation inside your house." Out of mercy, Amanda didn't declare the woman's home a crime scene in so many words.

"Okay," she dragged out. "What is Christine doing here?"

Amanda passed Trent a side-glance. This woman was a piece of work, but despite that, there was no easy way to tell her that someone was killed in her home. "Let's just walk up to the house." Amanda suggested this to get farther away from the crowds. A quick look over her shoulder, and she saw the PWC News van coming down the street. No doubt it had Amanda's *favorite* reporter, Diana Wesson, inside, arriving to break the story. Hopefully, by the time she and Trent left, Wesson would be gone.

Once they got closer to the house, Dominique pushed out a breath. "All right. I've been patient. Tell me what's going on."

"Detective Stenson and I came here after Christine's loved ones were concerned about her welfare. Since her vehicle was in the driveway, we tried ringing the doorbell. When that failed, we went around back and found the sliding patio door open."

Dominique crossed her arms. "There's no reason that should have been open."

"Which is what we thought, so we exercised our right in such a situation to enter your home. Before I say more, we may want to go around the back, so you can have a seat." Amanda was showing concern for Dominique's feelings.

"Just tell me. Trust me, I can handle whatever it is."

"We found a body inside your home." Amanda was going to elaborate, but Dominique gasped. "I realize this may come as a shock."

"Was it Christine?"

"It seems so, yes." Amanda felt comfortable in committing to that much. It wasn't official yet, which permitted a fine line of judgment. If the body was identified as Christine, her daughter deserved to be the first to know.

Dominique's eyes hardened. "But you don't know for sure? Dear God, was this person horribly disfigured? And all this happened in my home?" Dominique's voice became more shrill the longer she spoke.

Amanda must have misread her earlier gasp. It wasn't sprung from grief but irritation at the inconvenience this was causing her. "You miss the point that someone was murdered in your home, likely your real estate agent. Do you know when she was last scheduled to show your house?"

"She called Friday night, and I told her to go ahead."

It was just as they thought, but that didn't stop the verification from hitting. It was sad to think Christine had been dead inside for that long without anyone knowing. "And where have you been?"

"I left for Washington last Friday morning."

"Is that where you came from?" Sweat trickled down Amanda's back. She needed out of the direct sunlight, or she might find out if humans could melt due to global warming.

"It is."

"And why were you there?" Amanda kept the questions rolling while Trent recorded Dominique's responses in his notepad. Sometimes he was old-school. Other times he tapped them into the Notes app on his department-issued tablet.

"Business."

Trent stopped writing. "We'll need a bit more than that."

"Then I'll need to know why it's relevant. Even if Christine was murdered, it has nothing to do with me."

"A person was killed in *your* home. I doubt you want us to see you as interfering with a murder investigation," Amanda pointed out.

"I don't, but I also know my rights."

Amanda's redhead temper flared, but she remained silent as did Trent. He was scribbling away in his notepad. What he was writing, Amanda had no clue. Possibly *uncooperative*...

Dominique smiled. "I invented the silent card, Detective.

You can play it as long as you like, but I'm not saying more than I already have."

Another stream of sweat dripped down Amanda's spine. Her forehead was soaking wet. It was like nothing fazed Dominique—not the heat or a murder in her house.

"Hey! Get away from the Cadillac!" Dominique yelled down to the street, flailing an arm at the crowd that was encroaching on her precious vehicle.

Correction. She is obsessed with her car... Diana Wesson wasn't that far away from it, and she was waving at Amanda. *Think myself invisible...* Amanda faced Dominique again. "Ma'am, we need your focus here."

"What more can I tell you? I wasn't here and had nothing to do with it."

"Yes, but you can see why we might be interested in the fact someone was killed in your home while you were away?" Amanda served back. "You're going to need to tell us what took you to DC. Something more specific than *business*."

"I'm in the middle of acquiring a DC law firm."

"Was the trip to DC planned?" Amanda wasn't sure if this would factor into Christine's murder, but the more intel the better.

"Last minute. I decided I was going up on Friday."

Amanda squirreled that away. "Do you know who might have an issue with Christine Lane?"

"I have no clue. We weren't friends or anything. She worked for me."

The distinction was noteworthy. Dominique seemed the type to think of herself as above those she paid. "Does anyone besides Christine Lane have a key or the code for your security system?"

"I'm sure you noticed the realtor lockbox on the door. Christine would have passed along the code to any other agents who came to show the house."

"And did anyone else besides Christine show the house?" Dominique should know this because she would have had to step out for viewings to take place.

"Actually, no, I don't think so."

But Amanda's mind was still grinding on this. Selling this house would net a sizable commission. Maybe a rival agent let jealousy get to them that Christine had this listing. "Anyone else have a key?"

"Just my maid."

"What can you tell us about your housecleaner?" Amanda relabeled, not caring for the one that Dominique had used.

"Lucia is a sixty-year-old Spanish woman from Mexico. She'd have no reason to kill Christine. Honestly, I can't imagine her killing anyone."

Amanda felt comfortable ruling Lucia out, but there was one inconsistency. "If you have someone to clean your home, why do you have a robot vacuum?"

Dominique scrunched up her face. "Strange question, but okay, I'll play. Lucia only comes in twice a week, so I have two robot vacuums set up to run for the days when she's not here."

Amanda didn't understand how one woman living in such a large house would have a need for that much cleaning. The floors must be sterile enough to lick. "When are they set to go out?"

Dominique cocked an eyebrow but reached into her designer purse and pulled out her phone. "There's no way I'm remembering that. Again, I find it odd that you care."

"Please, oblige us," Trent said. "We're just interested in any set to run today."

"There is one upstairs and one down. Both do a section at eleven AM and another at four PM."

Amanda surmised they only had so much battery life, but that timing would explain why the one was still running when they'd arrived.

"Are you going to tell me why you care about my vacuuming?" Dominique slid her phone back into her purse.

"Open investigation, ma'am," Trent said and earned a groan from the lawyer.

"Uh-huh. What am I supposed to do now?"

"Well, your house is a crime scene and may be locked down for several days." Amanda didn't feel bad laying that out bluntly.

"Just great. And how will I ever sell it now? It's a murder house."

The sale of this house was the least of Amanda's concerns. "I can't say. But you'll need to find somewhere else to stay."

"Fine." Dominique started to walk back down the driveway toward her Cadillac.

"We'll need to know where you're going," Amanda told her. "In case we have more questions."

"I'm going to stay with my lover. Name's Joel Blackburn, and he lives in town." Dominique rattled off the address and phone number. Trent scribbled quickly in his notepad.

Amanda watched Dominique get into her vehicle after elbowing her way past several people.

Officer Cochran stepped in to get the crowd to stay back so Dominique could drive away.

Amanda turned to Trent. "If I don't get inside, I'm going to become a puddle of goo."

"Preach it."

They pushed through the front door and stepped into the air-conditioning.

"It's a dream in here." Trent snapped his mouth shut.

Amanda dismissed his comment with a wave of her hand. "Blame your poor word choice on heat stroke."

"It would be a valid excuse. Frick, it's smoldering out there."

Her phone pinged with a text message. "It's from Liam, and I'll pass along the highlights." She read, then summarized.

"Rideout's squeezing the autopsy in now. Prelim is two gunshots to the chest, one to the head... nine mil, fired at a distance of fifteen to twenty feet. No casings in the tarp, but it and the rope have been forwarded to the lab. The tarp and rope appear to be brand new."

"That's one novel-length text message."

"Don't knock it. I like all the detail."

"True enough, but if you ask me, it sounds like a hit. All that, and he didn't confirm ID?"

Three bubbles popped up in the thread, just before a new text showed up. She held the screen so Trent could read along with her.

Sorry that I missed saying vic is female, identified as Christine Lane. Compared driver's license photo to deceased, and there were business cards in her pocket.

"Just as we feared," she said to Trent and pecked back to Liam.

TOD?

Bubbles then...

Preliminarily a few days ago.

She showed this to Trent.

"That would place time of death sometime on Friday after her seven PM showing. Now to find out who requested the viewing here." Trent opened the closet for Christine's purse.

Amanda was moving slower, but it wasn't just the heat. Before Liam's message, a small part of her could cling to denial about the victim's identity. With one text, that was gone. Now before the day was out, Amanda would be breaking Spencer's and Riley's hearts.

ELEVEN

Amanda was still processing Liam's text. The way Christine had been murdered seemed surreal. And Trent's words, *it sounds like a hit*, kept ricochetting in her head. "What if you're right? That this was a hit or execution?"

"If it is, we need to consider the person who requested the showing may have lured her here to kill her. Even if Dominique Sharp was in town, homeowners step out during showings. If this person made the appointment, they would have wagered they'd have some time to do what they... well, what they did."

"Sure, but why target her here? And if this was the client, they took the chance she wasn't going to notify her office."

"Maybe they didn't care. They'd be gone before anyone would check on her."

"True enough." Amanda put on gloves and went into the closet for Christine's phone. She found the device right where they left it charging. After turning it on, she handed the phone to Trent. "You want to trace the pattern?"

Trent swiped the screen.

"Thanks." She looked at the call history first and saw that

Riley had called her mother at 9:44 PM on Friday night. The call lasted a minute, so Christine had answered. It was likely within moments of her death. She shared this finding with Trent. There were also calls that morning from Art Beasley with Best Homes Realty that came in after Amanda spoke with him. He must have wanted to try reaching her himself. Amanda also saw Spencer's attempts over the weekend.

Next, Amanda called in for the voicemails. She did this on speaker and entered the code of thirty-six twenty-three that Spencer had given them.

"You have twelve new voicemails," the automated voice greeted them.

Amanda glanced at Trent as they prepared to settle in for a bit.

There were a few messages from Spencer, five from clients requesting showings on various properties or following up, and one from Art Beasley. But four flagged for Amanda. Three were from the same caller and had taken place over the weekend.

"Christine, I need the code for the box and alarm system for Charmed Court. I have an interested client."

This message was attached to a contact in Christine's phone, and it was a name Amanda recognized. "Wasn't Marcy Maxwell the top agent for Best Homes Realty last year?"

"Uh-huh."

The next message played out from Marcy, sounding more hostile.

"You can't just ghost me, Christine. Call me back."

By the third, Marcy resorted to a whiny voice.

"Hello? Christine? Why aren't you calling me back? Are you threatened by me?"

Amanda stopped the voicemail from playing out. "We'll need to have a chat with Marcy, find out the story between her and Christine."

"Agreed. It doesn't sound too friendly."

Amanda shook her head. Could it be as she thought earlier? That a rival agent had targeted Christine?

The other message that had Amanda's attention was from a woman who wasn't in Christine's contacts. It was left at ten thirty on Friday night.

"It's Melanie. We're at the house. There's a Lexus in the drive, but there's no answer at the door. If you're inside, call me back. We'll wait around for five minutes, but after that we need to leave."

Amanda saved the message and looked at the call log attached to the number. "There were two calls on Friday from this number. Presumably, one requesting the viewing, and the follow-up that landed in voicemail. But there is also one from two weeks ago and a return call from Christine the same day."

"They've been in touch for a bit, but that doesn't necessarily exempt this person from suspicion. I say we track the number back to who it's registered to and follow up."

"Easy enough. Did you notice the woman said *we*? There were at least two people here to see the house."

"Right. Well, a partnership could be responsible for this."

"From the call history, Melanie never tried reaching Christine again. Leaving this message could have been a defense ploy." She offered this, realizing it was what Malone had said about Spencer. "Whatever the case, we need to track these people down and have a chat."

"Same goes for Marcy Maxwell, but we have two other stops to make first."

"Yes, I know. But I'm not notifying Spencer until we've gotten a hold of Christine's daughter, and this isn't news I want to give her over the phone."

TWELVE

Amanda shared the update on the victim's identity with the CSIs, and she and Trent were on the road again. Their first stop took them to Christine's house to see if Riley was home. When that failed, Amanda called her and had to leave another voicemail. "No answer again."

"So I gathered. What are you thinking we should do next? Want to head back to Best Home Realty to have a chat with Marcy Maxwell, or speak to this Melanie who requested the viewing?"

"Considering it sounds like Melanie was there around the time of Christine's murder, I say we start with her. In the least, Melanie might have seen something that could help with the case."

"I can get behind that. But I really need something to eat before we do anything. You all right with that?"

"Why not?"

A handful of minutes later, they had hit a drive-thru and were eating fries and chicken strips in the car. She with plum sauce, and he with honey.

Trent's phone rang, and he pulled it out. "It's Kels. I can let it go or..."

"Answer it. We don't know where this night is going to take us." If they were fortunate, they'd wrap this up and get Christine's killer in the next hour. That's what Amanda would love to believe, but life had taught her not to surrender to hope with a freefall.

"Hey there." Trent was smiling when he answered, showing his relationship was going strong.

She pushed a fry into her mouth and shut the container, abandoning some. Just unable to eat any more. Her phone rang, and her caller ID told her it was "Dr. Handsome." *Becky!* Her best friend must have gotten a hold of her phone and updated his name in her contacts. Amanda would change that before Carter saw it. She picked up his call.

"Wow. Is this Amanda in the flesh? Not a recording? I half-expected to wind up in voicemail."

She heard his smile from the other end of the line, and unlike her ex, Carter knew what it was like to have a demanding job that didn't adhere to fixed hours. His commentary on the voicemail was just a sign that he respected her busy schedule. "Well, you've got me, so what can I do for you?"

"Ooh, you know what you can do..."

She knew what he liked, but she flushed with heat thinking about his mouth over her ear, his breath on her neck. Then the way he'd nibble on the lobe, sending her into... She pulled herself out of the tailspin. "All right. Mind out of the gutter."

"But it's fun there."

Amanda laughed, and it caused Trent to look over at her and shake his head. Was that the hint of a smile, or a scowl? *Whatever...*

"I'm getting off work for the night, miracle of miracles, and was wondering if I should come over," Carter said.

Amanda had told Carter that Zoe was at her grandparents'

this week. "I'd love that except that Detective Stenson and I picked up a new case today. We'll be at this for hours yet."

"Oh, that's never good. It means someone's dead."

"Murdered, to be more precise."

"I have faith you'll bring the victim justice."

She appreciated his confidence in her abilities, but this one cut so close to home. Their relationship hadn't yet developed strong enough roots for her to share that much. Instead, she responded with, "Well, that's always the plan."

"You'll do it. I know you're a night owl, so if you get in late and want some company, just call me."

"Will do." She ended the call and found Trent watching her, his phone away and a smile resting on his lips.

"What?" she asked him.

"Nothing at all." He pointed at the container on her lap. "I can take it to the garbage with mine."

"Nah, I'll do it. You bring up the background on this Melanie and get us an address."

Amanda took their garbage to the closest trash can, thankful for a few seconds of fresh air. Even if that air was heavy with heat and humidity, it was preferable to being stuffed in a tight space with Trent right now. She didn't want to field his questions about how her relationship with the doctor was going. It was awkward enough that Trent knew Carter, the two of them meeting during a previous investigation. It was also when Amanda and Carter met each other.

She came back to the car and dropped into the passenger seat, sucking in the cool air coming from the vent. "So what have we got?"

"Melanie and Kent Schaefer, both in their late forties. No criminal record. On paper, they look clean. She doesn't have a job, but he's a chiropractor. Good-looking couple." Trent switched screens to show their photos from their driver's licenses.

"Sure, but if he's the only one who works, how could they afford the house on Charmed Court?"

"I'd say that's a question we need to ask. Their address is just a few streets over. Buckle up, and I'll get us there."

* * *

Amanda was ringing the Schaefers' doorbell at five forty-five. The heat still hadn't let up, and any advisories to stay indoors were being ignored. The excited screams and laughter of young children rang through the neighborhood. Amanda was propelled back in time to when she was a kid during summer break. Every waking hour, she was running under a sprinkler, splashing in a friend's swimming pool, or sliding down a slip and slide. That was until she developed and that experience became painful.

The smell of barbecued meat had Trent sniffing the air like a hound dog.

"One would think you didn't just eat," she said to him.

"Well, you can't say it doesn't smell heavenly."

The door opened, and the woman in the license photo stood there. Amanda held up her badge, as did Trent.

"Melanie Schaefer?" Amanda asked her.

"Yes." She was leery and appeared to strengthen her grip on the edge of the door.

"Detectives Steele and Stenson. We'd like to speak with you and your husband about Christine Lane."

Melanie let go of the door and backed up.

"Is your husband home?" Trent asked her.

The woman nodded and went deeper into the house, leaving them in the entry. "I'll go get him."

The house was modest, something one would expect to be the home of a chiropractor. Again, Amanda wondered how they could afford the house on Charmed Court. Though it was possible one of them came into an inheritance that allowed them to upgrade their living arrangements.

A man came from the back of the home. "Detectives? My wife says this is about Christine Lane?"

"It is," Amanda said. "Is there somewhere we could sit and talk?"

"Yeah, in here." Melanie gestured toward a side room. There was a television in there, but Amanda suspected it was a secondary location as the furniture style and layout spoke more to encouraging conversation than getting cozy and watching TV.

Amanda sat on one end of a powder-blue fabric couch, and Trent sat on the other. The Schaefers each took a chair across from them.

"Did something happen to Christine?" Melanie asked. "We were supposed to meet her Friday night at a house, but she never showed up, and well... now you're here."

"Well, we thought it was her vehicle in the driveway," Kent put in, correcting part of what his wife said.

The calls on Christine's phone with Melanie went back two weeks, so it seemed logical they'd be able to identify her Lexus. "How long were you working with Christine?" She just wanted to verify.

Melanie narrowed her eyes, seemingly noticing that Amanda hadn't answered her question. "For a couple weeks. She showed us a few houses, but when the one on Charmed Court came up for sale, my heart leaped."

"Is that why you wanted a late-night showing? You couldn't wait?" Trent asked, pulling out his notepad and pen.

Melanie shook her head and gestured for her husband to answer.

"I had a conference that took me out of town for the weekend," Kent said. "Melanie fell in love with the pictures. She was confident we'd be putting in an offer on Friday night."

"The house just spoke to me," Melanie weighed in.

Amanda glanced at Trent and shook her head. They hadn't been here long, but there wasn't one thing suspicious about this couple. And what would be their motive for killing Christine? The only anomaly was their financial situation. "It is a beautiful house. Well out of my price range." Amanda hoped it would entice the Schaefers to open up. If not, she'd go at it from a more direct route.

"It was just time," Melanie said.

"For what?" Amanda volleyed back.

"Kent?" Melanie said to her husband, and he nodded. "My husband is a wonderful man and an excellent chiropractor. I admire him and what he's built." She returned her husband's smile. "He has his own office and loves what he does, but it's not a huge moneymaker. He helps people though, and one can't put a price tag on that."

Amanda agreed that a chiropractor's work was honest and needed. She'd follow up and see if Malone called hers. She wasn't yet sure why Melanie had said what she did, but she had a feeling she was building up to the point.

Melanie went on. "It was just time for me to get my dream home. You see, I come from family money. I just never wanted Kent to feel I was stepping on his toes."

And there it is...

Kent reached for his wife's hand and squeezed it before retracting his arm again.

Amanda's curiosity was satisfied, and the Schaefers were safely off the suspect list. That didn't mean they still couldn't be useful though. "When was the last time you saw Christine?"

The couple looked at each other, and after a few seconds, Kent said, "She showed us another house on Tuesday last week."

"It was nice but not what we had in mind. You never answered my earlier question. Did something happen to Christine?" Melanie drew her gaze back and forth between Amanda and Trent.

"Unfortunately, Christine was found murdered this morning." Since there was no more putting it off, Amanda set that out there as delicately as possible.

Melanie's eyes widened. "Oh my goodness, that's horrible. That poor woman, but why are you here talking to us about this?"

"Christine was found in the house on Charmed Court," Amanda said. "And your call came in within the timeframe of her death."

"Were we there when…?" Melanie's eyes welled with tears.

"It's likely she was killed in the moments prior to your arrival." Amanda wasn't sure how much that soothed the Schaefers, but added, "Your voicemail mentioned you didn't understand why there was no answer at the door. Did anything stand out when you were there? Maybe you saw someone hanging around?"

Melanie snapped her head toward her husband. "Kent." The woman blanched.

"Mel thought she saw someone inside," Kent said.

"I assumed it was Christine," Melanie rushed out. "I didn't understand why she wasn't answering the door."

It sounded like Melanie hadn't lost respect for Christine despite thinking she was being ignored. She also hadn't called her cell phone again. "Did you call the real estate office this morning to try reaching her?"

Melanie shook her head. "I assumed something must have come up, and she'd get back to me as soon as she could. I certainly never imagined this." She rubbed her arms as if frozen by a sudden chill.

This woman had likely seen the killer. That was enough to give anyone goosebumps. "Where did you see the figure?"

"All the lights in the house were on. I just saw them moving around inside through the glass in the front door, but it's obscured so..."

"You didn't get a good look?" Amanda guessed.

"No."

Amanda's mind regurgitated what Melanie had said a moment ago. *I assumed it was Christine.* That was one thing that might keep Spencer off the suspect list. "This person looked like a woman, though?"

Melanie bit her bottom lip. "Yes, that's why I thought it was Christine. Now, I'm not so sure. It could have been a man about her size."

Because of the obscured glass... Amanda's stomach sank because Spencer was of comparable size to Christine. "And when you rang the bell, this person did nothing?"

"Nope. Not even when I banged on the front door. They just walked upstairs."

Melanie had witnessed the killer after the murder, possibly when they were cleaning up. Just for the record, Amanda asked, "Can you tell us where you went after Christine didn't answer the door?"

"We came straight home," Kent said. "I still had to pack some things for the conference."

"And can anyone corroborate that?" Trent asked.

The couple shook their heads.

"Please know we'd have no reason to want to harm Christine," Melanie said. "She was just helping us find a new home."

Amanda glanced at Trent, and he seemed to read her mind. He folded his notepad and tucked his pen away.

"Thank you for your time," Amanda said while she stood. "If you could please keep any of what we discussed to yourselves for now."

"We will."

"And if you recall anything after we've left, please call me." Amanda pressed her business card into Kent's palm.

Back in the car, they did up their belts, and Amanda's phone rang.

"It's Riley Lane," she told Trent before answering. "Detective Steele."

After she said her name, Riley added, "I'm just returning your call."

"Thank you. Would you by chance be home right now?"

"Yeah."

"All right. Stay put, please. My partner, Detective Stenson, and I will be there soon."

If Riley questioned how they knew where *home* was, she didn't ask. Amanda had to wonder if the girl had a sixth sense of the devastating news coming her way.

THIRTEEN

Amanda and Trent said little on the way to the Lane residence. They were in quick agreement the Schaefers were off the suspect list and that the mystery figure Melanie had seen was Christine's killer. "Is it just me, or did it give you chills to hear Melanie say this person just ignored her and continued upstairs?"

"You're not alone. Whoever this killer is, they are composed."

"That's for sure. They would have killed Christine and been in the process of cleaning up, yet it still didn't seem to faze them that someone was at the door."

Trent parked in front of the Lane house a few minutes after seven, and Riley was standing in the open front doorway before they reached it. Without a word, she stepped back to let them inside.

"We're Detectives Steele and Stenson," Amanda said, feeling it was appropriate the girl at least get their names before they crossed the threshold.

"Riley Lane, but you know that. Should we sit somewhere?"

"That would be best." Amanda felt for the girl, thinking about the news they had come to tell her.

Riley's cheeks flushed before she turned to lead them to the living room. It was a modest space with new leather furniture. The smell of it was hard to miss.

The three of them sat down. Amanda was the first to speak. "Unfortunately, we have some bad news..." She paused when tears pooled in Riley's eyes. *Your mother is gone, sweetheart...* "It's about your mother. She was found dead today, in a client's home."

Riley gasped out a sob but otherwise remained silent.

Amanda imagined there were a million questions rolling through her mind, even judgments against herself. How did it happen? Was it an accident? And how could she not have known as she went on with her life? "It was murder, Riley. She was shot." Amanda made the method abundantly clear to counteract one effect of grief. It had a way of impeding comprehension.

Riley's eyes snapped to Amanda's. "She was shot?"

"She was." Amanda would leave out the other details at the scene, like how her mother was shot *three* times and then wrapped in a tarp.

"But who would do such a thing?" A few tears splashed onto her cheeks, and she swiped them away.

"We plan on finding out." It wasn't the ideal answer, but it was an honest one.

"Ah, when did this...?"

"Friday night."

Riley got up and rushed from the room.

Amanda looked at Trent and found he was looking back at her. "We'll just give her a few minutes," she told him.

Witnessing this girl's heartbreak brought back her own loss. How ten years ago, she had to bury her husband, six-year-old daughter, and unborn baby. Like Christine Lane, they were taken suddenly without warning, but unlike Christine, they were killed in a car accident caused by a drunk driver.

A few minutes later, Riley returned wearing a plush, cream knit sweater with round wooden buttons over her T-shirt. The cardigan swallowed her frame, and she burrowed into it. The move reminded Amanda of how she'd spent many days curled up in bed wearing her late husband's sweater while hugging one of her daughter's stuffed toys.

"We're very sorry for your loss," Amanda offered as fresh tears squeezed from the young woman's eyes.

"I called and talked to her on Friday night. She sounded good. I don't understand." Riley shrugged deeper into the sweater and deeper into the chair she had plopped back on.

There was nothing Amanda or Trent could say to mend Riley's heart. Only time could make the effort. "What did you talk about?"

"Oh, she just wanted me to confirm I made it to the cottage with my friends. We rented a cottage on the lake, about six hours from here, for the weekend. I just got back today. Maybe if I'd stayed home..."

Amanda shook her head. "No. None of this is on you, Riley. Please know that."

"But she is my mother, and I rushed to get off the phone. If I had known, I never would have... I never even felt she was..." She stopped there as another batch of tears made their way down her cheeks and dripped off her jaw and chin.

"We don't always feel it. That doesn't mean they meant any less to us." The sentiment was to reassure Riley, but it also accomplished the same for herself. It was an old wound, and one that she thought she'd put to bed. After the accident, denial may have temporarily blocked out the reality that her husband and daughter were gone. That didn't stop the self-chastisement from hitting over the years. That she should have known regardless. That the light in the world had dimmed.

"I appreciate you saying that. Mom gave me a lot of freedom, even more after she and Dad divorced. But that didn't stop her from being protective of me. Like asking me to call when I reached places."

"The divorce must have been a tough transition," Trent said.

Riley shrugged. "I was thirteen when they split, and fourteen by the time the divorce went through. Dad's still in my life though. Mom's, too, on a limited scale."

"Then things are amicable between them?" Spencer had told her the marriage ended five years ago. But they'd talk with the ex-husband to feel him out. Some motives were buried deep.

"Yes," she said. "But don't go thinking he had anything to do with this. He'd never. He's going to be heartbroken. They were each other's first. No one can replace that." Riley nuzzled farther into the sweater, pushing the fabric to her earlobes. "I can tell him, right? Or do you need to? I've seen crime dramas on TV. You'll want to gauge his reaction to the news. After all, it's always the husband or the ex."

Amanda would like to handle the notification, but this case was a special situation. The father was this girl's support system. "You can tell him, Riley."

"If you're going to suspect someone"—Riley jutted out her chin—"look at the boyfriend."

The boyfriend... Riley's words ricochetted in her head. Amanda became cold and dizzy. Her mouth, thick cotton.

"Your mother was dating?" Trent asked, stepping up and playing dumb.

"Yeah. She's been seeing some guy for a while now."

Some guy... And a year was longer than *a while*. Amanda wasn't liking this turn in the conversation. But she'd assured Malone she would remain objective, that flesh and blood were nothing more than biological with Spencer. And Steeles honored their word. "His name?"

"Spencer Blair. He's a volunteer firefighter, and he's all right but..."

Amanda cleared her throat. "What do you mean by *all right but...*?" Requesting an elaboration had her feeling like she was betraying Spencer. She should have told Riley that pointing at someone in a murder investigation was a serious thing without justification. She just hoped whatever came out of Riley's mouth didn't make Spencer a suspect.

"Just that. Though no one's my dad. I don't much care for Dad's new wife either."

It was possible the ex-husband had moved on, but Amanda wasn't letting a new marriage alone convince her of that. They'd still need to talk with him. But she was relieved that she hadn't heard anything incriminating about Spencer. Yet, she pushed, "Is it just that, or is there more you need to tell us about Spencer?"

"It might be nothing, but Mom was pissed off at him. Honestly, I thought she was going to end things."

Amanda stood, trying to disguise her discomfort by making it look like she were stretching. Spencer hadn't mentioned any of this. He'd painted his relationship with Christine with brushstrokes of rainbows and lollipops. Trent shot her a look, seeing through her anxiety. Hopefully, Riley wouldn't. "That's what your mother told you? That she was going to end things with Spencer?" She was impressed she'd found her voice. As determined as she was to keep neutral, she was struggling to maintain her ground.

"I guess not in so many words."

"But you think it's possible that Spencer may have killed your mother?" Trent shot the direct question, which had Amanda briefly placing a hand over her heart.

"I don't want to think that, but..."

Riley left the sentence dangling for long enough that Amanda's stomach filled with acid.

"But, what?" Again, it was Trent taking on the burden of the unpleasant questions.

"He has a bad temper. I've seen it for myself."

Amanda walked a few steps but stopped herself and returned to the couch where she had been sitting. She was making herself anxious, and the last thing she wanted to do was make this moment worse for Riley. As she sat down again, she said, "Can you give us an example?"

"He came over after fighting a raging warehouse fire. He was tired and pissed off at the squadron leader. Mom gave him a beer, and he seemed fine. Then he was cooking us steaks on the barbecue, but the propane ran out before they were finished. He roared and threw them in the trash. That ticked Mom off. Steaks aren't cheap. She asked him to leave and ordered us pizza."

Amanda was feeling a touch feverish, but she was also ticked off. Spencer could have mentioned this, but he hadn't. So why not? After all, sometimes people blew up, couples fight and disagree. Was there something different about this time? "When was this?"

"Two weeks ago."

"Was that their last fight?" Trent asked.

Riley nodded. "I don't think they've met up since. They could have. I'm mostly in my own world. Will you be talking to Spencer?"

Spencer told them he'd seen Christine last Wednesday, but as Riley just admitted, she might not have been privy to that information. It didn't mean that he had lied to them. "We will be talking with him." As Amanda said this, her resolve kicked in. She'd look at this case like any other, as she'd intended from the start. It was always a possibility that things would point at Spencer. She'd deceived herself into thinking she could handle it if they did. It turned out facing that reality was more challenging.

"I'm sure he's going to be heartbroken. I should have kept quiet. He's not all that bad. Mom had a real shitty... Sorry, I didn't mean to swear."

"It's fine," Trent told her. "Nothing we haven't heard before."

"Her boyfriend before Spencer was an ass. Quite controlling."

"And how was that?" Trent's voice took on a menacing tone, which Amanda recognized as his inner white knight stepping up. He had zero tolerance for men who abused women whether it be physically, mentally, or emotionally.

"She's a real estate agent. It's not like she has set hours. He got it in his head that Mom was cheating on him." Riley shook her head, grimaced.

The teen spoke about her mother in present tense and would do so for a while yet until the loss sank in. Before Amanda could respond, Trent did.

"What did he do about that?" he pushed.

"Just bitched. If you're wondering if he ever hit her, then no."

"Abuse is more than fists." A small pulse ticked in Trent's cheek.

"What is his name?" Amanda asked.

"Wes Galloway."

All the guys named Wes that Amanda knew were slimy womanizers, though she was sure there were nice ones out there. Not that Galloway sounded like a trophy. "When did they break up?"

"Mom ended it about six months before she and Spencer met. I only know that because she read in some book that you should give yourself at least that amount of time after a breakup to be with yourself. Something about allowing a person time to rediscover themselves. Apparently, we lose ourselves in our relationships, or some such nonsense."

Amanda smiled at the teen, but what Riley saw as nonsense, Amanda saw as practical advice. It just so happened she broke things off with her previous boyfriend six months before she started seeing Carter.

Trent leaned forward. "You said your mom ended things. How did he take it? You know?"

"Fine, I guess. Mom said he moved out of state. California, if I remember right."

Based on what Riley told them the relationship had ended eighteen months ago. Healthy people would have long moved on, but Riley had described Wes as controlling. What if he wasn't happy that she'd ended things, and he'd kept tabs on her? "We're going to leave now, Riley. Is there someone we could call to be with you?"

"Just my dad, but I can call him."

"Okay, if you're sure," Amanda told her.

Riley nodded, and Trent closed his notepad and stood. Amanda followed his lead and handed Riley her business card before leaving. "The Prince William County PD also offers counselors who can be with you, to listen and talk. Would you like me to get someone from Victim Services to come over?"

"Okay."

"All right. You need anything, call me at the number on the card." Amanda turned to leave then, feeling as she often did after serving notifications. There was a gnawing in her gut that while she'd be moving on with her life, those in her wake would need to cobble together a new normal without their loved one in the picture. But as she was leaving the Lane residence, she was also full of dread. There was the ex-boyfriend, sure, but based on Riley's words, Spencer might have been headed that way. But was Spencer the possessive and controlling type? Riley said he had a temper. Did he get angry at the imminent dissolving of his relationship with Christine and become violent? To the point of murder? And if so, how had he known Christine would be at Sharp's house on Friday night? Amanda went cold with the answer. He'd know if he was stalking her. From the sound of it, he was guilty of holding back their recent troubles, so what else was he hiding?

FOURTEEN

Amanda made a quick call to Victim Services for Riley. Afterward, her thoughts turned to Spencer and how things would go with him. Would he lash out at her full of venom and denial, leveling accusations she was overcompensating by painting him the villain to prove she was doing her job? Or worse yet, would he confess? Either way, she and Trent had to question him. The ex-boyfriend was cleared with a quick background check.

Wes Galloway had a clean record, which didn't sway her, but his California address was more convincing of his innocence. Even if she could dismiss that, what would be his motive to kill Christine? Also, how would he have known where to target her? Riley said he was controlling, not a stalker, and it sure sounded like he'd moved on after the breakup. And while he might not have killed Christine, that relationship could have primed her to be more reactive to Spencer's explosive outburst.

Trent parked in Spencer's driveway and looked over at her. "Are you sure you're okay?"

"Not in the least." Amanda had called Malone just after

his relationship with Christine and become violent? To the point of murder? And if so, how had he known Christine would be at Sharp's house on Friday night? Amanda went cold with the answer. He'd know if he was stalking her. From the sound of it, he was guilty of holding back their recent troubles, so what else was he hiding?

FOURTEEN

Amanda made a quick call to Victim Services for Riley. Afterward, her thoughts turned to Spencer and how things would go with him. Would he lash out at her full of venom and denial, leveling accusations she was overcompensating by painting him the villain to prove she was doing her job? Or worse yet, would he confess? Either way, she and Trent had to question him. The ex-boyfriend was cleared with a quick background check.

Wes Galloway had a clean record, which didn't sway her, but his California address was more convincing of his innocence. Even if she could dismiss that, what would be his motive to kill Christine? Also, how would he have known where to target her? Riley said he was controlling, not a stalker, and it sure sounded like he'd moved on after the breakup. And while he might not have killed Christine, that relationship could have primed her to be more reactive to Spencer's explosive outburst.

Trent parked in Spencer's driveway and looked over at her. "Are you sure you're okay?"

"Not in the least." Amanda had called Malone just after

leaving Riley, wanting to get him in the loop from the start. A uniformed officer was expected to join them shortly. Spencer would be taken into Central for a chat in an interrogation room just like anyone else in his position. She had no choice but to approach this from an impartial standpoint. She tried to convince herself it was for her good and Spencer's. Once she cleared him of the murder, there would be no doubts to circle back on.

Amanda knocked on Spencer's door. When he opened it and saw her standing there with Trent, his knees buckled.

Trent moved in to assume some of Spencer's weight, to save him from falling.

"She's dead, isn't she? That's why you're back. The body that you..." Spencer went limp again, but Trent retained his hold on him.

"Spencer, we'll talk inside." Amanda wanted him seated before they got into the nightmare conversation they needed to have.

"Just tell me, Amanda," he spat, and batted Trent away from him. Spencer grabbed the doorframe to support himself.

Amanda also didn't want to deliver the news on his doorstep. Not when she knew what the future held. That the plan was to take him to Central and put him through an interrogation like any other suspect. "It's best we—"

"Amanda, talk to me."

It was just the way Spencer looked at her with round, expressive eyes that she didn't think she had much choice. "She's dead. I'm sorry."

Spencer cried out and wrapped his arms around her so tightly, it was as if he were holding on for dear life. She hugged him back, finding that she needed to buoy his weight, or he'd crumple to the ground. Only once she felt his legs steady beneath him did she draw back.

"Come on, let's go inside," she told him.

A police cruiser pulled up in front of the house, and Amanda cringed at its timing.

Spencer's arms fell to his sides while his gaze traveled over her shoulder. "Amanda, what's going on here?" His eyes met hers.

"It would be best if we spoke inside." This time she used her firm cop tone. It made anything she said sound less like an option and more of an order.

Spencer turned and went into his home, and Amanda followed. Trent held a hand up to the officer behind the wheel to motion for him to stay put.

Amanda, Trent, and Spencer returned to the living room where they had been earlier that day and even claimed the same spots and sat.

Spencer rubbed his forehead. "Tell me what happened to her. Do you know who..."

"Christine was shot three times. Twice in the chest, once in the head." Getting to the point might seem harsh, but it was kindness in disguise.

"Holy shit. So this... *this* really happened." He swallowed roughly. "Someone killed her."

"Yes. I'm sorry for your loss, Spencer." Her heart was pounding as she debated her next words. How to put it to flesh and blood he was a murder suspect? She'd stick to some facts first. "She died around ten PM on Friday night."

"I shouldn't be surprised by any of this." Spencer had the blank stare of shock. Even though adrenaline would be flooding his system and cushioning him from the full impact of this news. "I mean you had her car, her purse, her phone..."

"I need to ask where you were Friday night at that time." There was nothing easy about making this request of her half-brother. But by putting it this way, it shifted some of the onus from her to the badge. At least she hoped he would see it that way.

"Are you being serious right now, Amanda? You think that I... *that I...*"

She went rigid. "Please, answer the question."

"Here. And, no, no one can corroborate my alibi."

She overlooked the snark in his voice, saddened by what this meant. His whereabouts couldn't be verified and rule him out. "We spoke to Riley, Spencer. She told us you and Christine have been fighting." She'd leave out the part that Riley said she didn't think they had seen each other for two weeks. After all, by the young woman's own admission, she couldn't be certain.

"It was nothing. We would have gotten past it."

"Her daughter seems to think Christine was going to end things with you," Trent wedged in. "Did that happen?"

Amanda appreciated Trent handled the tough question with compassion, but Spencer seemed to miss it. He shot Trent a frosty glare.

"No. And I had no idea she was considering ending things either."

"It hurts when you're on the wrong side of a breakup," Amanda empathized, but she was also trying to draw him out.

"Except we didn't break up. Why aren't you listening to me?"

"I guess you lost your temper after a bad shift, and Christine sent you home. It was an incident with some steaks and the barbecue..." She hated being in this position, but she only had herself to blame. She had told Malone she could handle things if Spencer became a serious suspect. It was just time to live up to her word.

"You never have a bad day?" he tossed back at her.

Today ranks high among them... "They happen, but most of us don't lash out or toss steaks in the garbage."

"Was that the extent of it, Spencer?" Trent asked without allowing time for Spencer to respond to Amanda's comment.

"Of course it was. It was nothing."

Amanda wanted to believe him but didn't have the luxury of doing so. "You ever lose your temper before? Do something more violent?"

Spencer shook his head. "I don't need to sit here and listen to this."

Amanda stiffened. "You do, actually. Why didn't you mention any of this to us, Spencer? You made it sound like your relationship with Christine was solid. By not speaking up, you can see how that complicates things? A lie by omission. Did you kill Christine? Maybe she told you it was over, and you didn't agree?"

"You could have thought if you couldn't have her, then no one could," Trent said.

"It's nothing like that, and if I killed her, that would be something I'd remember," Spencer said.

His attitude was rousing her redhead temper. "Don't get smart with us. We're on your side."

"It sure doesn't feel like it."

"We're just doing our jobs," she defended.

"I called *you*, or are you forgetting that? Why would I do that if I killed her?"

There were a few seconds of silence.

"Ah, I see. You think I did that to make myself look innocent," Spencer eventually said, piecing it together.

She blinked slowly. Trent said nothing.

"Unbelievable," Spencer muttered. "So that's why the police car's out front? Are you arresting me?"

"Not yet, but you are a suspect in the murder of Christine Lane." Amanda stood. "You're going to need to come with us for further questioning."

"Go with you? Or be fed into the back of a police car like a criminal?"

"I'm sorry, Spencer, but we'll need to talk in a more official manner. For the record." The latter bit slipped out.

"Sure. Yeah, I get it, I'll go with you. But once I'm cleared, promise me you'll start putting your time and energy into finding her actual killer."

Amanda would let go of the fact he made it sound like going to the station was a choice he was making. "We'll need to collect your phone and laptop, as well. Stand up."

Spencer let out a huff as he got to his feet. "I don't know how we recover from this."

She pinched her eyes shut. "You have pride in your job, Spencer. So do I. And you might not see it yet, but my treating you like any other suspect, in any other murder investigation, is my doing you a favor."

"Excuse me for not seeing it that way."

"Come on, grab your electronics and get your shoes on. Time to go." Trent was standing there, shoulders squared.

The following moments broke Amanda's heart. Guiding Spencer out the door and into the back of a squad car. Watching Officer Wyatt drive off with him. But the worst was when Spencer turned his face away from her.

FIFTEEN

It was ten o'clock when Amanda was walking down the halls of Central toward Malone's office with Trent at her side. She was looking forward to talking to him about as much as she hated the thought of questioning her half-brother. Both were cranky, with their nights taking a turn they hadn't expected. But it was just getting started. Spencer had demanded a lawyer, and while they waited for him to show up, they dug into his record, phone, and laptop. The discoveries they made in the last hour and a half didn't make things look any better for him.

Sergeant Malone was seated behind his desk and waved them in. "His attorney here?"

"He arrived about fifteen minutes ago. He's with Spencer in Interview Room One," she told him.

"Good. I'm already late for my pillow. Nine o'clock is my typical bedtime on a school night. Lay out where we're at."

He was to the point, just as she expected from Malone at this hour. His cheeks were sagging, and he'd rather be curled up in bed than behind his desk. But who wouldn't? She'd trade being there instead of here in a heartbeat. "Trent and I have found some things..." She laid out their discoveries.

When she finished, Malone sat back and ran his hands over his short, trimmed beard. "I don't need to say it, right?"

He'd leveled his gaze on her when he asked the question, so she responded. "You don't. This doesn't look good for Spencer."

"And no alibi?"

"None that can be verified."

"Not good."

"Nope." She sighed.

"You don't need me to say this either, Amanda, but I'm going to anyway. I don't want you doing the questioning."

His statement landed like a punch in the stomach. "What?"

"This isn't up for negotiation. Trent will handle it. You can be in the room if you keep quiet. Can you promise me that?"

It felt like she was watching this take place from outside of herself. She'd proven herself thus far. She wasn't sure why he didn't trust her to go all the way with this. Even if it came down to a formal charge.

"Amanda?" Malone prompted.

"How could I just sit there?" There was no way she could promise to remain mute.

"That answers my question then. Trent will go in alone, and you'll watch from the observation room. I'll stick around with you."

As if he doesn't trust me...

Malone pushed out from his desk and pulled an ice pack from behind him before he stood, and the three of them went down the hall. Trent popped in for a look through the one-way mirror.

Spencer was seated with his arms crossed and a scowl on his face. The body language suggested defensiveness. Why couldn't he see that his being here was just procedure? If he was innocent, it would be a standard Q&A session followed by his release. Then just like he had said, they could pursue other suspects. Or more to the point, *the actual killer*, as he had put it.

But he must have known what they'd find and how it would look.

"I'm ready to go in." Trent looked at her as he spoke. She could tell he hated that Malone had benched her, but she trusted Trent with the questioning.

She nodded, still speechless.

When Trent entered the room, Spencer shook his head. "Where's Amanda?"

"Detective Steele isn't available for this interview. I'm Detective Stenson," he told the lawyer. An older gentleman whose glasses were sliding down his narrow, ski slope nose.

"Jerome Thornton," the attorney said. "It seems we're here under prejudice."

Amanda bristled, wanting to break through the glass and set the lawyer straight.

"We're here because evidence led us to your client," Trent pushed back.

The lawyer smiled tightly. "The way I understand it, the lead detective is a blood relative of my client. He feels she may be overcompensating, making a show of doing her job by accusing him of murdering his girlfriend. Surely, that's a conflict of interest and a perversion of justice."

"If any of that were true, we wouldn't be here. Detective Steele would have disregarded what we've discovered, made excuses for your client."

Amanda's heart warmed at how Trent had held his own while standing up for her.

"But isn't it more accurate to say that Christine was your client's ex-girlfriend?" Trent turned to Spencer.

Spencer's gaze shot to the one-way mirror, and it felt as if he were looking right at her. "What the hell are you—?"

His lawyer reached out with a cautionary hand.

"—talking about?" Spencer finished in a slightly softer tone while still looking at the glass.

"My client doesn't seem to know what you're talking about," Thornton said, echoing Spencer's response.

Trent reached into the folder he'd brought into the room and produced a printout. He pushed the sheet to the opposite side of the table. "That's a text message from Christine to your client last Thursday. I'll allow you time to read it." Trent sat back while Spencer picked up the page.

The message was sent from Christine to Spencer and was just one damning piece of evidence against him. CSI Keller had found it on Christine's phone and passed it along.

Spencer let go of the piece of paper. "This is... No, it's not what it looks like."

"You told us the last time you saw Christine was last Wednesday."

"Yes. And that's the truth."

"Well, I'm going to guess it didn't go well based on her message. If you haven't read it yet, I can—"

"I read it."

"For the record, Mr. Thornton, Christine told your client in a text message, 'I'm not sure how we move forward from here.'"

"So what? She changed her mind. This isn't proof she broke up with me."

"How could you know if she changed her mind? You just confirmed you haven't spoken to her since she sent the message. And there's the fact she didn't call you back or respond to your text messages. She ghosted you."

Spencer opened his mouth like he was going to say something, but snapped it shut again, clenching his jaw. His cheeks flamed red as he glared toward the one-way mirror again. Like before, she felt the gravity of his stare and felt like an ass for putting him through this. Not that she should assume that burden alone; the evidence led them here. All she was guilty of was doing the job she'd vowed to do.

"Another strange thing about all this is this text wasn't in the thread on your phone, Spencer. Can you tell us why?" Trent asked.

Spencer rubbed his forehead. "I don't have an answer for you other than I delete messages sometimes."

"Why this one?"

"You want to know? The truth is it made me angry as hell. I didn't want to see it or look at it. We've been together for a year, and she acted like she could just throw that away. Throw *me* away."

The attorney flinched at the fire of Spencer's speech but remained silent.

"But you can see how that might look? Like you were trying to make your relationship with Christine something it wasn't, so you wouldn't appear as a suspect in her murder?"

"If that's the case, I failed, didn't I? And I didn't even know she was murdered. I just couldn't reach her." Spencer added the latter part at a lower volume.

"We're just following the evidence," Trent said, matching Spencer's tone. "If you have nothing to hide, it will clear you in the end."

"It will," Spencer volleyed back, "because I didn't do this."

Trent pulled another page out of the folder, which he again set in front of Spencer. Amanda couldn't see it but knew what it would be. "This is your nine-mil Beretta, right?"

Spencer blanched. "It looks like it. I can't say if it is mine."

"It is," Trent told him.

Amanda put a hand on her stomach and cursed herself for the slip the second Malone touched her shoulder. "I'm fine," she assured him, and he retracted his arm. Finding out that Spencer had a gun registered to him had sent cold sweats over her entire body. She blew out a breath and saw Malone look at her through her peripheral vision. She hadn't been able to meet Malone's direct gaze since he blocked her from the interrogation.

"Christine Lane was shot with nine-mil rounds. Did they come from your gun?"

Spencer shook his head. "Unbelievable."

"Detective, it's on you to prove guilt, not for my client to do your job for you," the lawyer said. "After all, most American citizens exercise their right to bear arms."

"Don't worry, we will be running ballistics from this gun and comparing the markings to the bullet fragments retrieved from Christine Lane's body."

She had received an email from Rideout earlier with the full autopsy report. Most of it was a reiteration of what Liam had already told them. The addition was that Rideout had retrieved some viable bullet fragments and forwarded them to the lab.

Tears fell down Spencer's cheeks, and he swiped them away.

Amanda tried not to let herself be swayed by the display. If he were any other suspect, she wouldn't conclude such an action was one of grief. She'd entertain the likelihood it was remorse.

"We also found your membership card for a local gun range in your wallet." Trent produced the card from the folder.

"It means nothing!"

The lawyer touched Spencer's arm, but he pulled out of reach. "You're seeing what you want to see. I didn't kill Christine."

"How long have you been a member?" Trent rolled ahead as if Spencer's outburst hadn't fazed him.

"Five years."

"And do you practice often?"

"Whenever I can. I find it relaxing." Spencer was talking in a monotone like a robot.

"Then you could pull off a shot to the chest and the head from twenty feet?"

Amanda crossed her arms and hugged herself. She was the one who found the membership card.

The lawyer smiled again. "Detective, we have been patient, but just because my client may like to fire guns in his personal time that doesn't mean he shot his girlfriend. I've failed to hear any evidence that places him at the murder scene."

The attorney had struck the weak underbelly of their case against Spencer. All they had was circumstantial evidence and a potential motive. The crime scene had offered little forensically.

"As you know, Mr. Thornton, we have more than enough to hold your client while we continue our investigation."

"Why? So you can try to build a case against him? From what I've heard, you don't have enough for a foundation."

"Hardly true, but we're within our right to hold him for twenty-four hours without laying a charge."

That would allow them time to compare the markings from Spencer's gun to the fragments recovered from Christine's body. It was nauseating that Spencer would need to spend a single night in holding, but there wasn't anything she could do about that. And if he was guilty, he'd need to get used to life behind bars. *Behind bars*, her mind reiterated. When she'd brought him in she hadn't expected things would go this far.

"Would your client comply to providing a sample of his fingerprints and DNA?"

"That's a hard no, Detective," Thornton said.

"Your client's refusal doesn't make things look good for him. It would be easier if he cooperated with us—"

"Like hell," Spencer spat. "I know how the system works. There's no way I'm handing any of that over."

Amanda flinched. That's likely how he viewed her now. As part of *the system*. From the sound of it, one he saw as corrupt.

"Suit yourself then," Trent told him.

"Don't you get it? You find an iota of my DNA on Christine, then you'll pin her murder on me. But we were together. It's possible you'll find one of my hairs... or something. Everything will be twisted. I'll be one of those innocents serving life in prison."

"Have it your way, then. We'll need to get a court order," Trent said.

"Good luck with that," the lawyer said.

Trent gathered everything from the table. In the doorway, he said to Spencer, "An officer will be in to take you to a holding cell for the night."

Spencer glared at the one-way mirror again. Although he couldn't see her, she still couldn't bring herself to meet his eyes. She was numb as she headed for the door.

"Amanda?" Malone called out to her.

She waved her arm over her head and ignored Trent in the hallway. She needed to get out of here, go home, and let tonight sink in.

SIXTEEN

The heat the next morning was slightly less aggressive than yesterday, but it was still quite humid. It accentuated Amanda's headache from a horrible night's sleep, but neither the weather nor pain was going to hold her back. She walked into Central ready to tackle whatever came her way. If Spencer had killed Christine, she had confidence in herself to see this through.

She dropped behind her desk and found a to-go cup from Hannah's Diner there, along with a sticky note.

Figured you'd appreciate the coffee. We have a search warrant for Spencer's house. You can meet me there, if you wish. Trent.

The sentiment was nice, but she didn't appreciate he felt the need to coddle her. Not that she had it in her to turn down a Hannah's coffee. A free one, at that.

She got up, taking the coffee she'd brought in and the new one, and headed toward the station's lot. *There are worse things than double-fisting Hannah's...*

"Detective Steele," Malone called out, stopping her steps.

She turned around to see him curling his finger at her in a

come here motion. She took a steadying breath and followed him to his office.

Malone sat at his desk just as she cleared the doorway. "Shut the door."

She did as he directed. When she woke up that morning, she expected she couldn't put off a conversation with Malone for long. She had just hoped it was after another coffee or two. She set the two cups on his desk.

He pointed at the coffees. "One for me?"

"You can have this one." She pointed at the one Trent bought her. "It's black, so you can add your milk and sugar."

Malone gave her the flicker of a smile. "I shouldn't. Too much caffeine, my heart starts pounding and my stomach turns to acid."

Amanda was smarter than to suggest it might have to do with his age.

"I'm guessing you didn't get a good night's sleep," Malone said.

"Not really." She'd leave it at that.

"How are you feeling this morning?"

"Better than last night." Not exactly enthusiastic sounding, but it was what she could muster.

"Glad to hear it. Trent's over at Spencer's right now with a couple CSIs, executing a search warrant."

"He left me a note to join him."

"Depending on what we find there, we'll determine if a warrant for his financials is supported."

"To see if we can confirm the purchase of a tarp and rope?"

"Precisely. Spencer's DNA and prints have also been collected and forwarded to the lab."

"Trent got a warrant approved for that?"

"Nope, he ended up convincing Spencer to volunteer it."

"Oh. Wow. He sounded dead set against it last night."

"I think he wants this all over with, sooner than later."

He's not the only one... Just knowing was better than existing in limbo. But they were at the mercy of the lab while they waited for the ballistics testing to be done.

"There is no shame in backing out of this case, Amanda. No one would blame you."

"I'm fine, Scott. I promise." She didn't dredge out her sergeant's given name often, but his concern felt personal.

"Should that change, I want you to let me know."

"I will," she told him and stood. "How's your back, by the way?"

"I've got an appointment with your chiropractor this morning. I'll let you know."

She nodded. "Are you sure you don't want the coffee?" She hadn't missed how he'd continued to ogle it when he thought she wasn't looking. With her calling him out, he didn't bother trying to hide the fact. "Here, take it." Amanda lifted the fresh one from Trent and gifted it to him.

"Thanks. Hannah's is the best."

"No argument here." She smiled at him as she left his office, but the expression was brief.

Emma Blair came through the doors and stormed down the hallway toward her. Spencer must have called his mother at some point overnight or had his lawyer notify her.

"How dare you drag my son in like a criminal," she roared.

Amanda's cheeks heated. The accusation wasn't much of a surprise, but the ambush was jolting. "Emma, please, listen to me." She reached out to touch the investigator's shoulder, but she drew back and held up her hands.

"Please, keep your hands off me."

There was no way Amanda could postpone this conversation. It didn't matter how much she would have liked to join Trent at Spencer's house and get on with following the evidence to wherever it led. "I think we should talk."

"What you *should* do is release my son," Emma spat.

Amanda wasn't doing this here in front of an audience. She gestured for Emma to follow her and took her to a soft interview room. It was normally used for questioning victims or their families. Once inside, she shut the door behind them.

Emma remained standing while Amanda sat on the couch.

"You're just going to sit there?" Emma said with heat.

"It seems you have things to say to me."

"You bet I do. You arrested him? He didn't do this."

"There haven't been any charges laid against him, but he is a person of interest—"

"A *suspect* you are holding in a cell."

"Which we are within our right to do."

Emma huffed out a breath.

"We follow the evidence, and if he's innocent, more will turn up that leads us away from him."

"*Leads you away*...?" Emma dropped into a chair.

"It pains me that we're here, Emma, trust me. But what we have so far doesn't look good for him."

"Then you're not looking at it right. I'll have you know I called your father during the night, asking him to talk some sense into you, but he wants to stay out of this. He says he trusts you to do the right thing. Now you're telling me to trust you. How can I?"

The question stung. It superseded the fact that Blair had gone to her father. That was crossing a line no matter which way one viewed it. "I've never given you a reason to doubt that you can."

"Not until now. Just let my son go, Amanda. Catch the real killer."

Amanda shook her head. "You know I can't release him at this point."

"Because you think he did this."

"It doesn't matter what I think."

"What do you have on him?"

"You know I can't tell you that."

Emma scrunched up her face into an ugly mask. "Doesn't it bother you, at all, that while he's in a cell, the killer is out there free?"

"Emma, I've told you all I can, but you must know that I'm just following where the evidence takes me."

Emma's shoulders sagged. "Then you're either on the wrong trail, or someone is framing him."

"He lied to us." It was the only thing that Amanda was comfortable disclosing.

Emma stiffened. "No, that's a lie."

"It's not."

"My son isn't a liar."

"He held back information from us, Emma."

"If he did, I'm sure he had his reasons."

It was clear no amount of talking would break down the walls of defense Emma had erected around her son. "I'm sorry that you can't see my side in this, and for how you feel..." *Like I'm the enemy... untrustworthy...* "But I need to go. Please let me do my job."

"Amanda, if you have any doubts, and I mean *any*, let him go. You owe it to him to see this through." Emma left the room.

I owe it to him...? She wasn't sure why. He was the product of an affair, an only child, alienated from his birth father, but how was any of that Amanda's fault? She sat there, staring after Emma, hot tears filling her eyes. She was quaking from the storm that moved in, assaulted, and beat her. All she was endeavoring to do was her job. She wasn't naive to think it would win her any popularity contests, but when it rallied against the personal like now it was hell.

No shame in backing out...

Malone's words resurfaced, but surrendering wasn't part of her makeup. She'd dig so deep that when this case was closed, the guilty would be behind bars. Even if that was Spencer.

SEVENTEEN

Amanda's phone rang as she turned down the street for Spencer's house. She answered after seeing Trent's name on the display.

"There you are. Did you get my note?"

"And your gift, thank you. I should be at Spencer's within the minute."

"Okay. See you soon."

He didn't sound surprised she was coming over. Though she had debated whether it was a smart idea after Emma's attack on her at Central. Amanda was still shaking. And how dare she talk to her father? As if he could wrangle her under control. She'd also be lying to say she wasn't insulted that Emma questioned her trustworthiness. As if she were one to preach from that pulpit. Emma had slept with a married man. Yet despite all that, Amanda hoped the hurt caused by the interaction would wash away and not fester for long.

Amanda parked in front of Spencer's house, just as Trent was walking out the front door. He met her halfway down the walkway.

"We're just wrapping up, but there's nothing in his house or vehicle that's incriminating."

"That's good news, at least."

"And there's still the hope his gun won't be a match. Hopefully, we'll know more later today."

"Hopefully," she parroted. "Malone brought me up to speed. You've been quite busy this morning, convincing Spencer to part with his prints and DNA, and getting them all sent to the lab."

"Just doing what I can." His voice turned soft, and she couldn't handle that. Like he was showing her pity. It was the coffee all over again.

"Speaking of, thank you for handling the interview with Spencer so well. I could have done it if Malone hadn't vetoed me."

He waved a hand. "I have no doubt, and there's no need to thank me."

His humble response made her all the more appreciative he was her partner. "I would have been here sooner, but Emma came into Central and basically cornered me." If Trent hadn't been so kind, she might have been able to keep this to herself, but he made her want to open up to him. It was crazy to think she had initially resisted being paired with anyone.

"My God, Amanda. I'm sorry I wasn't there."

"Don't be silly. It was bound to happen at some point, and I don't need anyone to fight my battles for me." She saw the irony considering he had fought one last night for her. Though not on her say-so.

"Oh, I'm well aware of that. Just if I were there, maybe she wouldn't have gone at you so hard."

"You know Blair. She's not exactly soft and timid. Your being there wouldn't have made an ounce of difference. I can only imagine what it would be like in her place. I brought her son in under suspicion of murder and had him spend the night."

"Technically, I did that part."

"If we're talking *technically*, then circumstantial evidence against him did it."

"Speaking of, she must know we're only following the evidence."

"I tried explaining that, but she didn't want to hear it or believe it."

"Well, I'm not sold on Spencer doing this. He explained deleting the text message, and I get that. I can even understand his pride holding him back from sharing how they were having a rough time recently."

"You should have heard him when he first called about Christine. He was genuinely upset that he couldn't reach her. I just can't see him shooting her three times, wrapping her in a tarp, and pushing her under a bed."

"Yeah, that's another level. And Spencer's not the only one who had a complicated relationship with Christine. We both felt we could eliminate the ex-boyfriend, but there are the ex-husband and the rival agent, Marcy Maxwell, we haven't fully considered yet."

"Not that the ex-husband sounded suspect to me. He's moved on from what Riley said, even married again."

"How a kid sees their father can be different from how things are."

"True enough." Amanda could agree from experience. She'd always idolized her father, wanted to follow his career path. Then she found out about the buried affair and the existence of a half-brother. Some underlying resentment remained at how he could do that to her mother, her siblings... her. "We're still waiting on ballistics, and we can't just afford to stall the investigation if it turns out Spencer is innocent. Let's talk with the ex-husband and Marcy Maxwell."

"I'll just let the CSIs know that I'm leaving."

"And I say we cut back to one car. Meet me at the station, and we'll head out together from there."

"You got it." Trent walked back into the house while Amanda headed out.

On her drive to the station, she thought more about her father's transgression. She'd say she'd forgiven him, but forgetting was the harder bit. It wasn't his fault that she'd put him on a pedestal, elevated him above being human. When it came down to it, he was a mere mortal of flesh and blood, capable of hurting even those he loved. The strength of his character was revealed in the aftermath. He'd ended things with Emma Blair and stood by his wife and five children. As she thought when speaking to Blair, Spencer had gotten the shaft. He was raised by Emma's husband, loved as his own from what she knew, but he'd never had a chance of developing a relationship with his biological father. This had to contribute to the underlying tension between her and Spencer. The one wedge that kept them apart. And that was before this case. Was it too much to hope their relationship could ever be mended and allowed to grow?

EIGHTEEN

Amanda rode shotgun while Trent drove them to Gerald and Stephanie Lane's address. "By the way, thank you for the coffee."

"You already said that, but you're welcome. I'm glad you got it, and Detective Hudson didn't steal it off your desk."

"I wouldn't put it past him, but I might have regifted it."

"You gave away a Hannah's coffee?"

"Well, Malone gave me these eyes..."

Trent laughed as he parked in front of a modest bungalow. "This is it."

The front garden was full of overgrown hostas, and it brought back a memory of digging some up with her late husband. Getting those suckers out of the ground sure had worked up a sweat.

Trent rang the doorbell, and Gerald Lane came to the door wearing a gray T-shirt adorned with some baby spit-up. While those days were long gone for Amanda, she remembered them well. That sweet, putrid smell was her signature scent for months.

"Detectives Steele and Stenson?" Riley wedged into the

doorway next to her father. He moved to the side to accommodate her.

"Hi, Riley," Amanda told her. To Gerald, she said, "We'd just like a few moments of your time."

"Ah, sure." Gerald stepped back into the home with a protective arm around Riley. "It's tragic what happened to Christine. When Riley told me, I was shocked. Still am, truth be told." He spoke while taking them to the living room. "Sit wherever you'd like."

Father and daughter sat on the couch together. The faint cries of a newborn baby traveled from another part of the house. They were desperate and strangled, as if the baby was still experimenting with their voice.

"She'll be fine. Steph's with her," Gerald told them as if he expected they'd know who Steph was.

Amanda and Trent each dropped into a chair. There was room for one more on the couch, and another chair, but it was covered with baby toys. A playpen was in the corner of the room.

"I assume Riley told you everything?" Amanda wanted to ascertain they were on the same page.

"Christine was shot." Gerald shook his head. "It's unbelievable that someone would do such a horrible thing."

And he doesn't know about the tarp or that she was shot three times... "I imagine it would be hard to think of anyone hurting someone you loved." She chose her words with intention, to gauge his feelings for his ex-wife.

"I loved Christine. We just weren't meant to be a couple."

Amanda noticed the past tense. "Then you stopped loving her at one point?"

Gerald shifted his gaze to Trent. When he faced Amanda again, Gerald's expression was pained. "Never. I'll always love her. She gave me Riley."

EIGHTEEN

Amanda rode shotgun while Trent drove them to Gerald and Stephanie Lane's address. "By the way, thank you for the coffee."

"You already said that, but you're welcome. I'm glad you got it, and Detective Hudson didn't steal it off your desk."

"I wouldn't put it past him, but I might have regifted it."

"You gave away a Hannah's coffee?"

"Well, Malone gave me these eyes..."

Trent laughed as he parked in front of a modest bungalow. "This is it."

The front garden was full of overgrown hostas, and it brought back a memory of digging some up with her late husband. Getting those suckers out of the ground sure had worked up a sweat.

Trent rang the doorbell, and Gerald Lane came to the door wearing a gray T-shirt adorned with some baby spit-up. While those days were long gone for Amanda, she remembered them well. That sweet, putrid smell was her signature scent for months.

"Detectives Steele and Stenson?" Riley wedged into the

doorway next to her father. He moved to the side to accommodate her.

"Hi, Riley," Amanda told her. To Gerald, she said, "We'd just like a few moments of your time."

"Ah, sure." Gerald stepped back into the home with a protective arm around Riley. "It's tragic what happened to Christine. When Riley told me, I was shocked. Still am, truth be told." He spoke while taking them to the living room. "Sit wherever you'd like."

Father and daughter sat on the couch together. The faint cries of a newborn baby traveled from another part of the house. They were desperate and strangled, as if the baby was still experimenting with their voice.

"She'll be fine. Steph's with her," Gerald told them as if he expected they'd know who Steph was.

Amanda and Trent each dropped into a chair. There was room for one more on the couch, and another chair, but it was covered with baby toys. A playpen was in the corner of the room.

"I assume Riley told you everything?" Amanda wanted to ascertain they were on the same page.

"Christine was shot." Gerald shook his head. "It's unbelievable that someone would do such a horrible thing."

And he doesn't know about the tarp or that she was shot three times... "I imagine it would be hard to think of anyone hurting someone you loved." She chose her words with intention, to gauge his feelings for his ex-wife.

"I loved Christine. We just weren't meant to be a couple."

Amanda noticed the past tense. "Then you stopped loving her at one point?"

Gerald shifted his gaze to Trent. When he faced Amanda again, Gerald's expression was pained. "Never. I'll always love her. She gave me Riley."

Tears spilled down the teen's cheeks, and she tucked into her father's side. Again, he wrapped his arm around her.

"We understand you got divorced five years ago," Trent began while taking out his notepad and pen.

"That's right."

"Did the marriage end amicably?" Trent held his pen over a blank page.

"I mean, it was rocky at first. Both of us had to figure out who we were apart. We were high school sweethearts. But we came to realize that we were better as friends than lovers."

"Then you stayed in touch, even until recently?"

"We spoke sometimes. The most recent was a couple of months ago. Christine came by with some of Riley's baby clothes and other things. That playpen was Riley's." Gerald gestured toward the one in the corner.

"Did the relationship you maintained with Christine bother your new wife?" Many families were torn apart and stitched back together in a different fashion. Stepchildren were a common reality in the modern world, and people made new relationships work despite baggage from previous ones.

"Steph and Mom got along," Riley said.

Amanda nodded but looked at Gerald for confirmation. It would be best if Riley wasn't here for this conversation, but Amanda wasn't about to kick her out of the room.

"Riley's right. Steph looked up to Christine, and she's having a tough time with her death too."

A woman with blond hair swept back into a loose bun stepped into the doorway of the living room, cradling a baby. She was in her late twenties. Gerald had traded Christine for a younger model, but that assessment soured Amanda's gut. It made more sense why the woman would look up to Christine though. She was older and had been through things that Stephanie hadn't encountered yet. Like being a mother.

Gerald rushed up and cleared the remaining chair of the baby toys. "Here you go, sweetheart."

"Thanks." She sat down with the baby. "Hi, I'm Stephanie. I overheard Gerald. Christine's death is hard to grasp. She was..." Her chin quivered.

Amanda gave it a few seconds before prompting Stephanie. "What was she?"

"Just such a nice, warm person. Active in the community and loved by everyone who met her." She grabbed her baby's tiny hand, letting the baby's fingers wrap around her thumb. The intimate moment caused Amanda's heart to pinch.

"How was she active?" Trent asked.

"She suffered an experience when she was younger." Stephanie's voice was low, and her gaze flicked to Gerald, who had returned to the couch. "Can I tell them?"

"Sure."

"She was mugged at gunpoint when she went on a trip to NYC. She was in her twenties then?" Stephanie looked at Gerald.

"Twenty-two," he confirmed. "Her sister still lives there."

"We never knew that she had a sister." Amanda remembered searching Christine's background for familial contacts and hadn't seen any siblings.

"Well, Lori isn't blood," Gerald said. "She was chosen family."

"So she was mugged...?" Amanda prompted Stephanie to pick up where she'd left off.

"Yes, and she saw a therapist about it, and they helped her see she could use her traumatic experience for good." The baby fussed, Stephanie swayed her, and soon after the child quieted again. "She volunteered with a local victims' group and was a sounding board for people."

"How selfless." Amanda was impressed by how Christine

had made the best out of an ugly situation. When Amanda had lost her husband and daughter, she detested people saying there was a silver lining in everything. To find one in the death of a loved one was near impossible. But if she dug deep, she'd say that she discovered her strength and resilience. Qualities that she'd have preferred remained secret if that meant she kept her family.

"Do you have any idea who did this to her?" Stephanie asked.

"Not yet." Amanda saw that as the truth. "We were wondering if either of you might know if Christine had any enemies or a beef with anyone."

"No one I'm aware of," Gerald said. "But I wasn't in regular contact with her."

"She never mentioned anyone to me," Stephanie offered.

"Or me, except for what I already told you," Riley put in. "Did you talk with Spencer?"

Amanda met the teen's eyes when she responded. "We have."

"And?" Riley dragged out.

"And that's all I can say at this time," Amanda said, standing behind the sanctity of the investigation and in defense of her half-brother.

"Riley, you can't think that Spencer did this." Stephanie was drilling Riley with a look that was hard to read. Her eyes were softened out of concern, but there was also judgment in them.

"They were fighting. He has a temper." Riley thrust out her chin and shook her head.

This was the first time Amanda witnessed any discord between Riley and her stepmother.

"It takes more than a temper to kill someone," Stephanie said.

Riley wasn't even turning the woman's way anymore. Her

eyes were fixed across the room, and from what Amanda could tell, on nothing in particular.

"It sounds like you might know Spencer," Trent said to Stephanie.

"I've met him on a few occasions. He seemed perfectly nice to me."

"And that's where you're wrong. You weren't always around."

Amanda felt Trent bristle from across the room. She recoiled. "You don't think Spencer's a nice person?"

"He has a temper. I told you that," Riley spat.

"That doesn't mean he's not a nice person. He must have made your mother happy. They were together for some time." That was Amanda keeping her emotions in check, sticking to the facts as she knew them.

"Yeah, I guess so."

"People do disagree sometimes," Stephanie wedged in. "Even your dad and I fight. We can get pretty loud too."

"She's right, sweetie." Gerald reached for his daughter's hand. Riley pulled back and stormed out of the room. "You'll have to excuse her," Gerald said.

Amanda shook her head. "It's fine. She's going through a lot right now. All of you are. We appreciate your time and are sorry for your loss." She stood to leave, and Trent followed.

She loaded into the passenger seat and did up her belt while Trent turned on the vehicle.

"Well, we can rule them out," Trent said. "There's no apparent motive for them, and they don't seem to think Spencer killed Christine."

"Nope. They also made it sound like Christine was an incredible person. She helped victims of crimes despite her full schedule as a real estate agent. Which brings us to our next stop..."

"Best Home Realty? You got it."

NINETEEN

Sierra looked up when Amanda entered the Best Homes Realty office with Trent. Her eyes were wide and wet, and her complexion was pale.

"Detectives? Did you find Christine?"

Amanda felt compassion for Sierra living in limbo, but yesterday had been nonstop. "Unfortunately, we did."

Sierra gasped a loud sob, drawing Art out from his office.

"What happened?" He walked up behind Sierra, with his hand hovering above his employee's shoulder shy of making contact.

"Christine was found murdered at the Charmed Court listing." To the point was always the best way to handle things like this.

Sierra looked over her shoulder at her boss and sprung from her chair, retreating down a hallway.

"You'll have to excuse her. She's young, and this is quite the shock." Art rubbed his jaw.

Amanda didn't think age had anything to do with how a person took this type of news. "We can imagine it is. No one is prepared for this. We're sorry for your loss."

"Thank you. But, just wow, this is a lot to process. How is Riley doing? I assume she knows."

Amanda nodded. "She was informed yesterday. The road ahead for her will be rough."

"I can't imagine all she's feeling. That poor girl." Art shook his head. "I'm going to have to figure out how to let Christine's clients know about this. How does one even go about something like that?"

"Just be honest. You can mention Christine has passed unexpectedly, but I'd recommend leaving out the part that she was murdered," Amanda suggested.

"I see how that might be best."

Amanda let a few beats of silence pass before she spoke again. "Since we're here, Detective Stenson and I would like to talk to Marcy Maxwell, if she's in." There was no reason to disclose talking with her was their primary reason for this visit.

Art's face scrunched up. "Marcy? Why?"

She could take advantage of this minor detour. "What was her relationship like with Christine?" She'd take what Art told them and compare it to what Marcy might say.

"Competitive."

Amanda's gaze went to the agent-of-the-year portraits, and it had Art glancing at them, back at her.

"You can't think that Marcy killed Christine over some title and a picture on the wall." Art's voice was low.

"I'm sure there's far more to being agent of the year," Amanda said.

"Well, there's the honor and prestige that goes with it. The accomplishment is also publicized in a realty magazine."

"Is there any monetary bonus?" If there was, it became even more understandable why the competition was fierce.

"No, but the top agent needs to have earned the most money for the firm."

"Mr. Beasley, could you elaborate on your answer to Detective Steele's question about Christine's relationship with Marcy, beyond competitive?" Trent asked.

"I'm sensing the real question you want answered is do I see Marcy killing Christine? If so, then no. Not at all. But that listing on Charmed Court was a sore spot for her."

Amanda glanced at Trent, curious if it was enough of one to motivate murder. The voicemails Marcy had left hadn't sounded cordial. "How so?"

"The homeowner is some high-powered lawyer, who is eager to sell her home, and she demanded the best. Sierra told her that Marcy was our agent of the year last year and put her through to Marcy. This call came on a Friday, though, and Marcy wasn't in any position to accept the call or return it."

"Why not?" Art had told Amanda yesterday that a real estate agent's livelihood depended on their phones.

"A random, fluke thing. Marcy left early on that Friday and took a last-minute flight south for the weekend. By the time Marcy returned to the office on Monday, the homeowner had called again. This time demanding to speak with someone who would get the job done."

Amanda could fill in where that had wound up. "Which is how Christine came to get the listing."

"That's right. I'm just grateful the homeowner called again. At least the firm received the listing. She could have gone somewhere else."

"And now that Christine's dead, who will handle the account?" Amanda gave herself one guess.

"Marcy." Art spoke slowly.

"Then Marcy benefits from Christine's death." Now *that* strengthened Marcy's motive to kill her.

"Yes, yes, I suppose so."

Trent angled his head, his gaze on Art. "Can you tell us how Marcy handled it when she first realized she missed out on the listing?"

"I can, and it wasn't well. But still, I'm going to repeat myself here. I could never see her killing Christine over it."

Amanda would determine that. "Is Marcy in the office?"

"Not at the moment. I could call her—"

"Don't worry about it." Sierra returned sniffling with puffy eyes. "Marcy should be here any minute."

As if on cue, the front door opened and a woman in her late thirties walked in with an aura of confidence and superiority. A huge purse was hooked over one of her shoulders, but it wasn't the weight of it that had her stopping in place. She'd set her gaze on Amanda and Trent while never meeting their eyes.

"Ms. Maxwell," Amanda said, recognizing her from the framed photo. "I'm Detective Steele, and this is Detective Stenson. We have some questions for you concerning Christine Lane."

Marcy adjusted the strap of her bag. "What about? Did you find her?"

"She was murdered," Sierra spat out, and Amanda winced. She'd have preferred to break that news herself.

"She was *what?*" Marcy's eyes widened before she turned them on Amanda. Her mouth parted. No words came out.

Art and Sierra remained quiet now.

"It would be best if we could speak somewhere private," Amanda told the real estate agent.

"You can use the conference room, Marcy," Art told her.

"Ah, sure, this way." Marcy took them to a fair-sized office with a table and six chairs. She set her huge bag on a chair and sank into the one next to it.

"We understand that you and Christine had a bit of a rivalry going," Amanda began.

"Sure. But you said she's dead... *murdered?* Are you sure it was her? Sometimes people get it wrong."

Amanda blamed shock for such an oddball reaction. "We are, yes. She was found inside the house on Charmed Court."

Shadows passed over Marcy's eyes, and she licked her lips.

"We heard that listing was going to be yours." Amanda laid the bait to see if it would get a nibble.

"It should have been."

"And why wasn't it?" It would be interesting if she told them the truth as they just heard it from Art or made up her own version.

Marcy gave them the same account, and added, "When Christine got the call, she should have put it over to me. But she didn't. It wasn't fair. Dominique Sharp tried to reach me first."

"But you weren't available, so Ms. Sharp did what she had to. She wanted to sell her house," Trent pointed out.

Marcy shrugged back into her chair and crossed her arms.

"Why are you so uncomfortable?" Amanda asked.

"Because I know what you're getting at here."

Amanda gestured toward Marcy. "Which is?"

She stared in Amanda's eyes. "You know what? Never mind. I know what I've done and haven't done. And I'm not going to candy-coat things just because she's dead. Christine took a lot of pleasure in nabbing that listing."

With what they'd learned about Christine, she didn't sound vindictive, but her relationship with Marcy may have brought it out in her. Amanda could imagine that Marcy would make quite a rival in selling homes. "And how did that make you feel?"

"Angry. But also determined. She might have gotten the listing, but I was going to sell the house. But I guess now I know why she never returned my calls. I'm assuming you heard them."

Both Amanda and Trent nodded.

"I admit leaving them didn't show me in the best light, but look at it from my side. She snatched the listing from me and then was ignoring my request to show the house."

"Not *ignoring*. She was dead," Amanda corrected.

"Which I realize now. I didn't know that when I left the voicemails. All I knew was she was AWOL yesterday... But I swear I didn't kill her."

"Yet you just admitted to knowing she was missing yesterday. Why not reach out to us and mention these voicemails? Get ahead of things? Were you hoping we wouldn't want to speak with you?" If Marcy had killed Christine, she had to know the police would get around to her. Had she failed to realize how keeping silent would make her look like she was trying to hide away?

"I thought about telling you, but why would I? I just figured she'd show up. Again, it's not like I knew she was murdered."

"Where were you Friday night between ten and eleven o'clock?" Trent asked.

Marcy slipped him a frosty stare. "You suspect I killed her?"

"We're just talking right now, Ms. Maxwell," Amanda cut in. "But we need to know your whereabouts."

"I was at my friend's place for an evening pool party. I got into the cocktails and ended up having too many. You can call her. She'll tell you I passed out and spent the night."

The woman was about Amanda's age, and she'd long grown out of getting drunk and crashing at a friend's house. But to each their own. "Her name and number?"

"Caleigh." Marcy took out her phone and rattled off the number. "Try her now. I swear, she'll confirm what I just told you."

Trent punched the digits into his phone. A few seconds later, he was announcing himself as a detective with the Prince William County PD and asking about Friday night. He ended the call with a "thank you" and pocketed his phone again. He nodded at Amanda.

"See?" Marcy flailed a hand toward Trent. "I told you the truth. Christine and I might have had a strained relationship, but I never would have killed her. It's not even something that's ever entered my mind. In fact, if anything, the competition between us made me a better agent, more ambitious. I respected her for that much."

Amanda stood. "Thank you for your time, Ms. Maxwell, and we're sorry for your loss."

With that, she left the room with Trent, and they returned to the car.

"All right, back to zero suspects," he said, starting the engine.

She appreciated he was now running on the assumption that the ballistics on Spencer's gun would clear him. "That we are. I say we go back to Central and dig through Christine's full call history. We track down all the numbers and read all her emails. It will take a lot of work, but…"

"It could be worth it."

TWENTY

Amanda and Trent picked up cheeseburgers from Petey's Patties and brought them back to Central. Amanda savored every bite and was still thinking a couple hours later how the comfort food had hit the spot.

She and Trent combed through the data from Christine's phone history, which was sent over from her service provider. So far nothing had flagged. A closer look at Spencer's phone revealed several photographs taken of him and Christine. One as recently as two weeks ago. Christine was smiling next to him, the expression touching her eyes. Unless she was an award-winning actor, her happiness was genuine. There were likely to be many more such pictures on Christine's device, but it was with the CSIs in Manassas. And Gerald and Stephanie Lane made a solid point. Even if disagreements between couples became heated, both parties usually lived to talk about them.

"I'm not getting anywhere. You?" Trent looked over the partition between them.

"Nope." Movement on her screen caught her attention and had her looking. A new email from CSI Stuart had filtered into her inbox. "I might fall over..."

"What?"

"CSI Stuart emailed me, and I didn't have to follow up." Maybe that wasn't a fair judgment to make, as she'd only worked with the woman one other time. But it had been painful. She and Keller had taken their time processing a child's bedroom, and even after finding marks outside a window, Stuart had refused to conclude it indicated a break-in. Her argument was there were no scuffs or damage to the window itself. The way Amanda saw it, at some point one needs to use common sense and draw a conclusion.

"What is she saying?" Trent got up and joined her in her cubicle.

Amanda clicked on the message and read off the highlights. "There were no DNA tags on the brown hairs taken from the bottom of the vacuum, and the tarp was clean. No fingerprints, touch DNA, or footwear prints. The house, too, was clean. They searched the house for a chemical that matched the smell and came up empty."

"So the killer arrived with the tarp, rope, and cleaner. That's one premeditated murder right there."

"Yep. CSI Keller also told me that she found the victim's laptop on the back seat of her Lexus and accessed it. Nothing flagged in a search of her browsing history and emails as being relevant to her murder." Amanda sat back, having reached the end of the updates. There was nothing said about the bullet fragments. As she was about to shoot back an email asking about that, a fresh one came in from Stuart with the subject *Ballistics*. "Here we go..." She skimmed the message and sat back, letting out a deep breath. "Spencer's gun isn't a match. We can release him."

"That's great news."

"That it is." Though in one way it was bittersweet. He'd suffered all he had as an innocent man. But what choice did she have? "Stuart said that the markings on the fragments suggest they came from a Glock. She can't get more specific than that and provide a model because many of their guns leave the same rifling marks. There are also some other striations that lead her to believe a cheap silencer was used."

"I'm telling ya, something is off here. Three taps and now we have a silencer... Even a cheap one." He pierced her eyes with his.

She shook her head. "I know what you're thinking, but let's dig more into what we have."

"We don't have much. We haven't turned up anyone who had a motive to kill Christine Lane. Meanwhile, her murder suggests premeditation."

"We could speak to the people in her victims' support group, see if any of them offer a unique perspective. She could have pushed her nose in somewhere it wasn't appreciated. A perp felt threatened and came after her."

"That's one route that could involve a lot of time and get us nowhere. I say we start with reading reports from canvassing officers on Charmed Court. A neighbor they interviewed might have heard or seen something."

"We can check the system, see what's there."

Officers needed to enter their notes at the end of each shift before heading out.

"I'll call the uniformed sergeant on duty and get the officer names who went out." Trent returned to his cubicle to make the call.

"I'll get Spencer released." She got on the phone with Malone to get that put into motion. When she hung up, a weight lifted off her only to be replaced by another one. How was she ever going to mend her relationship with Spencer? Was it even possible?

Trent spoke over the partition. "Wyatt, Brandt, and Jensen covered the neighborhood. You review Wyatt's notes, and I'll take Brandt's. Whoever finishes first wins the prize of reading Jensen's interviews."

"You really know how to motivate a person," she teased before digging in. The first four people Wyatt spoke to had nothing to offer. She started the last one. Her stomach was sinking, hope leaving her, until she got further in. "Trent. We might have an eyewitness."

"Wow, really?"

"Get over here." Once he stood beside her, she pointed at her monitor and summarized the report. "A neighbor, Paris Dobson, saw a *late-night* jogger pass in front of Sharp's house and then double back and run in place out front for a bit."

"That's all?" His dry tone sapped some of her enthusiasm.

"It might be enough. This was around nine thirty. Not what I'd call late night, but..."

"It fits the timeline. Christine died within the hour. But a jogger?"

"Let me keep reading..." She'd stopped when she reached the description of this person. "It was a woman dressed in spandex shorts and a baggy T-shirt, with a backpack." Amanda scanned the entry and picked up a bit later. "Dobson never saw this woman around the neighborhood before. She didn't remember seeing any strange vehicles in the area either. But a woman, Trent." She wasn't sure why she felt the need to stress that when Spencer was already absolved.

"It seems absurd that a jogger would wear a backpack on a run through residential neighborhoods. If she was seen hiking through a long trail or woods, then, yeah, I might see it."

"So let's say this mystery jogger is our killer. A baggy shirt could conceal a gun and holster, and the backpack could hold the tarp, rope, and cleaner. Then upon her exit, she'd have a bag to carry out any evidence like rags or whatever she used to clean up after herself."

"But we can't overlook that."

Amanda was confused until he pointed toward the screen, drawing her eye to the last line of Wyatt's report.

The eyewitness seems wishy-washy about what she saw. Not wanting to commit to her statement.

That could explain why Wyatt hadn't called this in. "I still say we talk with this woman and feel her out for ourselves. Wyatt would have seen her when the situation was fresh. It would be a lot for anyone to take in. Dobson's nerves at the time might have prevented her from committing to her statement."

"Could be."

"Did you get anything from Brandt's report, or have you finished?"

"Just before you got me over here. According to him, none of the houses he visited had any doorbell cam footage for Friday night around the time of the murder."

"Which is strange. Wyatt noted the same. He also commented the neighborhood doesn't have CCTV."

"Even if there was, the county doesn't record. It's live feed only. So there's no way to verify this jogger even exists outside of Dobson's statement."

"It looks that way. We might get lucky with Jensen. He could have found a house with a working doorbell cam."

Trent's jaw tightened, and his body became tense. "I just can't help feeling like we're missing something here. Something huge."

She couldn't let herself get sucked into that feeling. "You know what? Leave Jensen to me. I'll call if there's anything earth shattering. You go home, call it a day."

"If you're sure."

"I am. Go." It didn't need to be said, but he'd clocked hours after she'd left last night and got an early start today. She owed him.

"Good night."

"Night."

After watching him walk away, she read Jensen's notes. Unfortunately, they offered nothing actionable or useful to the investigation. That left Dobson's statement as their strongest lead at this point. But even if there was a mystery jogger hanging around Charmed Court on Friday night, was she the killer they were after?

TWENTY-ONE

Amanda picked up a small pizza on the way home to carry on the tradition of Pizza Tuesdays as she and Zoe marked the day. For them it was an act of rebellion against the rest of North America's Taco Tuesdays. She ate two slices on the couch and considered calling Carter, but her body craved sleep. The sitting around only amplified that desire. She pushed herself until nine o'clock before turning out the lights and heading to bed.

She drifted off quickly but jolted awake from a vivid nightmare in the wee hours. A woman cloaked in black fired a gun on her three times in quick succession. She didn't even have a chance to respond. Then Amanda was outside of herself looking down on Christine Lane's dead body from above. There were two bullet holes in her chest and one in her forehead. Blood drained from the wounds, seeping from her chest and forehead. It trailed down the bridge of her nose and off the point of her chin.

Amanda was left catching her breath. It didn't matter that the sequences didn't make any logical sense. It didn't take a therapist to determine the source of the dream.

Three times... An execution... Like a hit...

Those words floated up from her subconscious. Phrases from the last two days of the investigation.

Three taps and now we have a silencer... Trent's words from yesterday.

What if his implication was closer to the truth than she wanted to accept?

She made out the time on her alarm clock. 2:05 AM. *The witching hour.* Chills spilled over her legs and arms and had her burrowing beneath the covers. She'd blame it on the energetic residue from her nightmare.

Amanda lay there, staring at the ceiling, letting her heart rate come down. But it was hard to shake the imagery or the message.

Three times... An execution... Like a hit...

Even assuming a mystery jogger existed *and* was the killer, how could she have known Christine would be in the house on Charmed Court Friday night? She could be a stalker they hadn't uncovered yet, but even so, why choose to target her there? This woman would know Christine was there to show clients the house.

But what if she and Trent had been investigating from the wrong angle this entire time? They hadn't been able to find anyone who wanted Christine Lane dead. What if someone else was the true target?

The homeowner, Dominique Sharp, was a lawyer. It was a career that made enemies more readily than a real estate agent. The woman was also abrasive, based on Amanda's first impressions, and she doubted that opinion would lessen with further encounters.

And Dominique's trip to Washington was last-minute...

If the mystery jogger was their killer, the timing would suggest she was around when Christine showed up at Dominique's house. She may have seen her pull into the driveway. Had she assumed Christine was Dominique arriving home?

When Amanda was looking at the photos on Spencer's phone, she thought Christine looked familiar in some. It took until now for it to click in as to why. The two women shared similarities. Same hair color and build. At nine thirty, it would have been dusky, but not dark. The house was a distance from the street though. Also, the jogger, presumably the killer, may not have seen Christine's face when she was driving in.

What if all of this was a case of mistaken identity? If so, that made Christine Lane collateral damage, and it meant that Dominique Sharp was still in grave danger.

Amanda jumped from bed and called Trent.

TWENTY-TWO

Amanda called Malone on his cell phone but had to leave a voicemail. It was a gift in disguise. If he didn't like being at Central after nine PM, he was guaranteed to be hostile in the wee hours. She met up with Trent at the station, and they headed to Joel Blackburn's residence. They brought along an officer as backup in case the night took a bad turn.

A background check on Blackburn didn't give any cause for concern, but Amanda still tried to reach Dominique a few times while Trent drove. Dominique never answered, and Amanda repeatedly met with a recorded professional greeting. She didn't leave a message. "Still no answer, and I have this sour feeling in the pit of my gut. Are we too late? I'm just sick that neither of us considered this before now."

"Don't go down that road. We've only followed the evidence in front of us."

Her head knew that, but her heart was refusing to grant her a pass. She tugged on the door handle to get out before the car stopped.

"Amanda," Trent said. "Please just wait until I've parked. You don't need to be rolling your ankle."

"Hurry up then."

Trent turned off the car, and she didn't waste a second getting out and rushing up the front walk. Joel Blackburn lived in a beautiful house in a beautiful neighborhood. It all looked idyllic from the street.

She ignored the large sparkling brass knocker on the black door and pushed the doorbell. It took three rings before there was movement inside the house. Soon after, a light inside turned on, followed by one on the front porch.

"Who is it?" a man's voice called out.

"Prince William County PD," she said.

The deadbolt was unlocked, and the door was eased open. Blackburn's face came into view through the opening, and she held up her badge to back up her claim.

"Detectives Steele and Stenson. We need to speak with you and Dominique Sharp. It's urgent." She made a small step forward, hoping the man would read the movement and ease back. He didn't, and Amanda stiffened. "As I said it's urgent."

"What is this about?"

Amanda felt eyes on her back, but when she turned she saw no one. "Dominique Sharp is staying with you, yes?"

"Yes." Dazed, confused, giving the first signs she had pulled him from bed.

"We believe she may be in danger. Let us inside, please," Trent put in this time.

Blackburn hesitated for a few seconds but backed up. Amanda made sure the door was locked behind them.

"What do you mean, in danger?" Blackburn's eyes narrowed, and his brow bunched up with wrinkles.

In the light of the entry, Amanda had her first proper look at Blackburn. Handsome, square jaw, black hair with a wavy strand curling over his forehead. He was wearing a navy-blue tracksuit, and his befuddled expression was only deepening. "Where is Ms. Sharp?" Amanda asked.

"She's in bed, where I suspect most people are at this hour."

Amanda didn't care for how this man was blocking them from Dominique. It had her questioning his motives. "We need you to get her for us."

"No need." Dominique slinked down the stairs wrapped in a silk robe with her arms tightly crossed. "What can I do for you at this time of night?"

"This conversation is better suited for sitting down." Amanda gestured toward the grand living room off the entry. With its coordinated grouping of chairs it resembled a lounge alcove in a luxury hotel.

"Why not? Should I put on some coffee too?"

"That's not necessary." Amanda responded as if the offer were genuine and not riddled with sarcasm. Once everyone was seated, she spoke. "Christine Lane has been identified as the person found in your home, but we have reason to suspect she may not have been the intended target."

Dominique's eyes widened a fraction. "What are you saying? That the killer was after me? That somehow Christine was mistaken as me?"

"You must admit that the two of you look similar," Trent said.

"I guess, but we're completely different people." This was spoken with the same condescending attitude she'd demonstrated when talking about Christine the first time.

"We haven't been able to find anyone who had reason to want Christine dead. There are also no explanations for why anyone would kill her at your house. We need to consider the possibility that you were the intended target." As Amanda said this it crossed her mind again that the killer would have realized their mistake when they wrapped up Christine's body, but by that point, it was too late.

Dominique shook her head. "Nah. What's to say she didn't

interrupt a robbery in progress when she turned up to prepare for the showing. You said the sliding door was open."

Amanda had to admit that it was a solid argument from the attorney except that it held no merit. "There is nothing to suggest that was the case."

Dominique angled her head, smiled tightly. "How could you know that with any certainty? You haven't consulted with me for an inventory of my things."

Amanda recalled all the opulence housed in that walk-in closet. Where would they even begin to catalog everything? And was it even necessary? Everything looked in order. More to the point, a fatal robbery doesn't result in the culprits wrapping their victims in tarps. A valid argument raised more than once. "Details of the scene sway us from believing any of this pertained to a robbery."

"The details of which I assume you're not at liberty to share?"

"Correct," Amanda confirmed.

"Well, if this person came for me, they failed big-time. It's tragic they got Christine in my place, but I'm still not sure how this brings you here at this hour."

"This killer will know they got the wrong person by now." *Technically, from the moment they wrapped Christine's body in a tarp...* "The threat on your life may not be over," Amanda stressed.

"Then you believe they'll come back for me?" Dominique looked at Blackburn, who smirked at her. "As you can see, Detective, I'm perfectly safe."

And arrogant... "For now. But whoever killed Christine is to be taken seriously. She was shot three times. Twice to the chest, once to the head." Amanda felt comfortable disclosing that much if that was what it took to convince Dominique of the threat hanging over her.

Blackburn shifted his position on the couch and cleared his throat. "Dom, that sounds like an execution."

"I'm perfectly safe, darling." The word *darling* dripped off her tongue like thick caramel.

"I'm not so sure you are," Blackburn said, and it had Dominique firing him a hot glare. "Can you protect her?" He was looking at Amanda as he asked the question.

"Unreal. If you think I'm going to be okay with a babysitter, you're sorely mistaken." Dominique flushed and crossed her arms.

"Don't be foolish, Dom," Blackburn petitioned. "This is your life we're talking about."

"That's right. *My* life. And it's always in jeopardy." She turned toward Amanda and Trent. "I'm a defense attorney. The job entails making enemies. If I didn't have them, I wouldn't be doing my job right."

"And that makes you feel safe and secure while you sleep at night?" Amanda raised her eyebrows, skeptical.

"It's just par for the course."

Trent took out his notepad and pen. "Do you have any names for us?"

"I have a lot. At my office. I don't bother myself with keeping track."

"We'll need those names," Amanda stated firmly.

"I'll get them for you. Just not right this minute."

It made sense Dominique wouldn't have a list handy, but she didn't even seem shaken by the request. Moving on, Amanda turned her focus elsewhere. Additional due diligence. Blackburn wasn't a big man. Through obscured glass he could be taken for the size of a woman. "Mr. Blackburn, where were you on Friday night?"

"You can't seriously think that..." Dominique chuckled. "There's no way Joel wants to kill me."

"She's right, though there are times I could strangle you." He gave her a mischievous smile.

She batted her hand. "The feeling's mutual."

Now they were both making light of the situation? "Your whereabouts, Mr. Blackburn?" she prompted. While they needed to follow through on the mystery jogger, they couldn't let assumptions block out other possibilities or they could miss something crucial. For all they knew the woman could have just been out for fresh air and exercise.

"He was in Washington with me."

Amanda stiffened. It rankled that Dominique answered on his behalf. "Is that true?" She made a point of leveling her gaze at Blackburn.

"It is."

Amanda was formulating another question when there was a thump followed by shattering glass.

"Did anyone else hear that?" Blackburn's eyes grew large.

Amanda jumped off her chair, as did Trent. Dominique and Blackburn appeared frozen in place. It sounded like it came from downstairs. "How do we get to the basement?"

Blackburn whispered his response and pointed the way.

"Okay, both of you stay right here. Don't move." Amanda felt it necessary to stress the importance of that request.

Amanda and Trent headed toward the staircase, with their hands ready over their holsters. She withdrew her Glock and flashlight, and Trent did the same. They used the beams to guide their steps.

There was more ruckus coming from the back end of the basement, and Amanda headed toward it. She went to the doorway of what looked like a guest room. She ran her flashlight over the window. A shadowed form was crawling through. They froze for an instant before raising their arm.

Amanda pushed Trent down and followed through herself just as a burst of light ignited.

The gun report was a dampened *thwack*. It was followed by two more rounds.

By the time Amanda was prepared to return fire, the person was gone.

"Go!" she yelled at Trent, as she scurried from the room.

There was a fourth *thwack*. Blackburn cried out.

"It sounds like Blackburn was hit," she said.

"You see to him, and I'll pursue the suspect." Trent raced up the stairs and out the front door while Amanda ran toward the back.

The sliding door was open, and Blackburn was lying on the deck bleeding from his chest.

Amanda holstered her gun and put away her flashlight and dropped next to him. She pressed down on the wound with one hand and punched in 911 on her phone with the other.

There was nothing but silence.

She pulled it back and looked at the screen. No bars.

Blackburn was panting loudly and groaning. Over him, she heard Trent's voice ringing out through the neighborhood, yelling at the backup officers.

"Where's Dominique?" she asked Blackburn.

He raised an arm but quickly dropped it. "Upstairs." There was a raspy, gurgling noise in his throat. Blood bubbled from the corners of his mouth.

Shit! All you had to do was stay put! Amanda looked at her phone again. Still no bars. Blackburn needed an ambulance now. His blood was hot against her palm and seeped through her fingers.

"Do you have a landline?"

Blackburn shook his head and winced.

"Just stay still, okay. Hang in there." She wanted to assure him that help was coming, but she'd feel more confident in saying that if she had a way of reaching 911. She could only hope that Trent told the officer to radio in.

Just as she thought all was lost, ambulance sirens pierced the night air. With the dense humidity, the sound was amplified.

"Help is on the way." *Please, let them get here fast enough...*

* * *

Trent's calves and thighs were burning as he ran through the subdivision. The mystery figure had a good start on him and was lithe and lean. Based on the size and how they moved, he'd say it was a woman of average height, somewhere around five-foot-five. Her hair was short, tucked into a skullcap or tied back into a bun. He made out other things too. She was wearing spandex shorts, an oversized T-shirt, and a backpack.

The mystery jogger?

She was smart and mostly stuck to the shadows, but Trent was afforded brief glimpses of the perp where the streetlights had a farther reach.

His heart pounding, he dug in deeper, searching for the resolve to keep going. But as they rounded the street corner, and Trent followed, he lost her path. It was like she just vaporized into thin air.

The backup officer, a man named Kendall, came up next to Trent and worked to catch his breath. Every part of Trent's body was ready to move. His muscles were pulsing, awaiting directions, but he had none to give them.

"We lost eyes on the suspect. I repeat, we lost eyes on the suspect," Kendall said into his radio.

A PWCPD cruiser drove by, lights flashing, and slowed next to them. The officer put the window down.

"Call in more units to search the area," Trent told him.

"Already done."

As if on cue, more cruisers with their strobing lights appeared along the street.

"All we know is she went that way." Trent pointed in the direction he'd last seen her go.

"*She*, sir?" Kendall asked.

"Yes, I'm sure it was a woman."

The officers spoke to each other, and the cruisers set out. Some parked down the street before getting out on foot to start the search. Trent headed back to Blackburn's house to check on the situation there.

TWENTY-THREE

Paramedics tended to Joel Blackburn. One handed Amanda a wet wipe to clean her bloody hand. She took it with a "Thanks" and set off into the house in search of Dominique.

"Amanda." Trent's voice had her stopping in her steps and turning around. He was walking through the rear sliding doors, making his way past the paramedics, who were now loading Blackburn onto a stretcher.

She bridged the distance to Trent. "Tell me you caught them."

He shook his head and filled her in. "*Her.* It was a woman. But, no."

"You're sure it was a woman though?"

"Uh-huh, and she was wearing the same apparel from that eyewitness account. The shorts, the shirt, the backpack..."

"And the gun used to fire on us had a silencer on it."

"Just like the weapon that fired the bullets at Christine," Trent finished her thought.

A heavy weight sank in Amanda's gut. "She's our killer."

"I'd say that's a safe assumption."

"Tell me you got a good look at her."

"Not really. Just that she's about five-five and slim. She can also move. She's fast," he added, as if his statement required further clarity. "What happened here? Dominique okay?"

"Joel Blackburn was shot in the chest. It's not looking good. I was just going to check on Dominique. I think she's upstairs." Amanda turned and went up to the second story, with Trent following. "Dominique? It's Detective Steele. You're safe now. Come out."

There was a thump from down the hall. Amanda pointed in that direction and set out with Trent.

"Dominique?" Amanda said ahead of them.

A door flung open, bouncing off the wall behind it. Dominique filled the opening, holding a raised gun.

Amanda held up her hands. "Dominique, it's us. You're safe."

No movement, no noise except for the sound of Amanda's pounding heart in her ears. *Ba-boom. Ba-boom. Ba-boom.*

Seconds later, Dominique lowered her hand, letting the gun lie against the side of her thigh.

"Let me take that from you." Trent moved in and relieved her of her weapon.

Dominique blinked slowly. "Where's Joel? Is he...?"

"He was shot—" Amanda stopped speaking when Dominique gasped. After allowing her a few seconds to absorb the blow, Amanda added, "But paramedics have seen to him, and he's likely on his way to the hospital now."

"Well, I need to go check on him." Dominique stepped toward the staircase.

"We can take you there, but first you need to tell us if you know of anyone who might want to kill you," Trent told her.

"Like I said before I wouldn't even know where to start." Dominique put a hand on her forehead. "Please, just take me to the hospital. I want to be there for him."

Amanda glanced at Trent and nodded. "We'll take you, but

you'll need to talk to us while you wait to hear from the doctors."

"Okay, fine, whatever it takes."

Amanda pulled out her phone to call for CSIs, not even thinking about the lack of bars from before until she had it out. Now she had them. "Okay, this is strange." She turned to Trent.

"Hello?" Dominique snapped. "Please take me to the hospital."

"One minute. If you could just stay right there this time." Amanda walked down the hall, putting several feet between herself and the lawyer. When Trent joined her, she said, "I tried calling nine-one-one when you were in pursuit of the suspect, and my phone had no bars. Now, they're back."

"So what are we looking at then? This person comes equipped with a signal jammer?"

"If you can think of another explanation, I'm all ears."

"If you're right about this, then I'm going to say this only gives more credit to our growing suspicions."

"Yep. We're looking at a professional."

TWENTY-FOUR

Amanda and Trent left the house in the hands of a uniformed police officer and called in Crime Scene. The perp had fired four rounds and didn't have any time to collect the casings. This could provide a potential breakthrough, letting the CSIs confirm if the rounds were also fired by a Glock. Of course, ideally, Amanda would put the shooter's gun in their hands for comparison. But short of that... Also if they were extremely lucky, there could be fingerprints or touch DNA that would lead to the shooter. But Amanda wasn't holding her breath. Not if their growing hunch was correct and they were looking for a professional hit woman. In that case, even if forensics existed, that trail wasn't going to get them anywhere.

Dominique was set up in a corner of the hospital waiting room. All they knew at this time was Joel Blackburn was in critical condition and had been rushed to surgery. They'd be questioning Dominique soon but stepped away to give her a few moments to herself.

Amanda was dealing with her own discomfort from being inside a hospital. The antiseptic smell triggered a sensory memory imprinted from the aftermath of the accident that claimed her family's lives. Also from the time Malone was hospitalized with a brain tumor. While hospitals provided moments of celebrations, like the birth of a baby, the painful memories outnumbered the good. She worked to push these thoughts away and focus on the last few hours. What a shitshow! She turned to Trent, who was standing next to her. "I tell you the evidence makes a lot more sense when you view it from a professional killer being behind everything."

"Except for that tarp. That bit is still strange to me," Trent responded. "Typical hit men knock out their targets as clean as possible and make a break for it. I'd say she enjoys killing and, as if to announce this to the world, has added her own flair to it. Her signature. She doesn't just take life. It's theater to her."

"There's also some compulsion to it all. She had to know that she got the wrong person when she was wrapping up Christine."

"Yet, she went ahead with it anyhow."

Amanda nodded. "Why not just walk away and leave her body there?"

"I see what you're saying. But she took a risk tonight. Breaking into a house when she must have known a few people were inside. That's brazen. Not to mention the lights were on."

"As they were at Dominique's house, but I hear you on the other part. She must have been watching the place. In that case, did she not see the backup officer?"

"Unless she was in the backyard when all of us showed up. Hard to know without asking her."

"Still, the lights were on. The curtains in the back of the house were open." This was something that Amanda had noticed. "She must have seen us inside. I'm sticking with brazen, but I also wonder if there's more to it. If we are looking at a hired gun, she'll only get her money when the job's complete. And Dominique's still alive."

"Which means she'll keep coming back until she finishes the job. That compulsion of hers may be her undoing."

"We can hope that will help us. And let's face it, she can't keep playing this game and not slip up eventually. Personally, I look forward to putting her behind bars. Well, I'm going to call Malone again, see if he picks up this time."

"Good luck. That's for if he answers." Trent smiled at her before walking over to a vending machine.

Amanda listened to Malone's line ring and cringed when it stopped partway through the third time.

"This better be good."

How to respond to that... It all depended on the angle.

"Steele, it's five thirty in the morning. I prefer to ease myself into the day with some coffee while I watch mindless TV."

She was blown away it was already five thirty. "Right, well, I wouldn't be calling if it wasn't important. Trent and I are at the hospital."

"Wait. Are you okay?" All irritation evaporated from his voice.

"We're fine, but Joel Blackburn is not."

"The name isn't ringing any bells. Let's pretend I haven't drunk a cup of coffee yet."

Amanda laid things out for him, even mentioned that she'd tried reaching him around two AM.

"It's a good thing I keep my cell phone out of the bedroom at night. But I'm going to need you to run through all of this for me again. Meet me at the station in two hours."

Before she could respond, the line was dead. Malone was gone. *Not up for debate apparently...* She pocketed her phone and joined Trent and Dominique. He was giving her a cup of coffee he'd bought from the machine and looked at Amanda. He nudged his head at her, which had her glancing over her shoulder.

Carter was walking toward her, lips curled down, his electric blue eyes intent, brows arched. "Are you okay?"

"I'm fine. Unfortunately, that investigation I mentioned a couple of days ago took a turn."

"Did you guys chase someone else into the side of a van?"

She nudged his arm and shook her head. "You're a brat." The occasion he referred to was how they met. And in her defense, the resulting injuries weren't her fault. The suspect who bolted was to blame.

"Well, other than another case bringing you here, how are *you*?"

"Tired."

"Not too tired, I hope." The devil played in his eyes and made her insides warm.

"I'm sure you could find a way to keep me up."

Carter leaned into her ear, and whispered, "You know I can." His warm breath spilled onto her neck, sending shivers down her chest.

Hello, headlights! She drew back and crossed her arms on instinct. Even though her light jacket would protect her modesty.

"I'll call you tonight, see where things are. Sound good?"

"Please." She was tempted to slap his ass when he turned to walk away but didn't dare. She was happy she hadn't when she caught Trent watching. He waved for her to come back over.

"For you." Trent handed her a cup of coffee when she got there.

"No, I couldn't."

"You will. I'm just going to get myself one now." He nudged his head toward Dominique, implying Amanda keep a close eye on her.

Trent wasn't gone for long. Amanda had braved a tentative sip of the vending machine brew. It wasn't half bad, but waged no competition against Hannah's Diner.

She sat beside Dominique while Trent sat across from them.

"We need to discuss your trip to DC," Amanda began.

Dominique lowered her cup from her lips. "There's nothing to say."

"Just that it was unexpected and last-minute?" It was curious why this woman was being difficult given what had taken place in the last few hours.

"That's right."

Amanda would play along. For now. "If it hadn't come up, would you have been home on Friday night?"

"Yes. Though, I would have stepped out if Christine had arranged a showing."

That seemed obvious, and it didn't sway Amanda from her conviction that Dominique was the true target. After all, tonight proved that she was. "You also told us before the trip was for business because you're acquiring another firm. Tell us more about this deal. Anyone not happy about the venture?"

Dominique shrugged and took another sip of the coffee Trent had bought her. "I'll have Casey gather all the threats against me together. It shouldn't take her too long. The office opens at nine. I'll tell her it's the priority."

That wasn't an answer to Amanda's question, but she'd revisit it in a minute. "Who is Casey?"

"My assistant."

"Her last name?" Trent asked.

"Branch." Dominique followed up by spelling it out, as if it weren't straightforward.

"Going back to the deal. You never said if someone wasn't happy with the acquisition," Amanda said.

"If anyone has a problem with it, they aren't saying as much to my face."

Given Dominique's formidable character that didn't

surprise Amanda. "Was there anyone you suspected of talking badly about you behind your back?"

"I don't pay attention to things like that. My work is important and demands my focus."

"Speaking of your work," Amanda began.

"Oh, no, I know what you're going to say."

Amanda proceeded anyhow. "Until we find this person, you'll need twenty-four-hour protection."

"I told you before that's not going to happen."

"This killer has made it clear they intend to follow through. They will keep trying until they succeed," Trent stressed.

"I refuse to let this person bully me into hiding away. As I told you, my work is important. Speaking of, if Joel's surgery doesn't wrap up soon, I'll need to leave for the office."

Was she using work as a distraction? Or was she really that heartless? Though, there must be some clue in how she referred to Joel as her lover. It was such a cold and clinical way to quantify a relationship. Even calling him her friend would be a vast improvement. "After what's happened, everyone at your firm would understand if you didn't go in today."

"Their understanding isn't something I need." She crossed her legs.

"An attempt was made on your life." It struck Amanda how often she and Trent needed to point this out to her. Was it denial or pure stubbornness? Or something else altogether? Her ego lying to her, telling her she had everything under control?

Dominique shook her head, waved a hand in dismissal. "They never got close to me."

But they got to Joel... The thought fired through, but Amanda wasn't heartless enough to voice it out loud. "It doesn't get much closer. They were in your home, in your bedroom. Then they tracked you down to Joel's house. Isn't this enough to let you know they're not going to stop?"

"I'm here. I'm okay."

It had to be shock. Amanda paced her reply. "Fine, if you insist on going to work, I can't make you stay away."

"Thank you." She flailed a hand.

Amanda would overlook the gesture of exasperation. As if she and Trent were the problem here, and not the person intent on killing her. "Listen, no matter what you are going to do, you will have police protection. It's not optional." Amanda had rushed out the latter at seeing Dominique's mouth open. She snapped it shut and drilled Amanda with a glare.

"Fine," Dominique pushed out with a not-too-subtle eyeroll.

"And you can't go home, or back to Joel's place," Amanda told her.

"Where am I supposed to go then?"

"We'll get you into a safehouse," Amanda said.

"Nope, no way."

"Then we'll arrange a hotel room for you, but there will be an officer posted at your door."

"Fine," Dominique hissed.

Amanda was far from *fine* though. There were questions that needed answers. The glowing ones were related to Dominique's business. Based on her own words, work was her priority. Possibly her entire life. If so, it could make sense that someone connected to the purchase of the DC firm wanted her dead. "When did you start the process with the acquisition?"

"Six months ago."

That wasn't long in the scope of time. "With you taking over, did some people stand to lose their jobs?"

"Yes."

Yet it didn't occur to this woman that might cause a problem... "Do you think any of these people are angry with you?"

An amused smirk as she shook her head. "It's just business. I'd expect professionals to understand that."

"Is that a no, then?" Amanda didn't understand why the woman was shirking her.

"That's a no. It's not even like I'm letting everyone go. Some aren't willing to come with me. As if DC isn't just a forty-minute drive away. It's not like they'll even need to uproot their life. Many people do that commute every day."

"Then you're shutting down your firm in Woodbridge?" Trent asked.

"You bet I am. It only makes fiscal sense, giving me one focus. Also DC has a larger population."

Amanda felt some compassion for the woman across from her, regardless of the tough barricade she erected around herself. But was that all it was? Or was it the woman? There is a saying that when people tell you who they are, believe them. Every time Dominique opened her mouth, selfish things came out. It would seem business trumped everything else. "What about the employees at the DC firm. Any staff cuts there?"

"Yes. Some will be replaced by my employees transferring over."

Amanda wasn't ready to give up on this angle. Her father taught her to look under every rock. He'd worn the phrase out for good reason. The effort often paid off. Same too, for following the money. "We'll need everything on the purchase offer."

"I think you're far too concerned about this deal."

"Are you willing to stake your life on that?" Amanda countered.

The woman remained unaffected and didn't rush to respond.

While sitting in a hospital emergency waiting room, no less!

"You don't get me," Dominique eventually said. "That's fine. Not many people do. But I haven't gotten to where I am by allowing myself to be bullied into compliance."

Amanda remembered she'd made a similar bold statement before. "No one is saying you have, and that's not what this is about. It is about staying alive."

"Fine, you want all the information on the sale? I'll make sure you get a copy of all the paperwork. For the sake of transparency, I'll also include the financial reports from my company and Gabay, Finch & Earnest, as well."

"Is that the company you're merging with?" Trent asked.

"Acquiring, but, yes, the very one. For the record, I just received their financial reports on Friday afternoon and haven't had a chance to dig in yet."

Amanda tensed. Was the timing key or coincidence? "Did you receive them when you were in Washington?"

"Uh-huh."

Amanda's mind was whirling. Could it be that someone wanted to prevent her from looking at the books? It was possible they expected Dominique to return home to Woodbridge that night and sent a killer for her there. Or was Amanda inching down the wrong path? All she knew was poor Christine Lane was collateral damage in all this, and Joel Blackburn was caught in the crossfire. It was too soon to know if he'd come out of this alive.

TWENTY-FIVE

Amanda and Trent walked into Central armed with coffees from Hannah's Diner. One for themselves and a third for Malone. They even brought him a freshly made blueberry fritter, which Amanda knew was his favorite. Trent got himself a double-chocolate dip, and she went with a French cruller. She'd take the added sugar in the glaze and hope for the insulin spike to kick in and wake her up. It might be a temporary rush, but it was better than nothing.

She rapped her knuckles on the doorframe of Malone's office, and Trent led the way inside carrying the tray of coffee. She held the bag of goodies.

"That's supposed to make up for the fact I'm at my desk at seven thirty?" Malone flicked a finger toward the coffee Trent was holding out to him.

"And this." She fished in the bag for Malone's donut and plucked it out wrapped in a napkin.

"Hmph." He looked at them with narrowed eyes while accepting their offerings. "Thanks, but don't think this makes up for the late night and the early start."

"We wouldn't dare." Amanda held back a smile. "How's your back?"

"Just fine. No need to worry about me." He took a substantial bite of his fritter, removing a chunk from the top corner.

Amanda's stomach rumbled as she held the bag for Trent to take out his treat. She happily reached in for hers when he was taken care of. She had just got her fingers on the sticky glaze when her phone rang.

"No one sleeps anymore," Malone mumbled around a mouthful of food.

Amanda dug out her phone and answered at the sight of *CSI Stuart* on her screen. "Detective Steele."

"CSI Stuart. Keller and I are working the scene here at the Blackburn residence. We've recovered four nine-mil casings. We'll run ballistics to see if they tie back to a Glock."

Amanda would take what she could get. The only true solution was catching this shooter and running ballistics on her gun. "Let me know."

"Will do. After all, you think the person from tonight killed Lane."

When Amanda called the CSIs, she filled them in on the direction she and Trent were leaning with the investigation. "We do." She passed a side-glance at Trent, who appeared all too content chomping away on his donut. He had a tiny smudge of chocolate in the corner of his mouth. Amanda tapped hers to let him know.

He mouthed, "Thanks," and wiped it. She gave him a thumbs-up.

"We also found some blood," Stuart said. "It was on a piece of broken glass that remained in the window frame. It may belong to the perp, so we'll be running it through the system."

"Thanks for calling me with this," Amanda told her.

"Yep." With that, the investigator hung up, and Amanda put her phone away.

Malone wiped his face with his napkin, then brushed some sugar crumbs from his shirt. "Good news?"

"Some news, anyway." She shared the details of the call.

"At least there is some forensic evidence from all this." Trent scrunched up his napkin and tossed it into the bag.

She was the only one left with an untouched donut. Her stomach rumbled as she reached for it.

"Fill me in on everything," Malone said.

Trent's phone rang, and he pulled it out of his pocket. "It will just be a second," he said, and answered.

"Unbelievable." Malone sat back with his coffee.

Saved by the ringing phone... Amanda scarfed downed her carbs, taking delight in every huge bite. Not exactly something to be proud of, but damn it, she'd earned the calories.

"Thanks." Trent sounded dejected as he put his phone away. "The search has been called off. There's no sign of the woman." He looked at her as if he expected her to say something.

Amanda couldn't have responded if she wanted to. Her cheeks were puffed out, full of delicious donut.

"All right, let's back up here," Malone said. "Amanda told me about a woman at the scene... Let's start at the beginning."

Amanda gestured for Trent to do the honors while she inhaled the rest of her donut.

After Trent caught Malone up, he leaned forward. "So, let me get this straight. You two think someone was hired to kill Dominique Sharp, but she messed up, so she's back to finish the job?"

She finished her treat, wiped her fingers off, and tossed her napkin in the bag with Trent's. "You can't dismiss that it seems someone is awfully intent on killing Dominique. A hired gun is something we need to consider."

"A female hired gun, at that."

"Why not?" She angled her head, challenging him.

Malone held up a hand. "It was just a comment. It's just not exactly something you run into every day."

"I'll give you that."

"We can't ignore the evidence. The murder method with the two taps to the chest, one to the head," Trent laid out. "And the rounds were fired from a gun with a silencer. Someone who wants to get in and out without being seen or heard."

"Huh." Malone shared his gaze with the two of them, going from one to the other. "So you're both stuck on this being a gun for hire?"

Trent nodded. "I am."

Amanda seconded that and added, "We need to get protection on Dominique Sharp, but she's not being what you'd call cooperative."

"Even though she must know her life is in danger?"

"Even though..." Not that it was something Amanda could understand.

"What is it with some people?" Malone shook his head. "Where is she now?"

"Set up in a hotel room with officers posted at her door," Amanda told him.

"That's something at least."

"*Something*, I guess." There was no way to hide that she wasn't impressed with Dominique's attitude about police protection. "She still insists on going about her life like normal. That includes going to work at her firm."

"Even after everything that happened? And the fact her boyfriend is under the knife?"

"*Lover* not boyfriend," Trent corrected. "She's put him into a box with a label that suggests the relationship is nothing more than a series of booty calls."

"To each their own. Still, the question remains. She's not responding like one would expect."

"Nope. Apparently, Dominique wears accumulating

enemies as some type of badge of honor. She's going to have her assistant gather all threats against her together. She's also agreed to share all the paperwork connected to the purchase of the DC law firm."

"The threats could present us with a bunch of rabbit holes, making it hard to know which one to go down." Malone grunted when he shifted in his chair and shot her a look.

With that, she didn't dare ask about his back. "They might, but I don't see what choice we have." She just hoped there weren't too many threats to wade through. Too many suspects could be just as problematic as too few.

"I agree with you both that Dominique Sharp seems to have been the intended target. It's tragic that an innocent woman is dead because of this."

Neither Amanda nor Trent said anything in response. There was nothing to say.

Malone rubbed his jaw. "If this is a hired gun, it's reasonable to think this person has a history of kills. Only thing is, she's messed up this time. She'll be getting more desperate. We can't afford to underestimate her."

"Speaking of not underestimating her, I believe she brought a signal jammer with her." She told Malone about the loss of bars for a brief time at the Blackburn residence.

"Huh, as if I weren't convinced already. Incorporating technology like that also suggests a professional."

Somehow hearing he agreed with them made the situation more stressful. *History of kills...* How many had she gotten away with? Meaning no one had stopped her before now. Amanda pushed both thoughts aside. It wasn't conducive to a productive mindset. Her focus needed to be homed in on being the one who would bring her down. "Once CSI Stuart is finished doing her thing, I'm sure she'll enter her findings into the system. It will kick back if the casings are a match to any previous crime scenes. But since we're thinking this is a professional, going about this from the gun standpoint isn't likely to lead us anywhere. I suggest we rope in the FBI and have them check ViCAP to see if our investigation shares any similarities with any unsolved cases." The Violent Criminal Apprehension Program housed records of major unsolved crimes in the US.

Trent was nodding. "Great idea. Since it's most likely this woman has killed before, her crimes are likely to show up there."

Malone shrugged. "You have my blessing."

"I'll reach out to my contact then." She could go to Brandon Fisher, who was with the FBI's Behavioral Analysis Unit and was also her best friend's boyfriend, but Amanda believed she had a number for Nadia Webber, an analyst who worked with him. She'd try her first.

TWENTY-SIX

Amanda invited Trent to join her in her cubicle for the call to Nadia Webber at the FBI. She made the call on speaker.

The line was answered after two rings. "Nadia Webber, speaking."

"Nadia, it's Detective Amanda Steele from the Prince William County PD."

"I remember you, but if you're calling me, it's not with good news."

"It's not, but I'll get to that. I have my partner on the line with us, Detective Trent Stenson."

"Trent." The analyst's voice softened. "It's been a long time."

"Hi, Nadia," Trent said, and his cheeks flushed.

Amanda raised her eyebrows. Was there ever something between the two or was he red because talking to Nadia reminded him of the time he helped the FBI with a serial rape and murder case? It hadn't been Trent's finest hour. He'd been an eager uniformed officer with the Dumfries PD, a much smaller department than the PWCPD, and inserted himself into the investigation. Hearing it from his side, he put the connections together before the FBI. Amanda was in no position to dispute his claim. What she knew was Trent's instincts had him running ahead of backup and paying the price. He almost became a victim himself and was left with bullet scars to remember the occasion.

"Whatever it is you need. Hit me," Nadia told them.

"We need you to look into ViCAP for us." Amanda ran through the details of the investigation, noting the tarp and rope and how pristine the murder scene was, including the strong cleaner. She also detailed the kill shots, two to the chest and one to the head, and the circumstances surrounding the failed attempt on Dominique Sharp's life. How Blackburn was shot with a nine-mil slug. Also that the perp had used a silencer and fled the scene, but not before they were able to confirm it was a woman dressed in spandex shorts and a baggy tee, wearing a backpack.

"None of this sounds like an amateur killer to us," Trent put in.

"Agreed. I would say from what you told me this woman sounds like a standard serial killer, aside from the brazen attempt on Sharp's life. She must also love killing. I mean, to wrap up the victim even when she must have known Christine Lane wasn't her intended target. She could have just left upon noticing her error, but she didn't."

"We boiled that down to a compulsion," Amanda said.

"I'd say. Makes sense too because it seems the tarp and rope are her signature. All of this is good news for us because it should make it easier to find similar cases if they exist."

If... Amanda realized the possibility was there, but found it harder to accept this woman hadn't left a body count in her wake. In that vein, Nadia's summary was bittersweet. While the method might help them track her down, it had taken more loss of life to get to this point. Hopefully, no one else would become a statistic before they shut this killer down. "All right. Let us know what you find out."

"You know I will."

"Thank you."

"No problem. Good luck in the meantime." With that, Nadia ended the call, and Amanda was left facing Trent.

"Anything you want to share with me about Nadia? Your cheeks got a little color to them when she said your name."

"It's nothing."

"I'm not letting you off the hook on this. Just tell me."

"It's just that whenever I talk to any of the team, that being Brandon's team, it takes me back to when I helped them on that case. And how I messed up. Running in, nearly getting myself killed."

"Though without your contributions, it's possible the killer wouldn't have been found and stopped."

"I don't know about that."

"And sure, you got ahead of yourself, but I think it's quite impressive that you were bold enough to insert yourself into an FBI investigation."

"I saw a pattern of missing women in the area, and I couldn't just ignore it."

"Law enforcement needs more officers like you who aren't afraid to take the initiative. Though don't let it get back to Malone that I'm encouraging such behavior. He might view it as disregarding authority or going rogue." She smiled.

"Well, I appreciate you saying that..."

"Hey, it's the truth. But moving on... What do you suggest we do while we wait for Dominique's firm to open?"

"I say we look up the principal players in her company and pull their backgrounds. I'm sure we could get their names off the firm's website."

"Works for me. At least we'll be going in familiarized with the players."

TWENTY-SEVEN

There were only two senior partners at Dominique Sharp's firm, along with a handful of associates and paralegals. Nothing flagged in any of their backgrounds. Sharp & Associates was described on its website as a boutique firm, and it seemed like Dominique had built her business on representing the downtrodden before turning to clients with deeper pockets. Criminals.

When Trent pulled into the parking lot for the firm, Amanda took in the new building and immaculate landscaping. The grass was trimmed short like a golfing green, and the gardens that lined the walkway and butted along the front were all well-tended. There were several varieties of plants and a rainbow of blooms.

Trent pulled into one of the five spaces allocated for visitors. Four were empty, but one was taken by a PWCPD squad car. Amanda waved at Officer Cochran behind the wheel. She wondered if Traci had ticked off her sergeant to get stuck with this detail.

On the way to the front doors, the closest parking spot was assigned to Dominique Sharp, Attorney at Law. Hers was the only space with a name and title. That and the prime location would remind Dominique's employees of the pecking order every single day they came to work and walked past. Her Cadillac Vistiq occupied the spot.

The lobby inside was fresh and minimalist with sleek edges and lots of chrome. A woman was seated behind a long reception desk. She looked up when Amanda and Trent entered, but didn't offer a smile or greeting until they got closer.

"Can I help you?" The woman was older than Amanda, mid-forties, and she took her job as the firm's gatekeeper seriously, judging by the rigid set of her jaw.

Amanda drew attention to the badge on her waist. "We'd like to speak with Dominique Sharp." She thought it was best they started there.

The woman stiffened and clasped her hands. "Do you have an appointment?"

Dominique must not have said a thing to this woman about the last several hours. "We appreciate that Ms. Sharp would have a booked schedule, but—"

"Detective Steele?" A woman's voice had Amanda turning around.

She faced a twenty-something with long, straight blond hair. "I am, and this is Detective Stenson."

"And I'm Casey Branch. Ms. Sharp told me to expect you. Come with me."

The woman at the desk narrowed her eyes as Amanda and Trent followed Casey, crossing behind reception to the hallways there. Casey took them to a spacious meeting room and gestured for them to enter ahead of her.

There was a credenza at the end of the room with a pod coffeemaker and everything necessary to make a coffee. A dozen white mugs with the firm's name printed on them were set out. There was also a pitcher of water with several tall glasses. On the main table, surrounded by ten chairs, was a stack of folders.

Casey pointed at them and said, "Those are the threats on file against Ms. Sharp. They are cataloged with the most recent on the top. Now I know that Ms. Sharp promised you the paperwork and financials related to the purchase of Gabay, Finch & Earnest. I apologize I haven't yet had the chance to gather all that together."

"That's fine, Casey. This is a great place for us to start." Amanda offered her a gentle smile. She understood Casey was just starting her workday. It was impressive she already had the conference room set up with the threats on hand.

Casey dipped her head and went to leave the room, but Amanda called out, "Actually," causing Casey to turn around.

"Is there something else I could get you?" Casey appeared flummoxed and overwhelmed. Her day's schedule was likely full before these added responsibilities.

"We don't need you to get us anything, but we'd like to speak with you, if you could give us a few minutes of your time." Amanda sat down and gestured at the chair across the table.

Trent parked next to Amanda with his tablet, prepared to make any notes on that.

"Ah, sure." Casey pulled out the indicated chair and dropped onto it.

It was all done in such a casual manner that Amanda suspected Dominique hadn't been forthcoming about the situation that morning. Or if she had, Amanda would like to know why Casey didn't seem at all concerned. But even if Dominique hadn't disclosed that her life was in danger, surely the word would have spread that a murder happened in her house. The news was public by this point. "Just to be clear, do you know why we're interested in the threats against Dominique and the sale documents?"

"Ms. Sharp told me you're concerned someone may be interested in killing her."

So Casey knows that much... "Did you know that a woman was murdered in Ms. Sharp's home?"

Casey nodded. "Her real estate agent. There are a lot here who keep up on the news, so the word got around pretty quickly."

"Yes, well, Detective Stenson and I are tasked with finding her justice and protecting your boss from any further attempts on her life." Amanda studied Casey for any sign that her words were making an impact. There was a subtle flinch in her left eye. "Before we look into this pile of threats, are there any that stand out to you, or any person in particular?"

Casey bit her bottom lip and shook her head.

Both actions came quickly and represented false timidity. Amanda would wager Casey was afraid of someone. "You're sure?" Amanda tried to ease the young woman into opening up.

Casey took a deep breath. "Ms. Sharp has a lot of people who dislike her."

"Why is that?" Trent asked, earning Casey's gaze.

"If she doesn't pull off miracles, some clients turn on her. We are in criminal defense, and it doesn't take much to upset our clients sometimes."

"Anyone specific coming to mind?" Amanda asked.

Casey turned away and shook her head, trembling.

"If you're afraid of someone, we can protect you," Amanda told the young woman.

"No, I'd just rather not point fingers at people when I don't know anything as fact. If that's all...?"

"For now. We will want to speak to the senior partners and the other employees of the firm though."

"There are almost thirty, though some are off today."

"That's fine. We'll just need five minutes a piece for the ones here. If you could send in one of the partners in first, that would be great." Amanda offered an encouraging smile to Casey, which was met with indifference.

"Okay."

Casey left, and Amanda turned to Trent. "I can't be alone in thinking she looked terrified to speak up."

"Oh, I'd say she was, and it's like she's fictionalized everything that is going on with Dominique. As if it's not really happening." Trent pulled the folders closer to them, took one for himself, and passed one to her.

Amanda opened it and was taken back by the sheer number. She read the first few, of which the most recent was from last month. None of the senders held back from speaking their minds, but they didn't disclose their names. Some of the threats were emailed, others mailed. If one of these people made good on their threats, it was going to take a lot more work to determine that.

"I wonder if we jumped ahead on this," she said to Trent, closing her folder. "After all, would a person who orders a hit advertise themselves as an enemy?"

"I see what you're saying, but you can't dismiss the possibility that hatred isn't always something that hits hot and fast. It can build over time."

Amanda looked at all the folders, and her stomach sank. She couldn't ignore the vast number of enemies Dominique had, but for now, it was best they stick to more obvious suspects. They could also return to these written threats if they found the case hit a wall.

There was a knock on the doorframe, and Amanda turned to see Bennie O'Neil. He strongly resembled his driver's license photo, which wasn't often the case. With a head of thick silver hair and sculpted face and body, he was the image of a gray fox. And being a lawyer, he likely took the analogy further and was sharp and cunning.

"Come in," Amanda told him. "And take a seat." She gestured to the seat that Casey had vacated. With O'Neil across from her and Trent, they'd be able to read his facial expressions and body language more clearly than if he sat farther away.

O'Neil closed the door before sitting where Amanda had indicated.

Formal introductions were made all around, and then Amanda got started.

"I take it you know why we're interested in speaking with you?" It was best to make sure they were on the same ground.

"Yes. It's insane if you ask me."

"What is?" Amanda wasn't sure if he was referring to their interest in speaking with him, or the situation with someone out there wanting to kill Dominique.

"All of it, I suppose. Her real estate agent was killed in her house. Like what are the chances? But Dom has a way of drawing strange scenarios."

"Unfortunately, the tally in this situation is even worse," Amanda said. "An acquaintance of hers was shot in an attempt to kill Ms. Sharp in the wee hours of this morning. He's in critical condition, and he might not make it."

O'Neil blanched. "That much I didn't know about. She just sent out a company-wide email telling us that detectives would be here today and may want to speak with us. We were already aware of the murder in her home the day the body was found."

It was interesting Casey never mentioned the email. Shock maybe? A minor detail she'd squeezed out of her mind, dismissing it as irrelevant.

"Ms. Sharp seems to be taking it in stride," Trent said, looking up from his tablet.

"That's Dom, and that's why she's an exceptional lawyer. You could light a bomb at her feet, and she wouldn't give you a reaction."

Complete hyperbole, but the suggestion conflicted with Amanda's observations. She'd witnessed a lot of heat with the lawyer, sourced from high emotions. Amanda couldn't imagine that quality would serve an attorney well. Though, it demonstrated the passion Dominique brought to defending her clients. This thought made it sink in they were protecting a woman's life who worked for the opposing team. She defended criminals while she and Trent fought for justice. "Mr. O'Neil, how long have you been working with Ms. Sharp?"

"Ten years here, five of that as senior partner, but I had dealings with her sometimes when I worked at a previous firm."

"What sort of dealings?" Trent asked.

"Ah, just lawyer stuff." O'Neil clasped his hands and sat stiffly.

His succinct response wasn't enough for Amanda to let him off. "Can you elaborate?"

"In this business, you need to build relationships with other attorneys. For the lack of a better word, let's call them favors."

"To settle cases?" Amanda asked.

"It doesn't hurt when clear-cut negotiations fail."

Amanda didn't care for the way the man's eyes shadowed, like he was shifty and hiding something. But she wasn't the biggest fan of lawyers. Never had been, but she respected they were necessary. "Any of these unsuccessful negotiations lead to ill will toward Ms. Sharp?"

O'Neil smirked. "Is that question a joke?"

Amanda remained silent, and Trent didn't move next to her.

"All right, you're serious. In answer to your question, yes."

"Do you have any names for us?" Amanda asked.

"No one comes to mind who would want to kill her."

"How about anyone who doesn't like Ms. Sharp, but is pretty good about keeping it to themselves?" The question was inspired by her conversation with Trent from a moment ago.

"That could describe most of the people in this building." O'Neil flashed another smirk that quickly washed out.

Trent leaned across the table. "Yourself included?"

O'Neil pulled back, straightened his tie, and stretched his neck from side to side. "Do Dom and I have our differences? You bet. But we sharpen each other."

Amanda wasn't buying his statement for a second. "Does one of those differences involve her purchase of the DC law firm?"

O'Neil tapped the table with a flat palm three times. Then he sighed deeply. "Her plans to up and move things to DC doesn't bother me."

"It seems like it might." She gestured toward his hand.

He pulled his arm back. "It doesn't," he stressed. "Some around here, sure, but I don't see them killing her. Personally, I'm ready to golf and travel more, and put decades of eighty-hour weeks behind me. It's time I retire and enjoy all that I've worked so hard for." As he spoke, the fine lines in his brow smoothed out, causing Amanda to believe him.

"Thank you. We appreciate you taking the time to speak with us," she told him.

O'Neil eased out of his chair and pushed it back into the table. He left the room without a word.

After allowing time for him to get down the hall, Amanda told Trent, "Interesting guy."

"Ask me, and he was too level about the whole thing."

"You heard him. He's been around. He's a little immune to threats of violence. Dominique seems to be."

"Well, there's no explaining her, and you could be right, but I just don't know if O'Neil was completely forthcoming."

"He is a lawyer, so I doubt he was." What she wasn't certain about was whether his lack of emotion was something they needed to worry about.

TWENTY-EIGHT

The time was moving along, and around eleven, Amanda made herself a black coffee. She and Trent had spoken with ten employees, leaving fifteen if it wasn't for the fact five people were out of the office today. Between speaking with employees, they flipped through the written threats. No one was flagging as incriminating, but could they expect it would be that easy?

One person they spoke with was the other senior partner, Dalton McClain. He was fifteen years younger than O'Neil and ambitious. McClain seemed more affected by the situation than any of the others they spoke to, but he was looking forward to the acquisition. He expressed excitement at the challenge of being in a larger market. Amanda swore she saw dollar signs come into his eyes more than once. McClain was also generous in his praise for Dominique. Amanda felt confident in concluding that McClain didn't hold any ill will against his boss, and therefore had no reason to order a hit on her.

A man in his mid-thirties entered the room without knocking, having bathed in cologne. He was dressed in a black suit that was snug on his frame. She'd guess he put on a bit of weight or muscle and hadn't bothered updating his wardrobe.

She offered him a tight smile and pointed at the chair across from them, but he dropped into the one at the end of the table.

Alrighty then... "We're Detectives Steele and—"

"I know who you are." The man undid the button on his suit jacket and laid a hand down the front to smooth the fabric.

She imagined their names had made several rounds inside the firm since their arrival. "You'll need to tell us who you are."

The man's face flinched, as if she'd wounded his pride by not recognizing him. "Chris Ritter."

"And your position with the firm?" She vaguely recalled his face from the firm's website.

"Junior partner. I'm the youngest the firm has ever had. I've been here since I graduated and passed the bar."

The website said the firm's doors opened seventeen years ago. "Which was when?" *It's like the guy set himself up to be questioned. Not exactly a strong trait to have if it translated to the courtroom. He'd always be batting away issues he raised himself.*

"Twelve years ago."

"And how do you feel about Dominique Sharp moving the business to DC?"

All the arrogance left his eyes and was replaced with fire. He clenched his jaw and said nothing. Though he didn't need to say a word when his body language spoke on his behalf.

"I'm going to wager a guess here that you aren't too happy about it," Amanda said.

"No." The small word sounded like it took effort to push out.

"Why is that?" Trent asked, beating Amanda to the same counter.

"I've worked my ass off for Ms. Sharp for twelve years, and now on the cusp of being promoted to senior partner, she closes shop here and moves on."

"Washington isn't that far. Many people commute," Amanda reasoned, noting how formally he referred to his boss.

"I'm not sure that's going to work for me."

It didn't seem that Chris held any warmth toward Dominique. "Why not?"

"Well, it's not so much about the drive, but Ms. Sharp has made it pretty clear she doesn't value my contribution to her firm."

Amanda's neck stiffened. There was a tinge of malice in his voice, but no wonder he wasn't a fan of Dominique if she made him feel that way. "She said that?"

"She didn't have to *say* it. She told me that once she takes over the new firm, she will be assessing everyone's positions within the company and deciding whether they will still have a job."

"I'm sure she meant in general," Trent said. "There would be employees on the other end as well."

Chris shook his head. "No. I asked her when I should get my promotion to senior partner, and she looked me in the eye and said it wasn't in the foreseeable future. I mean what a b—" He stopped talking and paled. "Don't go thinking that I would... No, I never..."

Amanda wasn't surprised that he'd rushed to his own defense, but it did little to sway her. "How did that make you feel? I mean you invested all those years in her company. You probably helped the bottom line."

"I *did* help it. My billings surpass the other junior lawyers. It's my turn to climb the ranks."

"Though it doesn't seem that Ms. Sharp is convinced of that." It was a hard reality check, but Amanda served it up, nonetheless.

Chris's face shadowed. "You know what? It's a good thing that I'm finally seeing her for the person she is."

"And what's that?" Trent's finger hovered over his tablet.

"She's sharp, just like her name, but she's also a shark. You turn your back on her for a second and she'll bite your head off. I've lost all respect for her. And this acquisition is more like a hostile takeover than a friendly agreement."

Amanda shifted and glanced at Trent. "What makes you say it was hostile?"

Chris shrugged. "I'm just basing that on her personality. There must always be something in it for her. She doesn't have qualms about equality or fairness."

"From the sounds of it, you've lost all respect for her since the announcement of the firm acquisition." *If not before...*

"You could say that."

"What would happen if Ms. Sharp were to die? Would the acquisition still go through?" She was striving to determine if retaliation for being denied advancement in his career would hold up as a motive. Though it was possible, regardless, that Chris could have had enough of Dominique's undervaluing his contributions to the firm.

"That I don't know, but ownership would pass on to the two senior partners, Bennie O'Neil, and Dalton McClain."

"But if the deal didn't go through, do you think the business would stay here?" she asked.

"I would suspect so. Both men live in town."

So Dominique's death could benefit Chris. Amanda remained quiet, and so did Trent. It took a few seconds for the impact to hit Chris.

"Oh, I see what you did there. You made me look like I'd want to kill her."

"You did that for yourself." She remained still as she watched him.

He met her gaze, his eyes cold. "Then ask for my alibis. I'll have them. I didn't kill anyone, and I didn't shoot Ms. Sharp's friend."

Amanda stiffened. They hadn't mentioned that much to Chris. "How do you know about him?"

He gave her a tight smile. "You don't think everyone's keeping quiet out there, do you? Word about you two and what's going on in here is all that's getting done today."

All right then... "Did you know about Ms. Sharp's last-minute business trip that took her to DC on Friday?" Amanda laid the bait to see what Chris might say.

"I think she ended up staying the weekend, and most of us around here knew that except maybe Bennie O'Neil. He was off last week."

Yet O'Neil was the least suspect of everyone they spoke to. And since Chris knew Dominique wasn't at home, why would he have sent a hit woman there? Though, it was possible he hadn't stipulated time and location. Still, Amanda didn't think he'd have the balls to hire a hit person to take out his boss or have strong enough motive. A lot of people hated their bosses but didn't order their murder. "Well, thank you for your time."

"Yep." Chris got up and ambled out of the room.

"He was a character," Trent said.

"You're still here? Unbelievable."

Amanda turned to the doorway where Dominique Sharp was standing. She'd changed since the hospital into a tight-fitting blue leather pencil skirt paired with a white blouse. She was wearing a strapless bustier vest over it, a few shades to the cream side of the spectrum. There was no explaining some people's fashion sense. Though Amanda didn't set the bar. "Have you heard anything from the hospital on Joel's condition?"

"He's out of surgery, and the doctors are cautiously optimistic."

That wasn't exactly something to celebrate, yet Dominique said it as if it were promising. The words of the senior partner came back to mind, about Dominique having a bomb lit beneath her without it raising a reaction. She saw O'Neil's point in action. Here, her lover, who she must have some feelings for, was lying in a hospital bed after taking a bullet, and she seemed fine. Amanda wouldn't have left his side in this woman's place.

"I'd like to know when you two should be wrapped up. My employees aren't getting anything done with you here." Dominique perched her hands on her hips and beckoned a response with an arched eyebrow.

"We're sorry to be a distraction," Amanda pushed out, impressed by her restraint. They were only there trying to determine if someone in this woman's camp had ordered a killer to take her out, but that made them a nuisance. "We shouldn't be much longer. But since you're here, could you...?" Amanda gestured to the chair across from them.

Like Chris, Dominique sat at the end of the table. "I don't have much time."

Even less if you don't cooperate with the police... The thought zipped through her, and it was hard not to let it slip out loud. "We were just speaking with Chris Ritter."

"Let me guess. He was bemoaning the fact I won't commit to giving him a promotion to senior partner. But there's no way that kid has it in him to take me on."

"You'd be surprised what people are capable of, especially the ones you least expect."

"I don't think so." She crossed her arms and jutted out her chin. "I've gotten pretty good at reading people over the years."

So have I... And what Amanda saw before her was someone so embedded in her own ego she didn't exist in reality. "Why deny him the promotion?"

"You met him. He's arrogant, and it impedes him from being a good lawyer. It makes him emotional and reactive."

"He said his billings are better than the other junior partners with the firm," Trent pointed out.

"Sure, but by comparison to the talent at Gabay, Finch & Earnest, Chris is found lacking."

Amanda cringed at Dominique's summation of a human being, no less an employee, who by his words dedicated his career to her firm since passing the bar. But she wasn't under any illusion the woman whose life they were trying to save was a saint. But the woman who died in her place had been. Amanda would do what she could to protect Dominique, but her primary motivation was finding Christine's killer and getting her justice. "Thank you for your honest answer."

"Honesty is the only way I roll. So? When should you two be leaving?" Her eyes drifted to the table. "Has Casey not brought you the sale and financial paperwork yet?" Dominique never waited for a response, got up with a huff, and left the room.

Trent leaned in toward Amanda. "We want to keep her alive, right?"

"It's the job," she muttered. "But I look at it this way. We find out who wants her dead, then we find justice for Christine Lane."

"I like the shift of focus."

"It's the only way I'm going to get through this." Amanda could have said more, like how Dominique Sharp was almost unbearable. She had a grating personality to be sure. But even though Amanda could justify her feelings toward the woman, she didn't deserve to get killed.

"I'm sorry for the delay." Casey came into the room holding a portfolio and handed it to Amanda. "This is a copy of all the sale paperwork and financials from both sides of the deal."

"Thank you. Before you leave, we just have a question for you."

"Okay." Spoken with the hint of a whine, like she'd wanted to hit and run. But Casey sat down anyhow, walking back to the chair across from Amanda and Trent.

"When we spoke earlier, you struck us as being afraid of something," Amanda said, easing into things. "Is there something you should be telling us?"

Casey licked her lips and nodded. "Though it's nothing serious, I'm seeing Chris Ritter. If this got back to Dom, she'd have a conniption. She's not a fan of office romances."

Amanda was disappointed that's all Casey had been holding back. "I can see her side. They often blow up." This was out of Amanda's mouth before she gave her response any thought. There were times her attraction to Trent seemed unavoidable, and he made no secret in the past that he had feelings for her too. They'd shared stolen moments a few times. A kiss here or there. But they had kept their relationship all business to avoid romantic complications.

"Yes, well, if I'm being honest, things have run cold between us. He's obsessed about Dom closing the firm here."

"So we heard. Thank you for the paperwork." Amanda pointed toward the portfolio.

"You're welcome." With that, Casey left.

"All these hours and no solid leads." Trent blew out a breath.

Frustrating as that was, it was how investigations worked. A step forward, several back. Sometimes it was just standing still while the clock rushed ahead.

TWENTY-NINE

Another hour and a half went by, and Amanda's stomach was grumbling in chorus with Trent's. It was going on one in the afternoon, and they'd had nothing to eat but the donut that morning. They had spoken with everyone at the firm they could except for the receptionist, who was due to come in at any moment.

"Did you want to break for lunch?" Trent asked her.

"Nope, we're here. Let's stay put and see this through."

"You wanted to speak with me?" The receptionist entered the room.

"Yes, please sit over there," Amanda directed, pointing at the vacated chair, which might as well have been a revolving door for the volume of traffic it had seen today.

She shut the door before following Amanda's direction.

"We're Detectives Stenson and Steele. We never did get your name," Trent said.

She licked her lips before speaking. "Minnie Yates."

Amanda offered her a smile, trying to calm her nerves. "How long have you worked for Dominique Sharp?"

"Since the doors opened seventeen years ago."

"It's always nice to find reliable employment. You must enjoy working here." Amanda would assume so given her duration at the firm.

"It pays well."

It seemed like a lukewarm response, and it had Amanda wondering about the reason. "Do you know why we're interested in speaking with you?"

Minnie nodded.

"Do you know of anyone who might want Ms. Sharp dead?" Amanda asked.

Minnie flinched, ever so slightly, and licked her lips again.

She was nervous or thirsty, or both. But if they were going to get anywhere with her, they needed to get her to relax some. "Would you like a glass of water?"

"Sure."

Amanda got up and poured her a glass from the sideboard and handed it over.

"Thank you." Minnie took a sip.

Amanda returned to her seat. "If there's something you need to say, please know that you're safe, whatever it is."

Minnie drank some more water and cradled the glass with both hands. "There are many people here who aren't happy about Ms. Sharp's decision to move the business to DC. And I'm not just talking about employees of the firm." Minnie's eyes flicked up and met Amanda's.

"You mean customers?" It wasn't even an angle Amanda had considered before. But this firm represented criminals. It could be someone who didn't want to risk her breaking attorney-client privilege. The move could have been seen as disloyalty.

"Uh-huh." Minnie slurped some water, adding to the palpable tension in the air.

Amanda could guess that Minnie was building up to some reveal and didn't want to push her for risk of her clamming up.

Amanda spoke up only after several minutes of stretched silence. "Do you have a specific customer in mind?"

A slight nod. "This person is rather dangerous."

Minnie's hesitation already had Amanda assuming that. "As I said, you are safe to talk to us. This person's name?"

"He has been a client of Ms. Sharp's since not long after she opened her doors. He was her first multimillion-dollar client."

Amanda wasn't going to push her on the name again so soon out of fear it would shut her down. "Did something happen with this client?"

"Uh-huh. All because Ms. Sharp decided with the move to DC she was heading in a different direction. She wants to shift focus to fraud and financial cases."

"They're still criminal offenses," Trent filled in.

"Yes, but different from this specific client's needs. She fired them as her client, refunded their retainer, and gave them a referral. Other clients were fine with it, but..." Minnie drained the rest of the water from the glass.

"Their name?" Trent asked.

"Lucas Hernandez."

No wonder Minnie hesitated to provide his name. Hernandez was a big-time drug dealer, who continually got away with his crimes. The PWCPD staged a sting that cost three officers their lives. Some of his men went away for that, while Hernandez remained untouchable. Even federal law enforcement had failed to get charges to stick against him. Was all that the work of Dominique Sharp? If so, it made it harder to think about protecting a woman who slept soundly after defending a cop killer. "How did Lucas Hernandez react to Ms. Sharp dissolving their professional relationship?" She could only imagine not well at all. Hernandez was used to being the one calling the shots.

"I overheard him talking with Ms. Sharp the day she handed him a check to reimburse his retainer. It was late at night, but I was here working on paperwork for a case. I had just locked up and was leaving when I saw Ms. Sharp in the parking lot with Hernandez and two of his goons. They didn't see me, I don't think, but I saw and heard them."

Amanda's heart was picking up speed. Hernandez had people who did his dirty work. What was to say one of them wasn't a woman who liked to shoot people and wrap them in tarps?

Minnie continued. "The guy had a gun on her. At least I'm fairly sure he did."

Amanda noted the subtle distinction in gender. *The guy...* She followed a hunch. "Were they both men?"

Minnie shook her head. "One was a woman."

Excitement laced through Amanda. Was this woman who they were after? "When was this?"

"Last Monday. I heard Lucas say he wasn't going to go away silently. He ordered Ms. Sharp to remain his lawyer, but she refused."

It wasn't hard to imagine Dominique standing bold in the face of life-threatening danger. They had seen that performance already.

"He spoke to her in this most chilling voice. I've had nightmares about it since. He told Ms. Sharp that she could work for him or end up dead in her bed." Minnie's chin quivered, having made it through what Amanda imagined was the worst of the story.

Dead in her bed... That struck just a little too close. The victim might have been Christine Lane, but she was killed in Dominique Sharp's bedroom. Amanda would like to know why Dominique hadn't mentioned a word about this altercation. Had she not viewed it as a threat? They never did mention Christine was found under her bed, but still... "What happened after that?"

"He ripped up the check and took off with his people," Minnie added.

"And what did Dominique do?" Trent asked.

"She got into her Cadillac and left."

"And what did you do?" Amanda wanted to make sure they didn't miss any small tidbit.

"I went over and picked up what he'd ripped up. That's how I know it was the check."

"Thank you for telling us all of this." While this was a promising lead, Amanda wasn't eager about where it was taking them.

"If he finds out I told you this, he's going to..." Minnie blanched, her face becoming a mask of horror.

"There's no reason he ever needs to find out." She and Trent would talk to Lucas Hernandez, but there would be no mention of Minnie.

"Thank you." Minnie sniffled and bobbed her head toward the door. "May I leave now?"

"You can, and thank you for being brave and sharing this with us." Amanda gave her card to Minnie and told her to call anytime if she thought of something else or was concerned about her safety. "Could you shut the door behind you?"

When Minnie was gone, both Amanda and Trent swiveled to face each other.

"This Hernandez guy could be who ordered the hit on Sharp."

"Yep."

"You know him." He wasn't asking and leveled his gaze at her.

"I wish I didn't. Before we continue this conversation, I'd like to speak with Dominique." What she hadn't yet said to Trent was they'd need to talk to Malone before speaking with Hernandez.

THIRTY

Amanda and Trent left the conference room and headed toward Dominique Sharp's office with all the folders and the portfolio in hand. She was in the room, door shut, talking *at* Casey with a raised voice. Through the window they could see that Casey was sitting across from Dominique, shoulders slumped.

Trent knocked. The berating stopped, and Dominique waved for them to enter. Casey stood and left. Amanda wanted to pass her a reassuring glance on her way out, but Casey's gaze was on the floor.

"Yes, Detectives. What is it now?"

Amanda didn't think she'd ever figure this woman out. Someone wanted to kill her, and she seemed more concerned about the inconvenience it caused to carrying on business as normal. "Were you going to tell us about Lucas Hernandez?"

"Tell you what?"

Amanda took a steadying breath and pointed at the vacated chair. "Would you mind?"

"By all means."

Amanda sat and broached Hernandez a little less directly.

"We heard that with the move to DC you are cutting some of your Woodbridge clients."

"What of it?"

This woman gave new meaning to the expression *cool as a cucumber*. Though if she didn't adjust her attitude, she might become *cold as a corpse*. The thought fired through and had Amanda chastising herself. "Not everyone was pleased with that decision."

Dominique leaned back in her chair as if she were involved in a casual conversation. "People resist change at first, but it all works out."

"We heard that Lucas Hernandez threatened your life." Amanda clipped right to the point now, tired of playing games with this woman. The longer they dragged this out and catered to Dominique's whims, the longer Christine Lane's killer was free.

"Again, what of it?"

No denial or question about where they'd heard the news. She either knew or didn't care. "Why didn't you mention this to us when we asked if you knew of anyone who might want you dead?" Amanda emphasized the last word and thought it might jolt some reaction from the woman. Nothing. Dominique was just as O'Neil described. Impervious.

"I can't remember everyone who has threatened me."

"This just happened last Monday. And within a week, there was a murder in your home, in your bedroom," Amanda stressed.

"And while that's tragic, why would I think to mention Lucas?"

Given the referral to him by first name, Dominique didn't seem intimidated by the man. "He said he could kill you in your bed." *Do I really need to remind her?*

Dominique smiled, causing Amanda to tense. The fact she dismissed a man like Hernandez was unsettling.

"He'd never follow through," Dominique said. "I know where the bodies are buried. That wasn't the first time he's threatened me, and it won't be the last."

Amanda couldn't get over the woman's lack of concern for her own life. Was she really that cocky, or was it as Amanda wondered before? Was there a reason they had yet to uncover? "Except that drug kingpins don't always subscribe to reason, and they aren't in the business of trusting people. You can't be certain he'll never come after you, knowledge of where the bodies are buried or not. But when you say *bodies*, are we talking about literal bodies?" The cop in her couldn't just let her earlier comment slip by. And really, wouldn't Dominique's knowledge make her a potential liability for Hernandez? One that he'd want to eliminate?

"Wouldn't you like to know?"

Amanda imagined the words *attorney-client privilege* rolling through the lawyer's mind.

"All this talk about Lucas reminds me I need to cut him another check." She pressed a button on her phone, and Casey's voice came over the speaker.

"Yes, Ms. Sharp?"

"Make sure that accounting cuts another check for Lucas Hernandez reimbursing his retainer. He mislaid his other one."

Mislaid... All those years working in defense, Dominique had wordplay down pat.

"I'll do—"

Dominique pressed another button, cutting Casey off.

Amanda saw little point in continuing to talk about Hernandez. Not when it felt one-sided. "Are there any other clients who threatened you when you told them you were referring them to another lawyer?" *Just for the sake of transparency...*

"No. Now, if that's all, you can see yourselves out. I have work to do." Dominique opened a folder on her desk and flipped her laptop open.

Unbelievable...

Amanda and Trent left the firm. The temperature had racked up several degrees, aligning more with the heat of her temper. "Does that woman have a death wish?"

"Not sure about that. I think she believes she is impervious to death."

"Impervious to everything, more like. But if she keeps up the attitude and independent streak, it might be too late when she finds out she's not."

They both loaded into the car. Opening the doors let some stifling air escape, but not a lot. Still, if Amanda had a choice between sweating in the car and going back inside with Dominique, the choice was an easy one. Both were uncomfortable, but being away from the lawyer let her temper cool off.

"So Lucas Hernandez is a drug kingpin?" Trent switched the A/C on. The warm air spilling from the vents only made the car feel like a convection oven.

"Yep, and to date untouchable. He always slips away scot-free. Before you transferred to the PWCPD, a sting operation was conducted on one of his warehouses, resulting in the deaths of three SWAT officers."

"And he still walked?"

"He did. Some of his guys were sent to prison, but they'll never roll on him."

"From the sound of this character, that would be a death wish."

"Most definitely. So trust me when I say I don't look forward to speaking with the man, let alone accusing him of anything. We'll have to watch how we word things. But before we do any of that, we need to clear this past Malone. I'm sure he'll want us to bring backup."

"I want backup."

Cool air wafted from the vents, and Trent got them on the road to Central.

THIRTY-ONE

"Lucas Hernandez? Are you mad? Have you lost your mind?" Malone was staring at Amanda and Trent from the other side of his desk. They had just run through everything that had transpired at Sharp & Associates, ending with the verbal threat against Dominique Sharp.

She understood his concern, though it changed nothing. "What choice do we have, Sarge? He threatened her life just days before Christine Lane was killed in Sharp's bedroom."

"Do you think someone like Hernandez would get this wrong?"

"We know he's not the one pulling the trigger," Amanda said.

"And one *goon* the receptionist saw was a woman," Trent put in.

Malone waved a hand. "Even if Hernandez sent one of his people, you can't go in there accusing the man. He'll lawyer up or worse..." He drilled Amanda with his gaze.

"I know the guy's dangerous. That's why we were just going to have a little chat."

Malone shook his head. "That might be your intention, but I doubt that's how Hernandez is going to see it."

Amanda flumped back in her chair. "Then what are we supposed to do? Ignore the fact he uttered a death threat? His people could have killed an innocent woman. A woman who helped people in the community in her downtime, found people homes, and was a mother. I couldn't live with myself if I just turned my back on this lead." She refused to let fear dictate her next moves, finding new appreciation for Dominique's viewpoint.

Malone's cheeks became bright red, and he clenched his left hand into a fist. "Fine. I get it. *But* you will approach this as a *chat* as you put it, and you will have backup. Am I understood?"

She could live with those stipulations. "You are."

"I can't stress this enough. This Hernandez is a serious fella, and not to be messed with."

There was a stretch of silence, during which Amanda's mind dipped to the past and the lost brothers in blue. She certainly had no interest in becoming another casualty.

"All right, get this over with. But use caution." Malone emphasized his last sentence, and it shot a cold shiver down Amanda's spine.

Amanda and Trent left Malone's office. Her steps were weighed down by this horrible feeling that something bad was going to result from speaking with Hernandez. She touched Trent's forearm to stop him, and he turned to face her.

"I can do this without you," she told him.

"No way am I leaving you to go talk to this psycho alone."

"Hernandez will make an enemy of us, just for questioning him. You don't need to get caught up in this."

"I seem to recall someone saying just a couple months ago that we don't intimidate easily."

Having one's words come back around was never fun.

"There is a distinction between those who hold powerful positions within the community and Hernandez."

"Sure, he's more likely to kill you if you piss him off than the mayor is."

"Hmm. I can think of at least a few powerful people we've taken down who were sick and murderous."

"All right, fair enough, but the point is there's no way I'm sitting this out, so get that through your skull." He pierced her eyes with adamant intensity. Even his posture became rigid. Feet planted, shoulders back and square. She might be witnessing the mindset that got him shot when he assisted the FBI with their case years ago.

"Fine, but don't say I didn't warn you." She resumed walking, and Trent matched her strides. She just wished she could shake the feeling that following this lead signaled the start of a storm.

THIRTY-TWO

Amanda turned down Trent's suggestion that they get something to eat before heading over to the latest address they had for Lucas Hernandez. Her stomach was too nauseous to accept food since Hernandez was mentioned.

Two uniformed officers were following them in a cruiser.

"Trent, pull over."

"We're almost there."

"Please."

He parked at the curb, and the cruiser pulled behind them.

Amanda got out of the car and went to the officer, laying out her directions. "I want you out of sight. If Hernandez sees you, this will change the friendly tone of the visit."

"We're supposed to be there to assist you. How are we supposed to do that if you have us posted down the street?" Officer Jensen was newer to the PWCPD, but not new to the badge. He was a transfer from another department.

"I appreciate your enthusiasm, but Hernandez can't feel threatened in any way." She couldn't stress that point enough. It struck her on the drive over, and it had her stomach roiling. *This is just a chat...* She reiterated her adopted mantra in her head.

She returned to the car with Trent. The cruiser pulled a U-turn behind them.

"Where are they going?" Trent's eyes were fixed on the rearview mirror.

She told him what she'd told the officers, and how they were going to set up on the closest side street to Hernandez's home. "They are still close enough to step in if things turn sideways, but Hernandez or his men can't see them."

"I'm not sure I'm comfortable with this, even if I get your point. This guy's that touchy?"

"I'm not willing to take the chance he's not and get my head blown off." She gestured toward the windshield. "Let's go."

Trent clenched his jaw and fixed his eyes ahead of him. If he was pissed off with her, so be it. Couldn't he see she was just looking out for both of them?

A few minutes later, Trent was pulling in front of a palatial two-story house with black trim that stood out in sharp contrast to the white stucco. The driveway was three car widths wide and long enough to fit four sedans. There was also a two-car garage, but two luxury vehicles sat in the driveway.

Amanda admired the sleek lines of the neon-green Lamborghini as she walked past it to the front door. It would seem her brother's love of cars had infected her. But she was also grasping for whatever would ease her nerves.

They walked under a double-story archway to reach a set of massive mahogany doors.

Amanda glanced at Trent, but he wasn't looking at her. She pressed the doorbell, shaking off his mood. She couldn't afford to let it affect her. Not now.

One door opened, and a man stood there with an assault rifle strapped across his chest. *Not trying to hide the fact he's armed and ready for war. Check.*

"We're looking to speak with Lucas Hernandez." She

grounded her posture, being careful not to come across as combative.

"Good for you." The man nudged his head toward the road, encouraging them to turn around and leave.

"We're just looking to have a nice, friendly conversation." She pushed that out with the trace of a smile while sweeping her jacket back to expose her badge clipped to her waistband.

The man lifted his gun an inch or two.

Trent flinched, but she stepped forward. If she was going to earn an audience with Hernandez, she needed to prove herself worthy. "It will take five minutes, and we'll be out of his hair."

"In five minutes, you'll be dead," the man hissed as he lowered his face to the height of hers.

Her insides were trembling, but she did what she could to prevent it from showing. It involved a lot of coaching herself to keep it together. "I'll need less than that."

The man stared her down while Amanda's heart pounded.

"Bruno, just let the fine lady and her friend in," a man called out.

The soldier stiffened, leaving Amanda to guess the directive came from Hernandez himself.

"Bruno!" the man barked and clapped his hands. This had the soldier backing up and leading them to a central seating area.

Crystals dripped from chandeliers overhead, and the expanse of the home swallowed them.

"Please, tell me who you are." Hernandez was seated on a long white sectional and patted the cushion next to him.

"We're both fine over here," Trent said.

"Oh, he speaks." Hernandez threw one of his arms over the back of the couch as an arrogant smile curved his lips.

"We're Detectives Steele and Stenson," Amanda said firmly.

"I thought I smelled pork." A slight woman entered the

area, and Trent did a double take. Amanda couldn't be sure if it was because she looked like the woman he pursued or if it was her apparel. She was wearing a black leather pantsuit that clung to her tight frame.

"Now, now, Nina, that's no way to talk about our guests."

Nina perched behind her master and stared at Amanda. She tried not to let it get to her as she dropped into a chair across from Hernandez while Trent stood at her side.

"We heard that you're searching for a new lawyer." Amanda started with neutral territory.

"I was expecting you might come by here. I heard someone was murdered in her home. It wasn't her though. How is Dom?"

"She's fine. Unfortunately, we can't say the same for her real estate agent. But we believe she was killed in a case of mistaken identity."

"How was she killed?" Nina asked.

"Three gunshots." Amanda relayed the facts without feeling.

"I prefer something a little more intimate myself." Nina pulled out a long blade from a sheath on her back. She stuck her fingertip against the point of the knife.

"That's enough," Hernandez bellowed. To Amanda, he said, "I sure hope you're not insinuating I had anything to do with this."

"Not at all. We're just here to talk. Dominique mentioned a few of her clients weren't too happy about her moving her firm to Washington." She phrased it this way to avoid being seen as accusing him again.

"I wasn't, but things never stay the same. I am disappointed by her lack of loyalty though."

It was as if he were trying to entice Amanda to mention his threat. With a man like this, though, she felt forced to say something. Hernandez could see the lack of a response as disrespect. "I can understand that."

A sly smile spread across the man's lips. "I like you."

His offering did little to soothe her nerves. "I'm pleased to hear that, and as a businessman, you can appreciate that my partner and I are here because... well, if we didn't come, our bosses might accuse us of not doing our jobs."

"I get that. Just doing what the boss tells you. I respect that. Obedience is an admirable trait in employees."

"If I had any, I'm sure I'd agree."

Hernandez laughed, but it died out quickly. "Well, if that's all..." Hernandez gestured to Bruno, indicating for him to walk them out.

Amanda stood. "Thank you for your time."

"Yes. Just remember the courtesy I've shown you today, Detective Steele."

Amanda's back was to him when he said her name, but shivers laced down her spine. There was something in his tone, in his choice of wording, that niggled.

Bruno shut the door behind them with a thud, and Amanda and Trent didn't say a thing until they got into the car.

"You did good in there," Trent told her, snapping his seatbelt. "You're very cool under pressure."

"If that's what you think, I should get an award for my acting skills."

"You earned one, but I'm worried to be honest. I didn't much care for what Hernandez said just before we left. He said *courtesy* as if he did you a favor and now you owe him."

It took hearing Trent saying this for her to understand why it had given her chills. There was also the way Hernandez made a point of saying her name, as if he were committing it to memory.

"You all right?" he prompted when she didn't reply.

She nodded, lying to him and herself. "I don't think he ordered the hit on Dominique."

"Not if Nina's his only female soldier. She's too petite for one thing."

And she seems fond of her knife...

"So what now? We still have a folder of threats against Sharp, but there are people at the other end of this acquisition. We haven't talked with them yet."

"Well, that's not happening today." She pointed at the time on the dash. 4:30 PM.

"Are you suggesting we clock out for five?"

"Since we clocked in around four this morning, yes, I am." She didn't have it in her to wade through the threats, hoping one would snatch her attention.

"I'm not going to argue with you. What do you think we should do with the financial paperwork for the sale and purchase?"

"We could look at them, not that we'll understand them. I suggest we pass them over to Financial Crimes to have them review all of it and see if they can find anything that flags. Not sure if I mentioned this, but I thought before that someone wanted to prevent Dominique from seeing them."

"I suppose anything's possible, and I'm with you about passing off the financial reports. Math and I aren't good friends." Trent got them on the road, and Amanda sat back and shut her eyes. Though she was far from relaxed.

Meeting Hernandez was like meeting the devil, or so Amanda imagined. Charming and enticing on the surface, scheming beneath. If he saw speaking with her as a courtesy, he would turn up one day to collect a favor from her. And when she refused...

Her eyes shot open.

THIRTY-THREE

Amanda and Trent dropped off the financial paperwork and parted ways with the agreement they'd set out for the DC law firm first thing. They also called the office and made an appointment for ten AM with the managing partner, Howard Gabay. That left her and Trent with the rest of the evening to enjoy.

But when she stepped into her house, she was blanketed with loneliness. Zoe wasn't here. To make the stillness worse, Hernandez's face popped into her mind with his smug smile. She shook aside the sudden chill that came with the image. That monster had no right to violate her peace, especially in her home, which was to be her place of refuge.

She flung her shoes off and kept walking through the home to the bathroom, where she ran a hot shower and let it blast her skin. She stayed there until the water ran cold, and even a bit after, trying to drown out all thoughts of the drug kingpin.

Her cell phone rang on the bathroom sink, and she turned off the taps and squeezed out between the curtain and the wall. She was dripping all over the floor, but whatever... If it was the job calling, she'd be there. She lit up at the sight of Carter's name on her screen. "Hello, there," she answered.

"Oh? Should I take the lack of a formal greeting as a good sign? Are you off the clock?"

"You should know better than to ask that."

"Right, you're always on the clock. I was calling to see if you're up for company."

"How fast can you get here?"

"Given how happy you sound to hear from me, maybe not fast enough."

"See you soon." She ended the call and dried off.

There was a knock on the front door.

Maybe Carter was just down the street when he called. She wrapped the towel around herself, deciding to greet Carter just like that.

"I'm coming," she said, prancing through the living room.

She'd come through the garage, so she hadn't dealt with the mail that was spread on the floor of her entry. It had been pushed with abandon through the mail slot. She gathered it up and tossed it onto the entry table. One envelope fell to the ground, maybe more than one. She didn't care.

She opened the door, wedging herself between it and the frame. It only took one second for mortification to hit. "Ah, Dad."

He smiled and turned away. "It seems I'm interrupting plans."

"No, no, it's fine." She gave an anxious look over his shoulder to see if Carter was pulling up. There was no one else in sight. "Ah, come in. I'll just go put something on." She held ever tighter on the top of the towel as she backed up and headed for the hallway.

She heard her father come inside and set the dropped mail on the table.

"You know you don't have to hide your boyfriends from me," her dad called out to her.

She was in her bedroom, desperately wanting to put the last

forty seconds behind her. Hearing him label Carter as her boyfriend had her freaking out a bit. That label landed as a blow to her chest and snatched her breath.

She shuffled through her drawer in search of a pale-blue shirt with the words BRING ON THE SUNSHINE. It was made of light-weight material and fit her curves perfectly. *Where the hell is that T-shirt...* And there it was! She snatched it and put it over her lacy bra. Then slipped a pair of capri shorts over lacy thong underwear. At least she was ready for Carter after her dad left.

"Should I leave? I mean, it's clear you have a guy coming over."

"No, it's fine. You're here now." She rushed back to the living room, where she found her dad on the couch. "Do you want water, tea, coffee...?"

"I'm good. I brought this for you, though." He held up a brown bag from Petey's Patties.

She'd been so self-conscious and shocked by him being on her front step she hadn't even noticed it before. "You're spoiling her, aren't you?" The burger joint was Zoe's favorite restaurant.

"You bet we are, but everyone at the house ate early. I drove by here on the way home with the order and saw you were here. I thought knowing you, you were starving yourself, so I made another trip to the place." He handed her the bag. "Bacon double cheeseburger, extra onions. That's the way you like it if I remember right."

"You did. Thanks, Dad, but you didn't have to do that."

"I wanted to."

The smells coming from the bag had her stomach rumbling, but she didn't want to devour a burger with all that onion before Carter got here.

"You can always eat it later. Though it might not be as good."

"Oh, they're even good cold."

An awkward silence settled between them. For most of her life, her relationship with her father was one thing that had come easy with two exceptions. When she turned her back on her family after losing Kevin and Lindsey and when the news came out about her father's affair with Emma Blair. Her cop instinct told her he was here to discuss the latter. "Right, so as you gathered, I am expecting company..."

"Let me get to the point then, and I'll be off." Her father wet his lips, and with that, the self-assured man she knew lost some of his power. "I wanted to apologize to your face."

"For...?" She was nauseous, not sure if it was latent hunger or anxiousness over where her father was going with this apology.

"I know you used to look up to me, even want to be like me and become police chief someday. I hope that my actions, namely the affair, haven't derailed that intention. You'd be an incredible asset to the department in that capacity."

"Dad, what are you saying?"

"I guess I'm trying to say that it eats me up that I've disappointed you, that I've hurt you. The affair I had with Emma Blair is unforgivable."

Amanda processed her father's words for a few minutes. "You're only human, Dad."

"Right. Well, that wasn't how you used to see me."

"I don't know what to say to that. You are flesh and blood." She offered him a smile, but he had his walls up. *Or is it me?* There was still a wound left from his infidelity.

"Hmm, Emma came to me. I guess there's a situation with Spencer."

Amanda felt her defenses rising. "You're not here to tell me how to work my investigation, are you? You told Emma you weren't getting involved."

"And I'm not. Hell, I'm going about this all the wrong way."

She could voice her agreement but gave him a pass, and offered, "Spencer's been released of all suspicion."

"Well, that's great news."

"Yeah."

Her father wrung his hands. "I also wanted to apologize for putting you in that position."

"Which position is that?"

"If the affair hadn't happened, then... well, there wouldn't be the recent complication."

"Spencer also wouldn't have life, Dad. The fact he does is a good thing." Not that she believed Spencer was going to talk to her again. She had her own apology tour to make.

"I just meant... Well, I hope you didn't go harder on him because you projected your anger at me onto him."

She never thought of it that way, but he might have made a good point. Her going hard on Spencer may have been more than overcompensating to prove herself free of bias.

Her father eased off the couch. "What I thought. I'm not sure how I can ever make this up to you."

Amanda stood, but she didn't know what to say. *Is there anything he can do?* "It will just take some time, Dad, but we'll get back to how things were." They'd had their conversations on the matter before, but this one carried the promise of being their last.

"You're right. More time." He turned for the door, but she wrapped her arms around him. He kissed her on the forehead. "Have a good night, Mandy Monkey."

She shook her head at the family nickname she detested. Not that her dislike for it discouraged her family from using it. They would probably have it etched into her gravestone. "You too."

Her father reached for the door handle at the same time there was a knock on the door.

"Maybe just let me..." Amanda went to wedge in front of her father.

Her father was smiling, clearly amused at her discomfort. She opened the door to Carter, and backed up, expecting her father to mirror her movements. Instead he bypassed her, said nothing to Carter, but turned around and shot him a glare for Amanda to witness.

"Who is that?" Carter pivoted to look at her father.

Amanda touched his cheek, and moved him to face her. "It doesn't matter. What does is it's about time you got here." She tugged on his shirt and yanked him into the house.

THIRTY-FOUR

Amanda heard Carter's phone vibrate on the nightstand and felt him kiss her cheek before he slipped out of bed around one in the morning. She would have called out goodbye, but she was down for the count. Even now, in the passenger seat of a department car on the way to DC at nine-thirty, it was a good thing she wasn't the one driving. At least Trent looked far more rested than she felt.

"How are you doing over there?" he asked.

It was unsettling he read her so well. It's like anytime her mind drifted, he knew it had left the present moment. She had a firm grip on a take-out cup from Hannah's Diner. The coffee was long gone but somehow just holding it helped keep her eyes open. "I'm just tired."

"Nah, there's more to it. We were home early last night." He glanced over at her, and their eyes met. "Oh."

He seemed to have read her mind again, but she spelled it out anyhow. "Carter came over." *And before that there was a weird incident with my dad...* She'd leave that out of her summary.

"I guess that explains it."

"Trust me. It does." No offense to her late husband, but she had mind-blowing sex with Carter. She'd feel accurate in saying he was the best she'd ever had. Memories from last night crept in and had her cranking the A/C. "The coffee's making me hot," she offered as an explanation.

Trent said nothing, but his facial expression tightened. Soon he was pulling off the highway and making his way down city streets to Gabay, Finch & Earnest.

After he parked, she set her cup in the console and got out of the vehicle. This firm was more impressive than Sharp & Associates, housed inside a large building and spread over four floors.

The reception desk was long with sleek lines and chrome. Two women sat there wearing headsets. One was speaking on the phone, but the second one greeted them.

"Welcome to Gabay, Finch & Earnest. Can I help you?"

"Detectives Steele and Stenson. We have an appointment with Howard Gabay."

The young woman looked at her computer, and a few seconds later, said, "Yes, I see that. I'll let him know you're here. If you wanted to take a seat while you wait, please do so."

"Thank you." Amanda backed up and walked over to the seating area. Her phone pinged with a text, and she checked it. The message was from Carter.

Sorry I had to leave in the night. Hope you slept well. You earned it. xo

Just his words had her catapulting back to their bodies entwined and tangled in her sheets. His warmth against hers and—

"Detectives?" A rotund man with gray thinning hair was walking toward them.

"Yes. Detectives Steele and Stenson," she said. "And you are—"

"Howard Gabay." He held out his hand, and she shook it. Then Trent did the same. "This way." Howard waved for them to follow.

After what felt like a mile of hallway, they arrived at a large office. It was outfitted with a couch, two chairs, a desk, and lovely views of the Potomac and the Key Bridge.

"Please, make yourselves comfortable." Howard sat on one end of the couch and crossed his leg, resting his ankle on his other knee. "I heard about the situation going on with Dominique. It's crazy."

That's one way of putting it... But how much did he know? "I'm not sure how much you've heard..." She left it dangling for him to fill in while she sat on a chair, and Trent sat in one opposite her.

"Her real estate agent was murdered in her home." Howard tilted his head, as if silently inquiring if there was something he'd missed.

"Yes, last Friday night. But I'm sorry to say there's even more to this."

"Well, I figured there must be for you to want to talk to me."

"Good instinct." The man blushed at her compliment, and she continued. "We believe Dominique was the intended target."

All the flush left his cheeks, but he remained silent.

"We also believe the same person who killed the agent returned yesterday for Dominique."

"Dear heavens, this is preposterous. But she's okay...?"

"She's fine, but her friend was caught in the crossfire. He's in the hospital, fighting for his life."

"Tragic. I had no idea about any of this." He was doe-eyed, and his mouth kept opening and shutting, like a fish gulping water.

"Though, why would you?" she countered. "Now we understand that Ms. Sharp was here, in DC, to discuss business on Friday. Was that so?"

"Yes. I sure hope she'll still want to go ahead."

"I don't think anything could stop her." Considering that a threat on her life wasn't slowing her down, Amanda imagined nothing could change her mind once it was made up. No matter what the cost.

"That's reassuring to hear. I'm looking forward to all this being over and done with."

Amanda would have expected more gumption from the head of a generational firm. Also the way he made it sound, he was washing his hands of the entire business. "I'm surprised to hear you say that."

"Because my great-great-granddaddy founded the place? Well, I've done my part for his legacy. Now, I'm looking forward to some peace and quiet. And lots of golf."

Howard seemed to say all the right things, but there was a false note in his voice. But if she was going to validate that suspicion, she'd need to finesse it from him. "Golf seems to be a favorite pastime among lawyers." Of course, she based this on *one* partner from Dominique's firm.

"It helps focus the mind."

That wasn't Amanda's experience the one time she tried it. *Slow*, *tedious*, and *mind-numbing* were all apt adjectives. She preferred something with a little more speed or levity. Though mini golf was fun. Speaking of, she needed to get Zoe out for that this summer.

"I enjoy it sometimes," Trent put in. "But it's not my sport. I prefer baseball."

Amanda glanced at him, learning something new. He nodded at her, so she took it to mean he wasn't just trying to relate to Howard. But she didn't want them to get too off topic here and steered the conversation back to the sale. "Mr. Gabay—"

"Just call me Howard, please."

"*Howard*, considering your great-great-grandfather's legacy, don't you have any children who might want to take over, step up in your place?"

"My son works here. He's an exceptional lawyer and a junior partner at the firm."

"What is your son's name?" Trent asked, now with his notepad and pen out.

"Sullivan Gabay. But you don't need to be writing that down." He wriggled a pointed finger toward Trent's hand as it was busy making the note.

"What will happen to Sullivan once the sale goes through? Will he stay on to represent the family name?" Amanda was reaching because she could see Dominique stripping the Gabay name off the letterhead in a blink.

"Sully's fine with whatever happens." Howard waved a dismissive hand. "Dominique has spoken of keeping him on, but if she doesn't, he'll be fine."

Amanda was unsettled by how easily Howard dismissed his son's feelings. In Sullivan's place, she couldn't imagine being too thrilled at the prospect of being kicked out the door. "I don't know a lot about these types of contracts, but I'm sure you could have worked it into a clause that your son would keep his job."

"I could have, but I assure you I'm no monster. Honestly, I'm doing him a favor. He pushed through law school for me. He's always had more of a shine toward the arts." Howard rubbed the arm of the couch. "I've been friendly and cooperative. Now, it's your turn, Detective. What really brings you here?" Howard's eyes narrowed, showcasing the analytical lawyer behind them.

"All right, I'll be frank." She settled farther into her chair. "Acquiring your firm is a recent event in Dominique's life, and it's a big deal. It involves a lot of people. Some of whom might not be too happy with the sale."

"So you suspect someone within my firm wants to kill Dominique to stop the sale?"

Amanda offered a slight shrug. "It's just one possibility."

"We'll I'm afraid you're bound to be disappointed."

"Then everyone here was pleased about the acquisition, including yourself? I know you mentioned golfing and a life of leisure, but are you happy with the terms of the sale?" She smiled at him, trying to set him at ease, trying to finesse an honest response.

Howard's eyes shot to Amanda's, and the look in them shoved a spike into her gut. A slight flicker answered on his behalf. If she was right, Howard wasn't pleased. But just what did that mean for the investigation?

THIRTY-FIVE

Amanda and Trent convinced Howard Gabay to let them speak with his employees and fellow partners. He told them one of the senior partners, Harris Finch, was in court today but the rest were in the building. They requested to speak with Gabay's son, Sullivan, first.

Howard took them to Sullivan's office and walked right through the open door, interrupting two men behind the desk. One was a close image of Howard in his early thirties, and the other was in his twenties with blond hair and green eyes. Sullivan was in the chair while the other man was on his knees next to him. He shuffled to his feet holding a computer drive in one of his hands. He must have been working on a CPU that was under the desk.

"Sorry to interrupt," Howard said. "Sullivan, this is Detective Steele and Detective Stenson from the Prince William County PD."

The drive fell out of the man's hand and hit the floor.

"Hell, Corey, watch what you're doing," Sullivan griped, still not paying any attention to Amanda and Trent.

Corey scrambled to pick up what he dropped.

Howard grimaced and resumed talking. "They're here with some questions about Dominique Sharp. If you could spare them a few minutes of your time, I'm sure they'll be in and out before you know it." Howard shot her and Trent a look that said he was doing them a favor. But he must know if he blocked them from talking to his son or others in the firm it wouldn't look good.

Corey shuffled out from behind the desk and went to step past Amanda. She moved in front of him and offered a pleasant smile. "What's your role here, Corey?"

"You don't need to bother him, Detective. He's IT." Howard shifted his focus to his son. "Let me guess. You click on something else you shouldn't have?"

"Whatever, *Howard*. Why don't you leave so I can talk with the detectives, then? That way they can be 'in and out before I know it.'"

Howard pointed a finger at his son, but turned and left without a word. Sullivan shook his head at his father's retreating figure.

Corey had slipped out during the standoff between father and son.

"We never got Corey's last name," she said to Sullivan.

"Why would it matter? As my dad says he's IT. He doesn't know anything about Dominique Sharp, aside from the fact her name's being flung around here."

"I like to be thorough. If you'd like, I could go after him and find out for myself." She jacked a thumb over her shoulder, not caring for Junior's attitude.

"It's Shea, but if you could just get on with your questions, I'm very busy." He gestured with a sigh toward two chairs facing his desk, and they sat down.

His office was much smaller than his father's, and there wasn't a secretary posted outside the door either. Regardless of the family name on the letterhead, it didn't seem nepotism held any power here. If anything, Howard might be harder on his son than his other employees.

"Yes, out of respect for your time, I'll get right to the point. There was an attempt made on Dominique Sharp's life yesterday morning." She skipped over the murdered real estate agent and Dominique's injured friend.

"That's horrible, but I'm not sure what that has to do with me."

Amanda crossed her legs, getting more comfortable. "We have cause to believe someone ordered a hit on her."

"Wow. Really? So a real-life hit man is after her?"

It was a touch disturbing he seemed fascinated by the idea. She didn't correct the gender and said, "Uh-huh. What do you make of that?"

"Clearly someone has it out for her. I mean, it's one thing to kill someone yourself, and another to *pay* a person to take care of it."

"That's what we think too," Trent told him. "Do you know of anyone who might wish Dominique Sharp dead?"

"I'm not the best person to ask about this."

"Why is that?" Amanda asked.

"Well, I don't know the woman personally, so I can't comment on who she might have wronged."

"We were thinking more along the lines of the acquisition. A professional slight," Amanda clarified.

"Ah, like me? Dear Daddy told you I was getting my walking papers. Let me clear this up right now." Sullivan pulled out his top desk drawer and dropped a small magazine onto his desk in front of her. "Go ahead, look."

She picked it up. A playbill for upcoming Broadway performances in DC.

Sullivan pointed at it. "That's what I'd like to be doing with my life. Onstage, singing, dancing, performing. That is my passion. Not this." To emphasize his point, he swept a hand across the spread of files on his desk. "Those performers affect people's lives with their work. Sure, by practicing law, I can help people, but it's not the same. It doesn't feed my soul. So if you think I have something against Dominique Sharp coming in here and taking over, think again. She's doing me a favor. She's giving me a way out. I'll be able to pursue this now without my father looking down his nose at me."

That was what Howard had told them. Amanda set the playbill back on Sullivan's desk.

He picked it up and thumbed through it. "You'll see my name in a playbill soon. By next year, with any luck." He popped it back into the drawer.

Amanda admired his ambition. "Well, good luck, or is it break a leg?"

"I'll take both. Anything else, or...?"

"No, that's good. Thanks for your time." Amanda led the way out of the office, and she and Trent headed for the front desk.

They spoke to several employees and the available named partner. He said he didn't have an issue with Dominique Sharp taking over the company, as he'd secured a deal to stay on board. Since no one was screaming guilt, Amanda and Trent were leaving DC around noon.

Once they were on the highway, she turned to Trent. "What did you make of Corey Shea?"

"Seems like an awkward kid. I'd also say that he and Sullivan are more than friends."

"Could be." She thought it was more than awkwardness though. He seemed twitchy to her. But if they had interrupted a stolen moment between lovers, that could explain his behavior. Corey seemed fine when they spoke to him later on. Maybe it was just that her mind was so desperate to close this case, she was seeing things that weren't even there.

THIRTY-SIX

Amanda and Trent stopped for a bite to eat before getting on the highway for Woodbridge. They were about ten minutes from Central when Amanda's phone rang.

"It's the hospital," she told Trent before answering. "Detective Steele."

"This is Dr. Prescott. Have I reached the lead detective in the shooting involving Joel Blackburn?"

"You have."

"I'm calling with rather unfortunate news."

Amanda's breath stalled, and her stomach sank.

"I'm sorry to inform you that Mr. Blackburn has succumbed to his injuries. He passed within the last hour."

A part of her expected this possibility from the moment he was shot, but the news still hit hard. Could she have somehow prevented this from happening? "Have you notified Dominique Sharp?"

"I haven't been able to reach her, but I left a voicemail."

One would think Dominique would pick up upon seeing the hospital's name on her caller ID. But she could have been in a meeting or nowhere near her phone. "I'll let her know. I'm quite sure I know where to find her."

"If you could do that, thank you."

"You're welcome, and thank you for letting me know." When she hung up, Trent was looking over at her.

"Joel Blackburn didn't make it," he said.

She shook her head.

"I got that feeling from what I overheard."

After he spoke, a silence set in. Her thinking twisted, putting the onus on Blackburn himself this time. If only he had stayed put in his living room, he'd still be alive. But this wasn't his fault, or hers and Trent's. The only one responsible here was that mystery woman, and Amanda was going to track her down and make her pay.

"We should let Malone know."

"I'll take care of it." She pressed his number and ran through all of it the moment he answered.

"What a mess."

"Uh-huh." Amanda was short on words. "I told the doctor that I'd notify Sharp."

"After you tell her about her friend, I want you to deliver her to a safehouse. I don't care if she protests like a cat being dunked in a tub of water."

That doesn't sound like any fun... "All right, just shoot me the address where we're to take her."

"Will do." With that, Malone ended the call.

She was left considering that things could have been even worse. If she and Trent hadn't been at Blackburn's house, they could have found two bodies wrapped in tarps, tied up with rope. Though that did little to soothe her. They had still failed Blackburn. And Dominique wasn't out of danger yet.

* * *

Amanda received a text from Malone with the safehouse address when she and Trent were walking into Sharp & Associates.

Minnie sat up straighter behind the reception desk at the sight of Amanda and Trent as they walked through the doors of the law firm. "Detectives?"

Amanda suspected Minnie wanted to know if her tip had paid off, but they weren't here to discuss Hernandez. "Minnie, it's urgent that we see Ms. Sharp."

"Certainly. One moment." Minnie lifted the phone, and soon after, she returned the receiver to the cradle. "You can go to her office."

"Thank you," Amanda told her.

Dominique waved Amanda and Trent in with an exaggerated sweeping roll of her arm. Amanda sat across from Dominique while Trent closed the door.

The woman's eyebrows kicked up for a second, as if she wasn't impressed they were taking over her space. "Have you found the person who is trying to kill me?"

"Unfortunately, that's not what brings us here," Amanda told her.

"I don't understand then."

Just coming out with it was the merciful and practical thing to do. Dancing around it only prolonged the agony. "We've heard from Mr. Blackburn's doctor, and we're sorry to inform you that Joel didn't make it."

"What do you mean? He made it through surgery just fine. I was told he was going to be fine..."

She seemed more irritated than accepting, which could be shock. "We're sorry for your loss."

"Sorry for my—" Dominique snapped her mouth shut and put a hand to her chest. Tears fell, and she rushed to swipe them away.

For the first time since meeting Dominique, she exposed a

vulnerable side. This shift might make her more compliant with going to the safehouse. "Dominique, we don't think this person will stop trying to kill you until they're caught or they succeed. For your own safety—"

"No. As I've already told you many times, I'm not going to hide away somewhere. It's bad enough the PWCPD has officers breathing down my neck. If you just caught this person, we'd be finished here, right?"

As if it were that simple... Amanda tamped down her frustration, appreciating that this woman was still processing a loss. "As I said, but until then—"

"There's a chance I will be..." Dominique let her sentence dangle there.

Killed... "Yes, there is, and I assure you the officers watching over you are there for you, to protect your life. Without them, there is nothing standing between you and the person who wants you dead." It might seem harsh putting added emphasis on that last word, but Amanda suspected it was necessary to breach Dominique's tough exterior.

"Very well then." Her voice was gravelly when she spoke. It would seem Joel's death had shaken her more than she wanted to let on. It must be the lawyer in her that was an expert at governing emotions.

Amanda nodded. "Good. Now our sergeant has instructed us to bring you to a safehouse for—"

"No, I'm not leaving my office right now. I have work to do."

Amanda saw this attitude as a slight improvement. At least she agreed to go with them, but she was just mistaken about the timing. "Given the threat level, it's imperative that you come with us now. You can bring your laptop and whatever files you need with you."

Dominique sat back in her chair, angled her head. "Why does the PWCPD care if I'm killed anyhow?"

Is she for real right now? "We take our vow to the badge and our community to protect and serve seriously."

"So I'm an obligation?"

Before Amanda landed on the right words, Trent replied.

"Ms. Sharp, if you are killed, that will cost taxpayers of Prince William County a lot of money in resources and manpower."

Dominique nodded. "Now, that I can understand. It's a business decision." She shut the lid on her laptop and tucked it along with some files into a leather case.

Amanda was impressed Trent had put it in a way Dominique could relate to. Even if to most people it would come across as cold and clinical.

The three of them left the office, only stopping for Dominique to tell Casey she was going to be working out of the office for the next while and would be out of reach.

Once they were outside, Dominique turned to Amanda. "She could have people call my cell phone or email me."

"Here's the thing. You can't be on your phone or connected to the internet."

"Are you kidding me?"

"Nope. This person could have a means of tracking you through either. We can't take any chances with your life. If you would kindly hand your phone over..." Amanda held out her hand.

Dominique shoved the device into Amanda's palm.

Amanda shut it off and waved for Officer Traci Cochran to come over. She was still assigned babysitting duties and had been set up in the parking lot. When Traci came over, Amanda told her, "We'll be taking Ms. Sharp to a safehouse. She'll need her things collected from her hotel room and brought there."

"No problem."

"First though, it would be great if you would accompany us, just as additional backup en route."

"Absolutely." Traci returned to her cruiser, and Amanda headed back to Trent and Dominique.

"All right, this is us." Trent gestured toward the department car.

"You must be joking. I'm not going with you in that," she spat with disgust.

Amanda opened the rear passenger door. "It's not any Cadillac, but it will work to get you from A to B. Hop in."

Dominique did so with a huff.

Amanda shut the door behind her and got in up front.

* * *

Amanda was surprised by the silence on the drive to the safehouse. She periodically looked in the side mirror despite not being able to see Dominique in the back given the sun's reflection on the window. Her grief could be felt though. It was a dense entity and one Amanda was all too familiar with.

It wasn't long before Trent was parking in the driveway of the safehouse. Officer Cochran pulled in next to them but remained in her car.

Dominique groaned at the sight of the rural property northwest of Woodbridge. "I'd ask about high-speed internet, but it wouldn't matter."

Amanda let it go, but couldn't Dominique see that what might seem like inconveniences were only for her protection?

An officer in his mid-thirties answered the door, and he wasn't someone Amanda had met before. He introduced himself as Officer McRoy, saying that he was new to the PWCPD. He let them inside.

The humidity from outside seeped through the windows and walls of the house, winning the battle against the rumbling air conditioner blowing through the vents. Amanda expected more complaints. To the lawyer's credit, none came. In fact, once she crossed the threshold, Dominique became subdued, sparking more of Amanda's empathy.

Officer McRoy gave them a quick tour. A dated living room, kitchen, and bathroom. He stopped outside a cramped space with a double-size bed and gestured inside. "That will be your bedroom."

Dominique poked her head through the door. Amanda imagined she must be cringing at the cheap pine dresser and nightstand. And the department store comforter on the bed.

The four of them landed back in the living room, where Officer McRoy excused himself.

"I'm going to make a coffee. Anyone else want one?"

Everyone declined, and he headed for the kitchen.

Dominique sat on the dated couch and crossed her legs. Amanda and Trent sat in a couple chairs.

"We've spoken to people at your firm and at Gabay, Finch & Earnest," Amanda began. "No one is standing out to us as a suspect, but we will keep digging and following evidence." She felt like a fraud even saying *evidence*. As if they had a lot to focus on. A misdirect at best. An omission or white lie at worst.

"Good. Thank you." Dominique crossed her legs the other direction.

Uncomfortable and self-conscious. Who would ever imagine themselves in a safehouse seeking refuge from a killer? It would seem not even Dominique for all the enemies she seemed proud to have amassed. Losing her friend must be impacting her greatly. Was she blaming herself, as if his death were her fault in a roundabout way? Amanda would be eaten alive by that guilt in her place. Even though it wasn't valid. "Is there anyone who has come to mind since we asked the last time?"

"Since yesterday? No." And there was the spark of defiance that Amanda had come to expect from Dominique Sharp.

"All right, well, Detective Stenson and I are going to head

out. You think of someone, call me. If you need anything, see Officer McRoy."

"Are you seriously taking my phone with you? I won't turn it on."

"Then it doesn't matter if you have it." Amanda hadn't returned it after turning it off and had no plans of doing so at this time. It just showed how Dominique wasn't her usual self not to ask about it until now.

"You can't just take my phone. I have rights. And anything on there is private."

"We will be getting a warrant, Dominique." Amanda figured it was best to level with the woman.

"Whatever for?"

"You're being targeted, and there might be something in your communications that can help us track this person down." *At least whoever hired them...*

"Well, I don't like this one bit."

"If you want, we can get that warrant right now." Amanda was prepared to do that if that's what it took.

"It's fine. Take it and go."

Amanda turned for the door, wanting to see what was on the device even more after Dominique's protests.

Before stepping outside, she and Trent let Officer McRoy know they were leaving. Officer Cochran was standing at the door waiting on them.

She kicked off the side of the house. "I feel comfortable in saying no one followed us here. Since you've been inside one car drove past, and that was just a few seconds ago."

"I was keeping an eye on the way here. I didn't see anyone standing out either. Unless you count this PWCPD cruiser on my tail." Trent smiled at her.

"Very funny, Stenson." Cochran rolled her eyes toward Amanda, which made her chuckle.

"Hey, I'm deeply wounded by the insult at my humor," Trent said, feigning hurt feelings.

"Oh, please." Amanda shook her head and got into their car, more than ready to leave here and get on with the case. If only it were that easy to leave Dominique out of her thoughts. "Is it just me or is that woman still hiding something?" she asked as Trent loaded in behind the wheel.

"Not just you." He turned the car on and got them on the road for Central.

"But if she has someone in mind, why isn't she telling us?" As Amanda voiced the question, she had the answer. "Dominique looks out for Dominique. Maybe she's holding back on a name because something in all of it reflects poorly on her."

"So she's looking out for herself by not naming her potential killer?"

"I realize how it sounds."

"Bizarre, yes. But it gels with what we know about her character. Still, though, to let her friend die and continue not to speak up, that is cold."

"Of course all this assumes we're right with our suspicions. Either way, I'm wanting an electronics warrant that covers her phone and laptop."

"We should have got her laptop when we were at the safehouse. Want me to turn around?"

"Not necessary. I thought about it when we were there, but didn't think there was any way in hell she was letting me leave with her laptop. It was surprising she let me take her phone."

"It was."

"We'll get the warrant and have her laptop dropped off at Central. That way we'll be in front of any argument she's going to make."

"I'll work on the paperwork and have a judge sign off,"

Trent offered. "What do you want to do with those threats we have against Dominique?"

Amanda would like to forget that stack of folders existed. If it wasn't for her father's admonition about turning over every rock, she might find justification. She might anyhow. "We can take an honest look at them. The thing is, though, if she received a threat from someone she's hiding from us, I doubt it would be in with what we have."

"True. But that's assuming..."

"We're onto something with that? I know."

They drove the rest of the way to Central in silence. Amanda was trying to untangle why Dominique wouldn't want her killer stopped.

THIRTY-SEVEN

It was midafternoon Thursday, and instead of an arrest, they had a second murder to add to the investigation. Amanda was frustrated by the lack of progress thus far, but at least there were a lot of threads to tug. It was just hanging in until the law of averages kicked in and their efforts paid off.

Amanda had ended up calling Judge Anderson about the electronics warrant to cover Dominique's phone and laptop. She just wanted to ensure he would sign off on the request before they compiled all the paperwork. He did better and gave them a verbal go-ahead. They'd still need to compile the paperwork, but this allowed things to get moving.

A phone call was made to Officer McRoy at the safehouse to collect Dominique's PIN for her phone and password for her laptop, and to have the latter brought to them at Central. Amanda didn't envy him that job. Time would tell if Dominique let him keep his head.

While they waited, Amanda and Trent each attacked a folder.

She rubbed her forehead. The dull pain of an impending headache was lingering behind her eyes. *Is it too much to ask for a break in this case?* Her cell phone rang. *No way.* Had calling out to the universe worked? She took out her phone and a rush went through her at the sight of the name on the screen. "Trent, it's Nadia Webber."

He left his cubicle and joined her, and she answered on speaker.

"Well, I've got some news for you," Nadia began. "ViCAP returned five similar cases within the last two years."

"You can add one more to her tally," Amanda said.

"Don't tell me Blackburn died."

"He did."

"Jeez, how horrible."

They faced so much death on this job it could desensitize a person. Amanda refused to ever lose sight of the fact victims were once living people with dreams and goals. "You said five similar cases. What can you tell us about them?"

"The FBI has flagged these cases as being linked to a serial killer investigation that tied back to the dark web and a site that posted ads for contract killers."

The fact such a thing existed didn't surprise her. Amanda just never expected to encounter one in her work. "What do we know about this woman? Anything?"

"Not a lot, but given how she wraps up her victims tightly in a tarp, agents on the case think she goes by the moniker the Anaconda Killer."

"Don't anacondas suffocate their prey by wrapping around them and squeezing?" Trent asked.

"They do. But you can see the parallel, yes? You said the word yourself, *wrapping*," Nadia reiterated.

"Is her profile on this site still active?" Amanda was hungry for more specifics, having seen her work up close.

"That site was taken down by the FBI, but there are active ones still out there. Our tech branch is always taking them down. For every one, there's five more that pop up."

"Has she turned up on any of them recently?" Amanda asked.

"Not with that username anyhow. So you know, though, I have already made a note in this file, but I would like to add your case to ViCAP. Of course, I'll need you to provide all the information in writing. I can provide you with the form."

"Not a problem," Trent said, beating Amanda to responding.

"I'll send it to you, then, Trent. Just the fact she seems to have resurfaced should be enough to move the file up the pile."

"Just *up*, not all the way to the top?" People needed to be focused on catching the Anaconda Killer even if that involved scouring the dark web twenty-four hours a day.

"You must understand there are a lot of unsolved cases, and agents can't be assigned to work every single one all the time."

Amanda hoped the FBI didn't have plans of sweeping in and taking over the case. She was all for collaborating with them though. "Tell us more about the cases on file. Are they identical to ours? And did you ever catch the people posting the ads?"

"Not to date. We can hope our luck changes. In all five cases, the victims were found wrapped in tarps, as was Christine Lane. Not always under beds, but they were killed in their homes or hotel rooms."

Amanda perked up at that last tidbit. "Hotels have cameras. Did any capture her?"

"Yes, and I was getting around to telling you that. Some homes had doorbell cams, but none of them caught anything. We got lucky at the hotel. We have two brief videos of her and derived a still shot from that. It's rather pixelated, but it gives you the general ID. It was run through facial recognition databases without success."

"We'll want to see all of that," Amanda told her. Trent saw this woman when it was pitch dark, but the potential eyewitness had seen her outside of Sharp's residence during twilight. They could show the picture to her and see if they could get confirmation.

"I'll get them over to you."

"I might have an explanation for the lack of footage from the doorbell cams. It seems she's using a jammer that affects both Wi-Fi and cell phone signals," Amanda said.

"Clever. Leaving the victim with no way of calling for help. Though, with that said, there is nothing to suggest the victims fought back either. Did they have time, or is this woman stealthy just like an anaconda?"

If it took Amanda's last ounce of strength, she'd find a way to slow this killer down. "Lane didn't have any defensive marks on her either to suggest a struggle."

"And the crime scene was pristine," Trent added.

"Same for the five on file," Nadia confirmed. "There is something I am compelled to say. The BAU is ready to take over from here if you'd like. All you have to do is say the word."

Amanda had read between the lines correctly. The FBI was ready to move in. There was no way she was handing the case off to the Behavioral Analysis Unit. She felt a responsibility toward the victims' families to get them justice. Spencer, too. And if she arrested his girlfriend's killer, it might go toward making amends for what she put him through. "No, absolutely not. But I assume we have the FBI's cooperation?"

"I can confirm you do. I will give you the direct phone number for an agent at the Science and Technology Branch. Her name's Lakisha Hester."

Amanda wrote the number down as Nadia rattled it off.

"Do I have your permission to pass along your number to her?"

"Absolutely, and thank you."

"Don't mention it, and good luck."

Nadia was gone, and Amanda turned to Trent. "Five other victims besides our two," she said, shaking her head. An email filtered into her inbox from Nadia. "No one can say she works slow."

"Never. Nadia is a bullet train. It's just how her mind works."

Amanda clicked on the message and found it had three attachments. She hit play on the first video and wheeled her chair back so Trent could see her screen.

A woman walked down the hall of a hotel, head down, until something behind her had her turning around.

Nadia was right about the footage being short. Less than thirty seconds.

"They couldn't have gotten a still photo from that."

"Nope. It must be from the second video." Amanda opened it up and let it play.

It seemed to take over from the last. This one showed her face, taken from a camera at the opposite end of the hall.

"And there she is." Amanda hit pause, freezing her face on the screen. "She look familiar to you?"

Trent leaned in toward the screen, and he shook his head. "It's rather grainy. Nadia said there was a still shot. Even pixelated, it would be better than this."

"Let's see." Amanda opened the JPEG.

"It's clearer, but still not great."

"Is it her?"

Trent angled his head left, then right, then left again. "It's a little hard for me to say. This woman's the right size anyway. I was fooling myself to think I'd recognize a face when I didn't get a solid look at her."

"I get it." And she did. If only positive thinking magically manifested things into reality. "We can go talk to Sharp's neighbor, see if she did."

"I'd just be happy if she was more certain about what she saw. But, wow, I'm still reeling from Nadia's update. A contract killer site on the dark web. There's nothing too depraved for some people."

Though should this really surprise them? Trafficking children and people was right up there, and she and Trent were given a front-row seat to that horror show a few years ago. "Nope. Time to update Malone."

THIRTY-EIGHT

Amanda and Trent stopped by Malone's office and filled him in. After telling him about Nadia's phone call, his thoughts tracked with theirs. It was unsettling such sites existed. Not that the depravity in this world should shock them working in law enforcement. He wished them luck with Sharp's neighbor, Paris Dobson, who had seen the mystery jogger.

The humidity was heavy in the air even at four o'clock as they made their way up the woman's front walkway.

Amanda rang the doorbell, and a woman in her forties answered, wiping her hands on a white apron she was wearing.

"Yes?" She spoke through a crack in the door, and only propped it open farther after Amanda and Trent held up their badges. Red stains were left where she'd wiped her hands. "I've been a little on edge ever since…" She nudged her head toward Dominique Sharp's house across the street.

"I understand." And Amanda did. Being back on Charmed Court days later, the air held a tangible feeling of darkness. "But you have no reason to worry. Just to confirm, you are Paris Dobson?" She'd seen her license photo, but a verbal confirmation never hurt.

"I am, but I would disagree with *no* reason to worry. A woman was murdered just feet away. What's to say the killer won't come back to this neighborhood again?"

Amanda considered what she was going to say. *It is just as likely lightning would strike the same place twice... Though that is possible...* She settled on, "There's nothing to indicate this person will be back." *Simple works...*

"If you're sure..." By the tone of the woman's voice, she wasn't.

"Could we come in for a moment?" Amanda asked. "We have a question about your statement to Officer Wyatt."

"I told him everything, but okay." Paris opened the door wider and stepped back to let Amanda and Trent inside.

The smell of strawberries and sugar floated to the front step and permeated the home. Amanda inhaled with great appreciation, as she was flooded with memories from living at home with her parents. "We shouldn't be long and value your cooperation. Are you making strawberry jam?" She tried to hold back the latter bit, but she was experiencing sensory overload.

Paris smiled. "I am. It's something I do twice every summer. I also pickle cucumbers and make blackberry jam toward September."

Amanda would love to share this experience with Zoe. It would be a fun and productive project they could do together. And it sounded amazing, until Amanda's imagination carried on. She could see red stains everywhere. Zoe was far from a baby, but she still often wore her food. And getting her to tidy up after herself was getting harder by the day. "Well, lucky you."

"Yes, well, you said you wouldn't be long. I need to get my jam in jars."

"Of course. Is there somewhere we could sit?" Amanda jabbed her gaze toward a side sitting room.

Paris took them in there, gesturing for them to sit wherever they would like. Both Amanda and Trent sat on the couch.

"I'm just going to remain standing, if it's all the same to you." Paris pointed at the mess on her apron.

Amanda nodded. "You told Officer Wyatt that you saw a woman on Friday night. Could you run us through that again?"

Paris recounted what Amanda had read in Wyatt's report, but it wasn't verbatim.

This went far in convincing Amanda that Paris was being truthful and accurate to her knowledge. But this also flagged a discrepancy in how Wyatt had interpreted her statement. "And you're sure that's what you saw?"

"Yes, she was just jogging in place out front of the house across the street."

"And you never saw this woman before Friday night?" Trent asked.

"Like I told the officer, I never saw her before. I'm sure I would have remembered if I had. Who runs with a backpack through town? And we rarely get joggers on Charmed Court anyhow. Janice at three-twenty-five sometimes. It depends on the week. She fluctuates between health kicks and bingeing on wine and chocolate."

And there's that... neighborhood gossip... "What about any unfamiliar vehicles driving through?" The hit woman could have staked out the house and area prior to Friday night to get the lay of the land. She was reminded of what Paris had said in the interview but wanted to see if any memory jogged loose.

"I can't say any stuck out to me."

"It sounds like you vividly recall what she looked like. If we showed you a picture, do you think you could tell us if it was her?" Amanda presumed she would and dug her phone out of her pocket.

"Yes, I think so."

Amanda would show her the photograph that Nadia had sent over, along with two others of similar-looking women. This way if Paris recognized the Anaconda Killer, the identification would be more reliable. Amanda got up and walked over to Paris. "I'm going to show you three photos. Let me know if any of these women are who you saw."

Paris met her eye and nodded.

Amanda held her screen up for Paris. "The first one. Is this the woman you saw?"

Paris took a few seconds but ended up shaking her head.

"The next picture." Amanda shuffled to the second photo.

"That's her!" Paris pointed at the screen.

The photo was the Anaconda Killer. "And you're certain?"

"One hundred percent, no doubt in my mind."

"Great, thank you." Amanda closed the Gallery app, put her phone away, and passed a look at Trent with a slight nod.

"Where did you get that picture of her?"

"We're not a liberty to say, ma'am." Amanda was preparing to offer the standard "it's an open investigation" line when Paris's eyes widened.

"You don't even know who she is, do you? It's a candid shot, something taken from a security camera, in a hotel hallway from the look of it. If you knew her name, you'd have shown me her license photo."

Amanda respected Paris's detective skills, but there were still rules they had to follow. Disclosing details of an open investigation would strip her of the badge. "As I've already said, we can't comment."

"All right, then, it seems there's nothing else to discuss. And I really need to get back to my jam. If you could see yourselves out..."

"No problem at all," Amanda said. "Thank you for your time."

"Uh-huh."

Amanda didn't know about Trent, but she was walking a little lighter on the way back to the car. An eyewitness had just identified the Anaconda Killer as being at their crime scene.

Now, to find this woman...

THIRTY-NINE

Amanda and Trent returned to Central and found Dominique's laptop, along with a note for the PIN for her phone. Both were sitting on Amanda's desk inside a clear evidence bag. Hopefully, the password to unlock the computer was here somewhere too. If not, she'd have to call over to the safehouse.

It was just after five, and she and Trent had the choice to stop for the day and or put in some overtime.

"What's your vote?" she asked him.

"I'd prefer to go home."

"Me too." The heat made the days feel longer and more exhausting. She'd still chastise herself for stepping out. After all, a contract killer hunting Dominique Sharp put a ticking clock on things. But she should be safe for now with officers watching over her.

"All right. See you in the morning then."

"Yep."

Trent practically skipped down the hallway toward the parking lot while she walked to Malone's office to let him know about their luck with Paris Dobson.

She found him at his desk, flicking his monitor off. His body sagged into his chair at the sight of her.

"I was just getting ready to head out."

She smiled and held up a hand. "And I'm not going to stop you. I just came by to let you know the eyewitness from Charmed Court identified the jogger. She was the Anaconda Killer."

"I'll be..."

"Yep, your well-wishing worked. Now, Trent and I have our work cut out for us. Not only do we need to find this woman and get her off the streets, we need to find out who hired her."

"I suspect the latter will be the easiest of the two. She hasn't operated for the last two years by messing up."

"Sure, but as you pointed out before, she is lately."

"True enough. Let's just hope there's something we can use that will lead us to her door."

"And that our luck has changed for good." Though she wasn't naive enough to believe that for a minute. It would take persistence and dogged perseverance to bring this woman down.

"We can always hope. Anything else?"

"Not really. I have the PIN for Sharp's phone, and her laptop is here. Trent's already left, and I'll be soon behind him."

"Good. Recharge."

"You too. Have a good night."

She left his office intending to do that, but the hallway presented her with another choice. Dominique's laptop was calling out to her, as was her phone. Either might hold the key to finding who hired the Anaconda Killer.

She walked to her desk and went for the laptop first. Opening the lid, she found a sticky note stuck to the screen with handwriting.

P: BossLadySharp$

At least that would save her a phone call. She powered up the laptop and typed in the password when the prompt came up, and she was in. Her first destination was Dominique's email. Based on the number of messages, Dominique wasn't good about archiving emails. There were over five thousand in total. Although these were organized into folders, there were at least a hundred of those. It would take Amanda forever to wade through all of this. And where would it be best to start?

Instead, she decided on a different tack. The sent mail.

She reasoned if someone was going to hire a killer, they would have been triggered to do so more recently. Clicking on the sent folder, she started with the most recent and worked her way backward. She stayed at it for an hour but didn't get anywhere for her troubles. No conversations carried a threatening tone or an underlying anger toward Dominique.

After looking back a month, Amanda powered down the laptop and put it back inside the bag. She pressed the sticky note to the outside. Since the device wasn't being logged into evidence, Amanda was comfortable leaving it on her desk when she left that night.

But before that, she wanted a quick look at Dominique's phone. She checked out the call history and text messages, and nothing flagged.

By the time she finished, her stomach was rumbling, and by the time she made it home, she'd spent the drive fantasizing about the pieces of leftover two-day-old pizza that were still in her fridge. She'd heat them up and enjoy her meal in her air-conditioning while watching something mindless on TV. Maybe one of those house renovation shows that Trent had told her Kelsey loved so much. It could be inspiring to see how people took a rundown place and turned it into their dream home. It was a plan.

But entering her empty house, her heart hurt thinking about Zoe again. She'd love to see the girl, give her an enormous hug. If only that wouldn't thwart her efforts to teach her independence and resilience. No, for Zoe's good, Amanda would let Zoe stay with her grandparents for the duration of the week as originally arranged. It just so figured that the week Zoe was away, the case Amanda was working afforded some flexibility. Meanwhile when Zoe was home next week, all hell could break loose, making it necessary to arrange care for Zoe.

Such an unfair world... But at least she wouldn't soon be burying a loved one, like Riley Lane and Spencer. Pizza could at least go somewhere toward healing her loneliness.

She started the oven, and while it was warming up, she changed into a pair of linen shorts and a breezy white tank top.

By the time she got comfortable, the oven was almost up to temperature. She laid out a piece of parchment paper on a pizza sheet and put the three remaining slices on top. Her meal was ready to go in the second the oven beeped. She set the timer for ten minutes, thinking that should be enough time to choose a home show to stream.

She headed to the living room, the couch as her goal, but her eyes drifted to the mail sitting on the entry table. Grabbing it, she took it with her. The show search would have to wait a few minutes.

Shuffling through, there was a lot of junk mail and flyers, including one for lawn care. One of these years, she'd pay someone to cut the grass. Zoe would be old enough in four years. If Amanda didn't want to wait, she could pass a few bucks to her teenage niece and nephew. Maybe she'd do that before this summer was out.

She tossed the unsolicited mail to the cushion next to her and was left holding a large pink envelope. The perfect size for a card. There were heart stickers next to the address label that noted Amanda's and Zoe's names. Amanda smiled because she knew then what this was and who had sent it.

She slipped her finger under the seal and took out the contents. Not a card, but an invitation.

It was printed on cream recycled paper with a gold border, and the image of a large rose in the top righthand corner.

Libby DeWinter and Penny Anderson request the honor of your company as they make their vows on September 21 at 4 PM.

The location provided was a small banquet hall in town. Elegant but not extravagant. Something that Amanda saw fitting the couple. And with that her thoughts daisy-chained to how she even came to know Libby and Penny.

It was four years ago, after Zoe's biological parents were killed. She and Zoe had an inexplicable bond from the start. Libby, technically Zoe's godmother, couldn't take her in, and Amanda listened to her heart. She needed Zoe as badly as the girl needed her. The adoption progressed at a fast pace, and Zoe became hers.

Libby and Penny had been together for as long as Amanda knew them, and they became engaged two months ago. They hadn't wasted any time setting a date.

Good for them!

There was a small card and an envelope for the RSVP, which Amanda would check off right now if she had a pen handy. But she also noticed there was another envelope addressed to her. She opened it and found a note.

Hi Amanda!

We want Zoe to be our flower girl! But we didn't want to presume, or put anyone in an awkward position. If you are okay with this, could you let me know? We'd love to ask her in person. There's also something we'd like to ask you face-to-face.

Love,

Libby XO

Libby wrote her phone number beneath the sign-off. Not that Amanda needed it. Libby was listed under Amanda's favorite contacts in her phone. She must have been trying to encourage a fast response.

Amanda was about to select her name when the oven timer beeped. In response, her stomach rumbled.

She jumped up to get her pizza and returned with the plan to pick the first home show that hit the screen. When she finished eating, she'd call Libby. Amanda was fine with Zoe being their flower girl, and Zoe would absolutely love it. But Amanda could hardly wait to find out what they wanted to ask her.

FORTY

As Amanda walked toward her desk at Central, she was still flying from Libby's question last night. She wanted Amanda to be her maid of honor. It was silly how excited she was by the prospect. But Libby sounded about as thrilled about Amanda's answer. This wasn't going to be Amanda's first time standing up in a wedding party, but it had been a while since the last time. It had been for her sister Kristen, nearing two decades ago. *Where does time go?*

She arranged a tentative date for them to get together with Zoe a week from this Saturday so that Libby and Penny could ask Zoe in person. Amanda just requested she be present because she wanted to see the bright smile on that kid's face. But for now, just thinking about Zoe's response would carry Amanda through the day. After all, who knew where it would take her?

Amanda set her Hannah's Diner coffee cup on her desk and eyed Dominique's laptop. She could take another look, this time at her browsing history. Maybe she'd find something there to point them in someone's direction. She was getting ready to do that when her phone rang.

Unknown showed for the caller ID, but she didn't have the luxury of disregarding such calls. She handed her card out to lots of people. "Detective Steele," she answered.

Trent walked past and waved. He must have seen she was on the phone.

Her caller wasted no time getting to the point of the call. "It's Detective Lola Lopez from Financial Crimes. I'm calling about the financial reports you sent over pertaining to Sharp & Associates and Gabay, Finch & Earnest, as well as the acquisition."

"One second, please." She motioned for Trent to come over to her cubicle. "I'm just going to put you on speaker. My partner, Detective Stenson, is here now. It's Detective Lopez," she added for Trent's benefit.

Lopez went on. "On the surface, Gabay, Finch & Earnest looks quite profitable. The income statements show a profit increase of twenty-five to fifty-five percent year over year for the last seven years. The anomaly that caught my attention happened in the current fiscal year. Gabay is set to make a seventy percent billable increase over last year. This got me digging into the customer and vendor accounts. Both showed an increase in numbered companies, which got me digging deeper again. Now, I have only gotten through so many but I've already uncovered twenty accounts, ten customer and ten vendor, that are shell companies. I suspect there are many more."

"Please lay it out like I have no idea what that means," Amanda requested.

"The short answer is someone is embezzling from Gabay, Finch & Earnest. False vendors are being paid money while counterfeit clients are being billed. The person doing this is siphoning the cash back into the business," Lopez clarified.

Amanda could see the flow in her head. Money out, money back. "So where was it going and coming from?"

"I can't tell you that, but Gabay paid out $1,175,100 to

these companies, and only a third of that has cycled back. Now all this started going out seven years ago, but it just started returning within the last six months."

Could it be a coincidence that was around the same time Dominique showed interest in buying the company? "Tell me we have a name tied to this." Amanda sat up straighter, seeing a motive for murder in this find.

"We do. Harris Finch."

"And Finch was *conveniently* out of the office when we went yesterday." They were told he was in court, but Amanda didn't trust a word of that right now. "Is there anything else we should know before we move in?"

"That's it for now."

"Could you send us those twenty company names you checked into?" she requested.

"I will."

"Thank you." Amanda ended the call and faced Trent. "We could have motive."

"Yep. Though I can't quite understand his standpoint. Sure, the sale was moving ahead. The books would be looked at. Did he think he could cover up the money he siphoned out by feeding it back in? And why do any of this under his own name?"

"There's no explaining some people. Maybe his anxiety got the best of him. As you said, the sale was going through. He'd know that would mean Dominique would get the financials, and she'd do her due diligence with them."

"So he'd want to kill her to prevent being exposed for fraud."

Amanda stood. "We've got to talk with Finch. You drive, and I'll call Malone from the road."

FORTY-ONE

The only delay in getting on the road was Amanda looking up Harris Finch. His license photo showed a handsome man with gray hair. His details said he was five-foot-ten, didn't need corrective lenses, and was sixty-four. Otherwise, his background itself didn't flag at all.

Amanda called Malone from the road and told him that the latest break in the case was taking them back to Washington, DC.

When she finished, he said, "Sounds like it's quite plausible this Finch guy hired the woman. I'm thinking we should bring the Metropolitan PD in on this, just to let them know we're in their territory. I mean based on what you got from Detective Lopez, this is more than a chitchat you're going to have with this guy. You'll be bringing him in?"

"That's how I see it at this point. MPD was going to be my next call. But they can't be moving in ahead of us. I want our showing up at that firm to catch everyone there by surprise," she told him.

"Which I understand. Keep me posted." He ended the call, and Amanda looked up the number for the MPD.

When she finished talking to the uniformed sergeant on duty, she turned to Trent. "They'll be sending out a couple of uniforms as backup should we need them."

"Let's hope we don't."

The forty-five minutes to DC flew by, and Trent was soon parking in the firm's lot.

The midmorning sun glistened off the glass of the building, making for a beautiful picture, but what they had to do wasn't going to be pretty at all.

There was only one woman at the front desk today when they turned up and asked for Harris Finch.

"He's in a meeting with a client at the moment," the woman said.

At least he's in... "We need to ask that you interrupt it. This is an urgent police matter." She and Trent had shown their badges when they'd first arrived, but a reminder of their position in law enforcement couldn't hurt things.

"I'm sorry, but unless you have a warrant—"

"Mr. Finch is the prime suspect in a police investigation." Amanda grounded her stance, prepared to stand there, hovering over the woman for as long as it took.

"I could have you removed by the MPD," the woman said, reading Amanda's energy.

"They came with us, but if you need me to get one of them, I can." She jacked a thumb over her shoulder where the timing of two uniformed MPD cops coming through the door couldn't have been better.

The woman sighed. "Fine, I'll see if I can reach Mr. Finch." She picked up the phone on her desk and pushed a few numbers.

"Thank you." Amanda pressed on a tight smile.

As the woman spoke on the phone, her cheeks flared a bright red. When she hung up, she said, "Mr. Finch will be down to see you in a few minutes."

"Thank you," Amanda told her.

"Uh-huh." She didn't say another word and put her attention to a folder on her desk.

Call it a hunch, but Amanda felt Mr. Finch was to blame for this woman's attitude. That seemed confirmed when Harris Finch stormed into the reception area. The woman didn't look up, even though there was no way she hadn't heard his soles slapping the floor.

"You're the detectives here to see me," Finch said, leveling this as if it were an accusation.

"Detectives Steele and Stenson. We'd like to speak with you someplace private," Amanda told him.

Two people entered the firm and looked at the three of them as they walked past to the desk.

"If you insist, but we need to make this quick. I have a huge client waiting on me upstairs. You've interrupted an important meeting." He led them to a small meeting room off the lobby.

Amanda waited until the door was shut to say, "Yes, well, you're going to need to send them away."

"Pardon me? What do you mean? And why would I ever do that?"

She gestured to a chair. "I suggest you take a seat, Mr. Finch." She took her own advice, and Trent sat down too.

"I don't have time for this."

Trent's jaw became rigid. "Detective Steele wasn't asking."

"Fine. But, as I said, make this quick." Finch dropped onto a chair.

"We never had a chance to speak with you when we were here yesterday," she began.

"No, I was in court. Do you need me to prove that?" He tossed out the question with a sardonic smirk.

"We might." This was said more to shake him. After all, he didn't need to account for his whereabouts yesterday.

Finch's face shadowed, and his eyes narrowed. "Do I need a lawyer?"

Lawyers could slow down the process, but they served a purpose. She had the choice to stoke the flames of the existing tension or pull back. The latter was the wisest course. She replied in a calm, level voice, "That is up to you."

"Just tell me what's going on."

"We spoke to some of your colleagues yesterday about the upcoming purchase of the company," Amanda began.

"I heard. Is that why you dragged me out of a client meeting? To get my opinion on the sale?"

"Not exactly, but if you could answer that question," she said.

"It doesn't much affect me. I've been interested in retiring for a while now."

"Then you didn't stand to lose from the sale?" Trent asked.

"Nope. Per the bylaws, I need to be bought out."

Wouldn't that be the cherry on top? Making off with a fraudulent haul *and* a payout? "Then it didn't concern you the company's books were being made available to the purchasing entity?"

"Why should it?"

"We had a detective in Financial Crimes look at the firm's financials. I'm sure you're familiar with the adage *Follow the money*? Well, they discovered several vendors and clients were opened within the last seven years that were numbered shell companies."

"I'm not sure what this has to do with me."

"Your name is on these accounts."

"What? No, that's preposterous. An outright lie. I did no such thing."

Amanda continued as if he'd said nothing. "You started putting money back into the company by forging billables in the last six months. Six months," she reiterated. "That was right around the same time that Dominique Sharp came around interested in buying the firm."

Finch remained silent.

"Come on, Mr. Finch. You would have known that Dominique Sharp would see your books, arrange for her own forensic accountant to comb through all of it," Trent said.

"You wanted to keep your embezzlement from coming out," Amanda added.

"No, no, none of what you're saying is true."

"Then how do you explain your name being attached to these fake accounts?" Amanda wasn't letting his repeated denial sway her. People would say anything to avoid prison.

"I've been set up? I don't know."

Amanda was disappointed in Finch's weak defense. "You can't just toss that out there on its own. Who and why?"

"Maybe I should get that lawyer because I swear to you, I didn't do any of this." The lawyer's posture shrank, but Amanda still wasn't convinced of his innocence.

"Not even order a hit on Dominique Sharp?" She laid the bomb and watched confusion sweep across his face, causing his forehead to become rows of wrinkles.

"I know nothing about that."

"The embezzlement is seen as a motive, Mr. Finch. It's only so long before we get into your bank accounts and confirm that you hired someone to kill Ms. Sharp." She spoke with a definitiveness the evidence had yet to support. He looked good for embezzlement. Conspiracy to commit murder was another thing altogether.

"You've lost your mind if you think I'm in on any of this."

"Did you know two people were murdered by this hit person just within the week? Christine Lane was a successful real estate agent and a mother. Joel Blackburn was a successful lawyer and left behind his parents and a brother." The latter was something she had looked up along the way.

"Listen, I'm sorry those people are dead, but I don't even know them."

"Collateral damage, caught in the crossfire, take your pick," Trent said.

Flinch rubbed his forehead. "Crossfire? Listen, we got off on the wrong foot here, but trust me, I'm as confused as you are."

"I'm not confused. Are you confused?" She faced Trent.

"Nope."

"We're going to need to ask you to come with us back to Woodbridge, Virginia," she told Finch.

Trent got up and started walking around the table.

Finch raised his hands in front of him, palms flat toward Trent, holding him off. "Please, just hear me out. I swear to you I never stole a penny from this company or ordered anyone's murder. I wouldn't even know where to start. Does one go to a sketchy part of town...?"

"In this case, we suspect the dark web," Amanda said.

"*The dark web*," Finch parroted. "How the hell does one even get on the dark web, let alone know where to look for a killer?"

"You could tell us," she countered.

"No, I can't. That's my point." Finch raised his voice, and color infused his cheeks. "You think I have motive because of the embezzlement. Well, I didn't do that, as I've already told you, and I'll do anything to prove it. As I've said, I must have been framed."

And we're back to that... "You still haven't told us who would want to frame you."

"Beats me, but all partners have the authority to request the accounting department open vendor and client accounts. As for which one would do this to me, I can't even imagine except for one person. And it pains me to say their name aloud." He paused there, but Amanda wasn't going to encourage him. He was a grown-ass man. Finch eventually spat out, "Howard Gabay."

"And why would the owner and founder of this firm steal from his own company? One that has been in his family for generations?" Trent asked.

"You'd have to ask him. But the guy is broke."

"Sales are up year over year, even taking out the false billables," Amanda said.

"His company isn't broke. *He* is broke. All his life working as a lawyer, and soon he'll have nothing to show for it. The offer from Dominique Sharp is a joke, but he signed on the dotted line, using his majority shares to justify the decision. There was nothing the rest of us could do."

Amanda leaned forward. "What do you mean it was a joke?"

"Just that. It was a lowball offer, only a fraction of what the firm is worth."

"Why would he accept the offer then?" Trent asked.

"I just told you. The guy is broke, and he ain't getting any younger. He thought this was his way out."

"Except you're missing one point here. If he embezzled over a million dollars, the guy isn't broke," Amanda reasoned.

"Listen, I don't know why he'd do it. All I know is it wasn't me."

"Detective Stenson." She stood and summoned him to join her on the other side of the room. "Let's say this is Howard Gabay. He's on his way out, and by *his* account"—she nudged her head toward Finch—"needs all the money he can get. It wouldn't make sense that he'd put money back into the company at this stage. Doing so could even draw unwanted attention."

"Which it did, but I have another question for our friend here." Trent walked back over to the table. "Why would Howard Gabay try to frame you?"

"His first wife left him for me."

"When was this?" Amanda asked.

"Seven years ago."

Back when the money started being siphoned out of the firm. Finch had struck on something with his accusation, but there had to be some way to prove it. Amanda wasn't going to rely solely on his word. "You said that all partners can authorize new accounts. Run us through how that works."

FORTY-TWO

Amanda and Trent let Harris Finch return to his client meeting while they set off to talk to the people in the accounting department. Finch had told them there was a paper trail for every new account. Each request had to be signed off by a partner, and Finch said they didn't use signature stamps. Amanda messaged Detective Lopez in Financial Crimes to remind her to send the list of business names as she hadn't seen it yet.

The accounting supervisor was Molly, a plain woman with brown hair. After they introduced themselves, she gestured for them to sit across from her desk.

Amanda was the first one to talk. "There have been several new accounts opened in the last six months, vendor and customer, attributed to Harris Finch. These are numbered companies, and he's denying that he made the requests. We'll need to see those signed requisitions and be provided with samples of each partner's signature for comparison." This would let them know if someone had forged Finch's signature, and if so, who.

Molly leaned forward and clasped her hands on her desk. "Right, well, I can't help you unless you have a warrant."

Amanda was afraid they would meet with that response but figured they should try it first. "We'll return with one." She left the room with Trent.

"I can call Judge Anderson about this," he offered, and when she nodded, he got on the phone.

A few minutes later, he was off and giving her the update. "We've got verbal authorization, and I'll get the paperwork through to my email soon. Have you received the list of business names from Detective Lopez yet?"

"Let me see." She checked the email on her phone and saw a message from the detective come in. "I do." She turned and knocked on Molly's door.

"Come in," she called out. The supervisor's shoulders sagged when she saw her visitors were Amanda and Trent again.

"We have verbal authorization for these requisition forms from Judge Anderson. A hard copy will follow soon," Trent told her.

"Okay. Once I get that, I'll gather the requisition forms."

"If I could get your email, I'll send you the list of businesses and Detective Stenson will forward you the warrant."

"Very well." Molly gestured to her business card in a holder on her desk. "My email address is on there."

"Thank you." Amanda plucked a card, and she and Trent returned to the hall. She forwarded the list to Molly's email and passed her card on to Trent. "For when you get the warrant."

"Yep. And while we wait?"

"We talk things out."

They settled back in the conference room where they had been with Finch.

Trent started the conversation moving. "I'd like to know why Howard Gabay would sell his firm to Sharp if she gave him a lowball offer."

"That's assuming Finch is telling us the truth about that.

But let's focus on the facts. The money started going back in six months ago. At the same time Dominique Sharp became interested in acquiring Gabay's firm."

"This could be about more than trying to cover the embezzlement. Whoever is behind this may have wanted the firm to look good on paper."

"Which would track for Howard Gabay if not for accepting a lowball offer. Supposedly," she added.

"Going back to covering up the embezzlement. If Finch was being framed, why would the real culprit care about feeding money back in? Finch would be the one to pay for the crime."

"Except for one thing. This person could have lost their nerve and panicked, thinking this would lead back to them. After all, the sale would have put more eyes on the books. We can't see those forms soon enough."

"I just hope they still exist." Trent checked his phone, and a moment later was pecking Molly's email in from her card. "The warrant's been forwarded."

"Good, that's one thing off the list. And while we wait on accounting to get everything together, we should consider another aspect of all of this. If the embezzlement is linked to the hit woman, who is most capable of accessing the dark web? I don't see Howard Gabay as being very techy."

"Makes two of us. The guy must be in his mid-sixties. But here's the thing. Where there's a will, there's a way. Howard Gabay could afford to pay someone to do this."

Her eyes widened. "Or he already is? He does have a computer guy on the payroll."

"Corey Shea," they said together.

"And he was rather cagey when we walked into Sullivan Gabay's office," Amanda said.

"So Howard Gabay, as we're presuming here, paid Shea to do this." Trent took out his tablet. "I'm going to pull a background on Shea right now."

He rarely used his device for this purpose, but it was police-issued and capable of accessing all law-enforcement databases.

Trent moved his finger around the screen and stopped a few seconds later. "All right. Here we go. Shea is twenty-five, graduated MIT."

"So he's a tech genius. Continue."

"He's single and rents an apartment..." Trent did more sweeping of his finger. "He has a new BMW X4 M. Registration records show he just got it two weeks ago."

"Okay, that's an expensive car for a law firm IT guy. I doubt his regular salary would allow for that extravagance. They cost close to eighty K."

"Right, so how could Shea afford that car unless he came into some sort of payday? He's young enough that he probably still has student loans to pay off."

"Although, there is the possibility that we're wrong here. He might have family money behind him."

"One way of getting a picture of his finances is a credit check."

"Which would require a warrant, and I'm not sure a judge would approve one based on what we have so far. It's nothing more than speculation and circumstantial."

"So close, yet so far away. It's maddening. I think you'll agree with me it's likely that Shea was paid to go onto the dark web and hire a contract killer."

"I can get behind that. So, I say while accounting is pulling the account requisitions, we have a chat with Corey Shea. See if we can get him to roll on whoever put him up to this." She just hoped they were on the right path with this.

FORTY-THREE

Amanda and Trent returned to the front desk for directions to Corey Shea's office and instructed the receptionist not to call ahead of them. The first time they spoke to him, they'd done so in a meeting room.

Corey's office was on the second floor, and it wasn't much more than a cubbyhole. Some storage closets were larger.

He was standing over a table in the corner tinkering with computer components, his back to the door.

Amanda knocked on the doorframe, and Corey jerked around and dropped the tool that was in his hand.

"We didn't mean to startle you." *Again...* The guy sure was jumpy.

"I'm fine." He ducked down to pick up his tool. "Detectives Steele and Stenson, right?"

"Excellent memory." Though if he was guilty of what they suspected him of, he'd remember them well.

Corey stepped to the side and gestured to the table. An array of computer parts was laid out. Amanda recognized a CPU casing and a fan unit, but that was all. "Is there something I can do for you? I'm just in the middle of a computer build."

"There is actually." This time she was the one motioning. She wanted Corey to take a seat at his desk. It had a bunch of computers stacked up on it too, with one front and center. It must be what he used for his work.

Corey sat down, and they stepped all the way into the space. Trent closed the door.

"Is that really... necessary?" Corey shifted in his chair.

"It is," Amanda assured him. "We need to have a private conversation with you."

"Okay." His leeriness had adrenaline flowing through Amanda's system. She'd been at this game long enough to recognize the signs. Corey was hiding something.

"Please know that whatever you say to us, you're safe. If someone manipulated you into doing something illegal, we can help you." She painted it as if Corey were helpless to resist this illegal activity in the hopes it would gain his cooperation.

"I... I don't know what you're talking about." His tongue darted out like a lizard.

"Then I'll make it clear. Detective Stenson and I believe you ordered a contract killer through the dark web to take out Dominique Sharp." She ignited the bomb, and the explosion lit in Shea's eyes. The light dimmed just as quickly though.

"No, that's crazy."

That isn't a denial...

"Is it?" Trent asked. "You graduated from MIT. You have a job in IT. Presumably you would possess the ability to access the dark web..."

Corey remained silent.

"Did you do this for someone else, Corey?" Amanda softened the tone of her voice to encourage a response. When Corey didn't speak, she added, "Maybe you didn't feel you had a choice, or were afraid to refuse them. Was your job threatened, or were you offered some extra spending money?"

Amanda didn't mention the BMW in so many words, but Corey paled, gripped the edge of his desk, and said nothing.

All right, it's time to mention the car... "You've got quite the nice, new, and shiny Beamer. How are you liking it so far? You've only had it a couple of weeks, right?"

Again, her question met with no response. She let the silence stretch out for several minutes, during which Corey repeatedly adjusted his posture.

"I could only dream of having a car like that at your age," Trent said. "Heck, that one's out of reach for me even now."

"Fine, I'll talk, but I need a lawyer."

"That's up to you, Corey, but it would go a long way if you work with us." She was walking a fine line here.

"I was made to do it. If I talk, will you give me a deal?"

We were right about him! She squared her shoulders. "We'd need to know everything. All that you did and where, and for whom."

Corey looked down at the floor.

She continued. "The clock is ticking, though, Corey. A killer is out there stalking Dominique Sharp as we speak. She won't stop until she succeeds. She's already murdered two people in her quest to kill Dominique. If anyone else is hurt, there can't be any deal on the table. Do you understand that?" She held back saying those two deaths were on his shoulders so as not to intimidate him into silence.

He rubbed his face and nodded. "My God, I can't believe this came back to me. How did you figure it out?"

A blend of cop instinct and him wanting to clear his conscience... "First thing you need to do is call her off."

Corey shook his head furiously. "I can't do that."

"Are you refusing to cancel the job?" Amanda required clarification.

"No. It's not possible. Once the hit is ordered, there's no going back."

"You're going to find a way," Amanda said, and Trent touched her arm.

"There's another option here," Trent said to her, and she received his unspoken message and nodded.

Set the bait and lure the Anaconda Killer out... "Tell us everything you know about her, where you hired her, when... all of it."

"I made an ad on this site. A person with the handle A. Killer responded. You're saying they're a woman? I didn't even know that much."

The Anaconda Killer hadn't wandered far from her original moniker. Though it was probably just enough to obscure any searches by the FBI. "What's the name of the site?"

"Death at Your Door."

Like they were DoorDash or the many services that offered home deliveries. Only instead of food or other products, a person could order murder. "Can you still access this site?"

"I think so."

"Good, because you're going to reach out to A. Killer. You'll be telling her when and where she can find Dominique Sharp." They were going to lay a trap for the Anaconda Killer she couldn't resist walking right into.

FORTY-FOUR

Corey Shea confirmed the site and A. Killer's profile remained active. He expected she'd stick around until she completed the job and was compensated, as it was the only means they had of communicating.

"And how much does a life go for these days?" Amanda asked, though not sure she wanted to know.

Corey looked away. "Thirty K."

"Thirty…" Trent snapped his mouth shut.

"Since I told you about her and the site, I get a deal, right?"

He'd failed to understand her earlier despite saying he had, and she couldn't care less how much he was given right now for his role. "Who paid you to do this?"

"No. I'm not saying any more until a lawyer is involved and a deal is on the table."

Amanda gave him a tight smile. "That's not how this works. You give us information and if it pans out, then we talk about a deal."

Corey crossed his arms, and Amanda stepped into the hall.

She called Malone to inform him of their conversation with Finch, serving the warrant on Molly in accounting, and their relative success with the IT employee. "He's refusing to tell us who paid him to do this until there's a lawyer involved and a deal on the table," she summarized.

"That's not how this works."

"That's what I told him. But we have something in mind that might help us catch the Anaconda Killer." She laid out their plan.

"Simple, but do you think it will work?"

"There's no reason it shouldn't. She's not getting paid until she finishes the job. We're going to set it up for tonight at eleven. We'll have officers on scene for immediate backup should things turn sideways."

"And you think that setting this up at Sharp's house is the best plan?"

"I do. It's believable. The killer must know that Sharp is a strong-willed career lawyer. It's conceivable she'd return home."

"All right, let's do it, but is there any way I can talk you out of being involved, Amanda? This is a contract killer."

"She's nothing more than a serial killer who gets paid, and I've taken on serial killers before. Besides, she's just flesh and blood and I'm going to help her remember that."

"Remember you are too."

"I never forget." Not the entire truth. There were times she made risky choices.

"And what are we doing about Howard Gabay? Are you wanting to wait around for the account requisition forms before you question him?"

"No. We'll be having Howard Gabay brought back before then. It might take accounting a while to get the paperwork together."

"Sounds like a plan."

Amanda next called Special Agent Hester in the FBI's Science and Technology Branch using the number that Nadia had given her.

"No wonder our system didn't flag her as active," Hester said. "The new name differs just enough that she'd remain invisible. I'm going to dig into this site and see what information I can get from it. Not that I'm holding my breath. The whole appeal of the dark web for its users is the anonymity."

"Well, do what you can, but whatever you do, don't shut down the site. It's our strongest link to her." Amanda shared their plan to trap the Anaconda Killer.

"That's as good a strategy as any, and let's hope it works. Good luck."

"Thanks." Amanda ended the call with the FBI agent and returned to Corey's office.

Corey and Trent turned toward her when she entered the doorway.

"He's ready if everything's been cleared," Trent said to her.

"It has been. Arrange it."

Corey swiveled toward his keyboard. "Just tell me everything I need to know."

Amanda did, and she and Trent leaned over Corey's shoulder while he punched everything into the site. Seconds after he sent the message, A. Killer responded.

Consider it done. Have payment ready.

Amanda glanced at Trent. As they were relying on, her intention was to complete the job and collect her money. Yet as frustrating as it was to be a screen away, the consolation was that soon nothing would stand between her and this killer.

FORTY-FIVE

Amanda and Trent left the DC law firm without the account requisition forms. The accounting department was still working on pulling them out, but Molly promised she'd scan them and email them to Trent.

Howard Gabay had a stunned look on his face when they had entered his office and informed him they needed to speak with him at Central in Woodbridge. But he hadn't resisted. Same too for Corey Shea, but he put in a request for a lawyer while Howard hadn't.

It was nearing midafternoon when both men were set up in interview rooms.

Corey was in one with his lawyer and being watched over by a PWCPD officer. They had him bring his laptop in case the A. Killer reached out to him, and he needed to respond.

Howard Gabay was next door, seated by himself, and Amanda, Trent, and Malone were watching him through the one-way mirror. He kept wiping his forehead with a handkerchief he pulled from the inside pocket of his suit jacket.

The MPD officer who drove the men here told her and Trent that neither of them had said a word to each other. It could be they didn't want to risk slipping out with something, or she and Trent had this all wrong and Howard was innocent.

"He's nervous about something," Malone said. "But the guy never even requested a lawyer. One would think if he was guilty of embezzlement and contracting a hired gun, he would have."

"Yes, and one would think calling a lawyer would be automatic for an attorney called in for questioning by police," Trent said. "Isn't the saying, a man who is his own lawyer has a fool for a client?"

"All of which makes me even more curious what we might learn from him. Shall we?" Amanda waved for Trent to join her next door.

Howard Gabay was tucking his handkerchief away when they opened the door. He said nothing, but his shoulders sagged, and he took a deep breath.

"Do you know why you're here?" Amanda asked as she sat across from him with a folder. It was stuffed with mostly blank paper to make it look intimidating.

"I'm too smart to walk into that trap, Detective. I've already waived a lawyer, but you're going to lead this conversation. There's no way I'm stupid enough to volunteer something that may entrap me."

Not the words of an innocent man with nothing to hide, but was it embezzlement *and* murder? "All right, I'll lay it out in a way that's clear. You're suspected of four felonies." Amanda listed them in her head. Conspiracy to commit murder, two murders, and one count of embezzlement.

Gabay didn't so much as blink, but fresh beads of perspiration popped on his brow.

"This doesn't come as a surprise to you?" Trent asked.

"I'm not sure where you got four."

Huh... It seemed he suspected to be considered for at least one. *The embezzlement?* "When Ms. Sharp decided to purchase your firm, she was given access to your books. Is that correct?"

"That's right. She was given these last Friday."

The way he responded so calmly was unsettling. How could he not see where they were headed with this? Unless *they* were the fools for believing Harris Finch when he pointed them in Gabay's direction. "Was that why she was in DC?"

"Yes."

"And she was there all weekend?" That was the story they had all along.

"I can't speak to her entire itinerary, but she was at the firm on Friday, and she called on Saturday for me to meet her for dinner in DC."

It was possible Howard had sent the hit woman to Dominique's house Friday night, thinking she'd have returned home. "Why was that?"

"She was feeling confident about the purchase." His voice sounded tight, the words strained, as if resisting coming out.

If Finch was right and the offer was a lowball one, had Howard felt forced to accept it? If so, what could make him do so? Amanda benched those thoughts for now. "Ms. Sharp was first interested in your firm six months ago. Why was she just receiving your books now?"

"Things like that take time to get together."

"Yet, you agreed to an offer she made. And she put one in without even consulting your numbers?" Amanda asked, finding that strange.

"She already knew she wanted the firm. I wanted to retire. Win-win."

"Despite the lowball offer?" Amanda treated what Finch had told them as fact.

Howard wiped his brow again. "Who said anything about it being lowball?"

She'd take his reaction as confirmation. "Regarding the firm's finances, we've had a look at them ourselves."

"Then you've seen our amazing growth over the last seven years. We're set to beat previous sales records this fiscal."

"The Financial Crimes Unit of the PWCPD saw something else." She scanned his eyes, and he was giving nothing away. His stare was blank in response. She ran through their findings, and added, "Several clients and vendor accounts are shell companies. You embezzled money from your own firm and fed it back in after you made some interest. Or was it to cover your tracks? The theft was in the amount of nearly one-point-two million dollars."

"Come again?"

He was either playing dumb or really had no idea. She'd sway to the latter.

"They must be mistaken," he rushed ahead. "There's no way someone at the firm would do that."

She noted how he shifted things from himself. "Not just someone. You."

"Nah, no way. The reports will tell you that. You said you have the financials? Well, the name of the person associated with those accounts would have been included."

"We spoke with that person, and they're why we're speaking with you," she told him.

"Who was it?"

"Harris Finch."

"Well, there's no way Finch would have stolen the money. Please check with accounting. Every new account needs to be signed off by a partner."

It was as if Howard forgot about the allegation against him. "They are getting the paperwork together."

Howard clasped his hands and circled his thumbs. He was biting down on his bottom lip.

"Mr. Gabay, is there something you want to tell us before we see it?" Amanda asked.

He pulled out his handkerchief again and wiped his brow. He shook his head.

"We believe the embezzlement and the attempts on Dominique Sharp's life are connected. Ms. Sharp's would-be killer has already claimed two victims trying to get to her." Since the embezzlement angle alone didn't seem to jolt him into talking, maybe bringing up the murders would.

"It's all very tragic, but it has nothing to do with me."

"Well if it wasn't you, and it wasn't Harris Finch...?" She left the question dangling there.

"I have no clue who." His voice turned hoarse.

"Are you sure it wasn't you? From what we heard, you have motive to set up Harris Finch," she said.

"What are you talking about?"

"He took your wife from you," she said.

Howard met Amanda's gaze and laughed. Actually laughed. "He can have her. Cheryl and I were never meant to last. We're so different."

Trent leaned forward. "Then you weren't upset by the divorce?"

"Not at all, and if I was, do you think I would have kept him on at my firm? I'd have paid him out and sent him packing a long time ago."

Amanda was stumped because his reasoning made complete sense. But if Howard Gabay didn't take the money and have Corey Shea hire a killer, who did? And why? Or had she and Trent made a huge mistake and pardoned Finch too readily?

FORTY-SIX

Amanda sat back and relaxed her posture, meeting Howard's gaze. "You came with us willingly. You've sat there, waiving your right to a lawyer. But you were surprised we suspected you of four felonies, as if you had at least one in mind. What did you think we pulled you in for?"

"I've been debating since I've been here whether I want to say. There's no obligation for me to do so, but I will say this much. I figured you'd discover something about me when you were looking into Dominique's life."

Amanda clasped her hands on the table. "And what is that?"

"Nah. I'm no longer in the sharing mood. The fact you pegged me as stealing from my own company *and* accused me of hiring someone to kill Dominique has me changing my mind. I can't trust either of you. Also, from what I see you have no cause to hold me, so I'm going to leave now."

Amanda stood and told him, "Please, just five more minutes."

She left the room with Trent and went next door to the observation room.

Malone was shaking his head. "Without those requisition forms, we have nothing on him in the embezzlement case, and without that, where's his motive to want Sharp dead?"

"Though he just admitted he feared we would uncover something about him when looking into Dominique's life. I, for one, would like to know what that is," she said. "I suspect it sheds light on why he'd accept a lowball offer on his family's firm. Because given the way he reacted to my question now and the first time we spoke with him, it feels like he was strong-armed into the deal."

"I'd like to know too, but we can't force him to talk, and we have nothing to hold him," Malone pointed out.

"What if Howard Gabay has an inkling about who was stealing the money from his company?" Trent said, taking things in another direction.

"Based on...?" Malone popped his eyes.

"Trent could be right, Sarge. He has been denying the embezzlement in general terms, saying no one in the firm would do this. But his speech was shaky when he asked what name was on the accounts, like someone came to mind. What if he's trying to protect this person? But who would demand such loyalty?" She met Trent's eye, and it clicked together. "We know Corey Shea hired the killer for someone. We don't know who."

"But Amanda and I believe that Corey Shea and Howard's son, Sullivan Gabay, are lovers," Trent wedged in.

"Could we be looking at the wrong Gabay then?" Malone asked. "If Howard suspects his son is involved in the embezzlement, that would be someone he'd want to protect."

"It could also explain Shea's silence. He'd want to protect Sullivan too. And Sullivan would have reason to set up Harris from another slant. He didn't destroy his marriage, but he broke up his family," Trent reasoned.

"Let's say that is the case. Where's his motive for killing Dominique Sharp?" Malone asked.

"He's not as happy about her taking over the family firm as he let on?" Amanda suggested one possibility.

"So he puts the money back into the company so it's certain to stand out," Trent said, talking this out. "Finch would take the fall and get sent to prison, and Sullivan would get his revenge for Finch breaking up his parents. Also, Sharp might lose interest in the firm."

"But she didn't. Maybe Sullivan didn't know she just received the books on Friday."

"It sounds like it's time to bring Sullivan Gabay in for a chat," Malone said.

"It does, but just give us one moment before we do that." Amanda was tired of smacking into corners and trying to feel her way out. She wanted to get this case wrapped up once and for all. "I'm going to pop in with Corey Shea to test our theory."

Trent and Malone followed her down the hall. Malone set up in the neighboring observation room while she and Trent went in with Corey and his lawyer.

"Detectives, it's about time. My client and I have been waiting here for an hour." The attorney clearly wanted to be seen as the one in charge.

Amanda didn't bother taking a seat or responding to the lawyer, and neither did Trent.

"Corey, we have Sullivan Gabay in the other room," Amanda lied and slowed her speech as Corey met her eye. "He's talking to us. Is there anything you want to say?"

Corey smiled. "Nah, Sully would never throw me under the bus."

The lawyer let out a deep sigh and shook his head. Corey didn't realize he'd just lost his bargaining chip for a deal, and it hadn't even taken much to get him to part with it.

She resisted the urge to smile. They had both of them. "Why are you so confident he wouldn't?" Amanda had an idea why but wanted to hear it from Corey.

Corey's eyes jabbed toward his lawyer.

"You don't need to be quiet now," he said in a huff.

"He loves me, and I love him. We've been together for a year."

"Is that why you did as he asked?" Though Amanda wagered cash had some influence in the matter too.

"I would do anything for him."

The lawyer shifted, again shaking his head. Frustration was coming off the guy, and she couldn't blame him. In his position, she'd be frustrated as hell. Corey wasn't letting him represent him or protect his rights. Instead he'd wedged himself into a tight corner.

"And by anything, you are admitting for the record that you hired a contract killer on Sullivan Gabay's behalf to take out Dominique Sharp?" Amanda perched her hands on her hips.

"Yes."

The lawyer was now doodling on his notepad, and Amanda didn't blame him for that either. He might as well entertain himself somehow.

"You are under arrest for conspiracy to commit murder, hiring a hit person, and two counts of murder. And this isn't over yet. The number of felony charges against you could increase depending on the course of the night." They could already add one for shooting at officers from the incident at Blackburn's house too. But Amanda left the room, leaving behind a gaping-mouthed Corey and a disgruntled lawyer.

"We've got him," Trent said to her once they were in the hallway.

Malone left the observation room and ran into them in the hall. "I'll get Sullivan Gabay brought in."

"Thanks." Amanda told the officer that he was to continue to monitor Corey's laptop, and to have another officer escort him to a holding cell. To Trent, she said, "Now it's time to catch our killer."

FORTY-SEVEN

Time passed quickly after leaving a stunned Corey Shea with several charges levied against him. Amanda took pleasure in the fact one aspect of this case was settled. The forms from Molly in the DC firm's accounting department came through to Trent and gave them a clear picture of the person behind the fake accounts. It wasn't Howard Gabay, and Amanda felt better about releasing him. It also wasn't Harris Finch, which came as a relief.

But Amanda's primary focus was on apprehending the Anaconda Killer. She had to put it out of her mind that the woman had evaded capture for the last two years. Maybe longer. If she dwelled on that, she'd get sucked down by negative self-talk that would have her believing she wasn't any different than any previous officer on this woman's trail. Rather, she had to put faith in the fact she was and that tonight would be a success.

Plainclothes officers were in position on Charmed Court and neighboring streets. They were all armed with the Anaconda Killer's photograph and a description of her signature apparel and tasked with looking out for her.

Amanda and Trent were to go inside Sharp's house and make it appear as if she were home. They even got her Cadillac and parked it in the driveway. Hopefully, the killer didn't take it as an obvious sign this was a setup considering the three-car garage. But they were counting on her desperation to finish this assignment and collect her money.

The house was cavernous at night. They turned on only a few lights, including the one in the primary bedroom. It was where they wanted to draw the killer. She might be eager, considering it was familiar terrain. Something else that might work to Amanda and Trent's advantage. That's if the killer even got this far. The plan was she'd be apprehended by officers while breaking into the home.

They had shown up at ten o'clock, an hour in advance, just to ensure they weren't spotted going inside the house. They walked through the home to get the entire layout, including a stroll through Dominique's home office. Amanda noted the wall safe fit Dominique's character. It would be more unusual if she didn't have one.

Amanda and Trent tucked inside the walk-in closet, so as not to cast their shadows in the windows.

"Five minutes," Trent told her, having taken out his phone and waking the screen.

"I just want this over with." To be so close to getting justice for Christine Lane and Joel Blackburn felt amazing. Not to mention her other five victims cataloged in ViCAP.

"Huh, and I think you'll get your wish sooner than later. Look." He pointed out that his phone had no bars.

This was something they were prepared for and why they were using tactical radios. They appeared to be active, so thankfully, the type of jammer being used didn't affect them. Each radio was also paired with earpieces and an attached mike, which kept their hands free.

There was a deadened thump downstairs.

"She's here," he whispered.

Amanda's heart picked up speed. "Why didn't we hear from the officers?"

"The perp is in the home," Trent said, notifying the lookout officers through the radio.

One responded, "We never saw anyone enter the home."

This sentiment was parroted a few times.

"Well, she's—" Trent started and stopped.

There were soft footfalls on the stairs.

Amanda held a finger to her lips.

There was one squeaky floorboard about five feet down the hall outside the primary bedroom, and Amanda heard it. She put her hand over her gun, ready to draw it.

The woman was coming into the room now, the sound of her shoes patting on the hardwood floor. She was headed toward the bathroom, where they had the lights on and the water running in the shower.

Just when Amanda expected her to carry on past the closet, all went silent.

What is she doing... Amanda was certain the woman might hear her heartbeat for how hard it was pounding.

A few seconds later, her steps continued. The handle on the bathroom door turned, and the door opened.

Amanda nodded at Trent, and they stepped out of the closet with their guns drawn.

Her shadow stretched into the doorway and showed she was approaching the shower.

Then three pops. Muffled shots through a gun with a silencer.

A second later, the shower curtain was pulled back, and the metal hooks scraped against the rod.

Then nothing.

All became silent.

The quiet stillness was more nerve-wracking than if she'd come out of the bathroom, gun blazing.

Amanda motioned for Trent to take one side of the door while she stayed on the other.

"You think you're smart," she said from inside the bathroom. "But I know you're out there. From the breathing, I'd say there are two of you."

Trent looked at Amanda, and she shook her head. They were under no obligation to announce themselves in this situation. It would expose their positions and put them in more danger.

"Fine, you want to play again. I love a good firefight. Tell me, is one of you that handsome detective who ran after me the other night?" Her shadow showed her moving closer to the bathroom door.

Amanda signaled to Trent that she would draw the woman's attention. He nodded, getting her implication. By doing this, they'd gain the upper hand. The woman would need to put her back to Trent to face Amanda.

He moved back along the wall, putting space between him and the doorway. Amanda set out in the opposite direction to the sitting area. Once there, she said, "It's time that you came out with your hands up. Prince William County PD."

Silence, then the door flung open, and the woman stepped into the room. She turned to the left where Amanda had spoken from. But Amanda was no longer standing. She had ducked behind the couch.

"I've got a gun on the back of your head. PWCPD! Arms in the air," Trent said.

"Sure. Why not?"

Amanda peeked around the side of the couch. Something was off. There was no way this woman would surrender without a fight.

"I'm just going to put my gun on the floor..."

Amanda braced herself to act. *Come on, Trent, please see through her...*

The Anaconda Killer bent over to make a show of setting her weapon down. But then she popped up, pulling a knife from a sheath. She spun and swiped at Trent, who juked out of her way. She must have nicked Trent's arm because he cried out. His gun dropped to the floor.

Amanda jumped up from behind the couch. "I'd stop right there. I won't hesitate to put a bullet in your head."

The woman turned around, eyeing a new quarry. She came at Amanda like she had Trent, not seeming at all deterred by the gun Amanda held on her.

"Stop right there, or I will shoot you," Amanda warned her again.

"Me too." Trent had reclaimed his gun.

The Anaconda Killer was undeterred and kept coming.

Amanda squeezed the trigger.

FORTY-EIGHT

Amanda's bullet landed where she had aimed. The Anaconda Killer's upper right shoulder. But she'd survive, unlike her victims.

She screamed out in agony and dropped her knife. "You'll pay for that."

"That's my line to you. And because of your compulsion to sign off on your kills, you can be tied to killing seven people. So, thank you for that."

"Screw you."

Amanda smiled at her. "You keep saying my lines."

Trent grabbed her arms behind her back and snapped on the cuffs so hard that the woman howled.

Officers moved into the room.

"An ambulance should be here soon," one of them said.

Another officer assumed hold of the Anaconda Killer from Trent.

"And I'll be going with her. I'm not letting her out of my sight," Amanda told them.

"I'm not *her*. I'm the Anaconda Killer," the woman said.

"Call yourself whatever you like, you're still going away for the rest of your life." Amanda looked over at Trent in time to see his eyes roll back and him buckle to the floor.

The next several minutes played out in slow motion. Paramedics swept into the room, and one raced straight to Trent and turned him over. He hadn't just been swiped by the blade. It had pierced his left side, and the wound was bleeding heavily. Trent must have been in shock to keep going as if nothing had happened.

It took a few minutes for the paramedic to bring Trent around, but he was then loaded onto a gurney and taken out.

"She's mine," Amanda hissed, grabbing the Anaconda Killer's arm and leading her out of the house to another waiting ambulance.

Amanda was torn between going with Trent or going with this murderous woman. She did what she knew Trent would want her to do, and Amanda loaded into the back of the ambulance that would shuttle the Anaconda Killer to the hospital.

She was restrained on the gurney in the back with two sets of cuffs, and a plainclothes officer went along as well.

After they arrived at the hospital, Amanda told the officer, "Stay with her every second. Do not let her out of your sight."

"Yes, ma'am."

Amanda went to check on Trent, who was being rushed through the emergency room with a slew of doctors tending to him. She jogged up to them. "What's going on? Is he going to be all right?"

"You need to stay back. Wait in the waiting room, and a doctor will let you know," a nurse told her.

As she watched Trent being wheeled down the corridor out of sight, warm tears fell down her cheeks.

* * *

Time was standing still as Amanda paced the hospital waiting room. She'd asked for updates on Trent several times in the past hour, but no one was telling her anything. She couldn't even pull on her relationship with Carter because she couldn't get a hold of him. But if he was home sleeping after a long shift, he'd have his ringer off, and she couldn't fault him for that. She left a message though, just in case.

"Tell me everything." Malone rushed toward her.

She told him what had transpired in the house.

"So back up. No one saw this woman enter the house?"

"Nope. And my mind's a mess right now, but all I can figure is she must have arrived before us and hid out inside the home."

"We know she has a way of getting inside without leaving a mark. But shit. What are the doctors saying about Trent?"

The swear word spilled from Malone's mouth like it was natural for him. She knew he only pulled one out when he was upset. "I don't know. No one is telling me anything." She raked her hand through her hair, spinning out. Nothing could happen to him. It just couldn't.

"Amanda?" Carter jogged toward her. He took her hands. "Talk to me, and I'll find out what I can."

"It's Trent. He was stabbed in his side. They took him in about an hour ago, and I haven't—"

"Detective Steele?" One of the doctors she'd seen taking Trent away was standing mere feet away. He took off the surgical cap he had on and held it in front of himself.

Her heart was pounding, and her vision was hazy. That posture... it wasn't good. Her head spun, and Carter moved in and wrapped his arm around her. Just that bit of support helped her find her voice. "I am."

Malone joined them.

"Trent should be just fine," the doctor said. "He'll be admitted, so we can monitor him for a few days. He should be able to receive visitors in the morning."

Amanda breathed only slightly easier. Nothing was guaranteed.

"Thank you, Dr. Ryan," Carter told him.

Ryan dipped his head and left.

Amanda turned to Carter. She wanted to hug him, but it didn't feel right celebrating Trent in the arms of another man. "He was lucky, wasn't he?" She knew things could have been far worse.

Malone put a hand on her shoulder.

"I don't want to leave this hospital until I can see him."

"You just heard that won't be until the morning. You should get some rest," Carter told her.

She couldn't imagine going home and crawling into bed like nothing happened, like her world hadn't spun upside down. "There's no way I can do that. The woman who did this to him is somewhere in this hospital, and I need to talk to her."

"Just tell me her name, and I'll track her down."

"I don't have her name." Then it was like her mind cleared. She had the officer's number, and she called him. He answered on the second ring. "Tell me you haven't let her out of your sight."

"I'm looking at her right now through the glass. They're just wrapping up her surgery."

"The diagnosis?"

"She's going to live."

"Good." *Because I'm going to make her regret it!*

FORTY-NINE

Amanda only left the hospital at both Malone's and Carter's insistence. Malone told her a search of Sullivan Gabay's DC rowhouse turned up incriminating evidence. He had a bank account in the Caymans. It was enough to bring him in, but Malone said he could get comfortable in a holding cell overnight.

Carter came home with her and spent the night. Though she felt bad for thinking she was keeping him up with all her tossing and turning. Whenever she drifted off, she had feverish dreams that replayed the hell that had transpired in that bedroom.

She gave up trying to sleep when her eyes opened at six AM, but she lay in bed thinking over everything. They had some answers but not all of them. Such as a solid motive for Sullivan Gabay to want Dominique dead. Then there was Howard Gabay, who alluded to doing something illegal that he thought would be discovered from their digging into Dominique. Whatever the hell that was...

And did any of this have to do with Dominique's lowball offer to buy Gabay's firm? If so, wouldn't Dominique suspect he'd want her dead for that alone? Or was there more to this? Howard's illegal transgression?

Her mind was just spinning, trying to make sense of the bare threads. Dominique's phone and laptop hadn't shed any light on things, so where else might she keep sensitive information? Presumably intel that would expose Howard's wrongdoing.

The answer hit and had Amanda throwing the sheets off herself and getting dressed as quietly as she could manage.

"Amanda, what are you doing? Is it time to get up already? What time is it?" Carter whispered across the room.

"It's only six. Go back to sleep, but I've got to go."

"They won't let you see him yet."

Trent... She felt a jab of guilt that Carter surmised she was running to her partner. "I know, but there's something else I must do."

"I'll come with you."

"No, you won't. It's a police matter. Please, just lock up when you leave. No rush."

"Of course. Be safe."

She walked around the bed and kissed him goodbye before setting out into the early morning.

* * *

The heat and humidity foretold of another blazing record-breaking day ahead. There was even a haze in the air when Amanda pulled up to Dominique's house. Officers were still posted outside.

Locked down as a crime scene... A flame lit in the pit of her stomach. *Trent...*

Amanda shook the thought of him aside, needing to focus on why she was here. She flashed her badge at the officer at the door, not having met him before. "Detective Amanda Steele. I was here last night when everything..." *Went down, and I could have lost my partner...*

"Yes, Detective? I'm sorry to hear that Detective Stenson was injured. Will he be all right?"

She pressed her lips and nodded, not trusting herself to speak. To do so would risk breaking her emotional dam.

"Glad to hear it. What can I do for you, ma'am?"

"I need to get in the house."

He had her sign into the crime scene and let her into the house.

Crime scene... The words assaulted her again, echoing in her mind and tugging on her sanity. But she kept moving forward. One step at a time.

She flipped on the light switches and headed to the staircase. Her steps were hampered by paralyzing flashbacks that had her pausing to catch her breath. *I'm overreacting... Trent is going to be just fine...* Not only that but she would see him in less than a handful of hours. She exhaled the stress and shook her shoulders before entering the home office and going right to the wall safe.

Where people keep sensitive information...

She'd arrived armed with the combination code from calling the safehouse on the way there. The officer on duty woke Dominique Sharp, and he told Amanda she had only parted with it when threatened with interfering in a murder investigation. And begrudgingly at that.

Hearing that only made Amanda more interested in seeing what was inside.

She punched in the code, swung the door open, and looked over the contents. It didn't take long to realize that Dominique Sharp had some explaining to do.

* * *

Sucking back caffeine would help Amanda carry on and see this day through. No matter what it threw at her. It baffled her mind how many conversations lay ahead of her though. Dominique Sharp was being brought over from the safehouse, and Sullivan Gabay was being pulled from the holding cell. She'd already spoken with Howard Gabay. Then, of course, she'd be chatting with the Anaconda Killer.

She missed Trent when she entered the interview room to speak with Sullivan, another coffee and a folder in hand.

Sullivan was seated across from the door with his lawyer, a man with a round face and brown eyes. He introduced himself, but Amanda didn't even make a point of remembering his name. This interview would be over as fast as it began.

"We all know why we're here," Amanda began.

"We do? Then maybe you can explain that to myself and my client."

"You will be charged with several felonies." She listed the charges against him, including the latest addition of assault on an officer. Since he instigated the felony that resulted in Trent getting stabbed, he was liable. Neither Sullivan nor the lawyer said a word. "You don't deny your culpability in these matters?"

Sullivan shook his head. "But I want you to leave Corey Shea out of this. Let him go."

"We can't do that. Because of what he did, two people are dead." *And almost a third...* The thought fired through and made her clammy. If Sullivan thought she was going to let anyone involved walk away, he wasn't too bright. "I'd like to know why you did all this, Sullivan. Why steal money from your family firm and order a hit on Dominique Sharp?" Seated across from him, Amanda remembered Sullivan had said he didn't even know Dominique. So how did they get here?

"The reasons don't matter," the lawyer said. "It's whether you can prove he's done these things, and I, for one, don't feel you have enough proof."

She could point out that his client didn't deny his involvement just a moment ago. But she also knew that wasn't enough. The justice system demanded proof. Which they had. "Corey Shea is speaking with us. He admits to taking payment from Sullivan Gabay to contract a killer on the dark web to kill Dominique Sharp. As for the embezzlement, we have plenty of evidence. For one, the requisition forms to open fake customer and vendor accounts were submitted by Sullivan Gabay." She produced printouts of what Molly had provided. One of these was a legit account requested by Harris Finch and another from Sullivan Gabay. She set these on either side of a form requesting the opening for one of the shell companies. The differences in the forged signature were subtle and easy enough to be missed by busy clerks. "As you can see, Sullivan, you scroll *I*'s like this. Mr. Finch doesn't. Yet, there it is on the forms requesting the opening of several fake accounts." She laid out more to support her statement.

Sullivan was refusing her gaze now.

Amanda steamed ahead. "We also found a Cayman bank account attached to you, Sullivan. The statements were in your home."

"So what?" The lawyer balked. "It's hardly against the law to have one."

"It is if the funds in it were obtained illegally." She turned to Sullivan. "Once Financial Crimes digs into the statements, are we going to find corresponding transactions that line up with the money taken from Gabay, Finch & Earnest?"

He said nothing, and his silence affirmed the allegation for her.

She continued. "You expressed your desire that we leave Corey Shea out of this. Is that why you bought your boyfriend a brand-new BMW? To get him to find a killer online instead of leaving a more obvious money trail? That was the only smart thing you did. It's too bad he gave himself away when he reacted awkwardly at the sight of myself and my partner in your office. He was uneasy. It soon became clear why. He was hiding something. But why frame Finch for embezzlement?"

"Why should I tell you?"

"You don't have to, but I'd like to wager a guess. You were pissed off at Harris Finch because he caused your parents' marriage to fall apart." There was just a slight tightening of his jaw. *Jackpot!* Amanda carried on. "You wanted to get back at him, so you had the idea to take money out of the company and frame him for it. What I don't understand is why you started putting the money back six months ago. Would you tell me?" Amanda was banking on the fact most criminals had enormous egos and loved receiving credit for their work.

"Dominique started sniffing around the firm then, and I saw my opportunity to make the embezzlement more obvious."

That worked against what she'd originally seen as motive for him to want Sharp dead. The fact he wouldn't want the embezzlement found. Though given what she had taken from Dominique's safe, she had another theory on motive. Time would tell if it was spot-on. "Why did you order a hit on Dominique?"

"I hate Dominique Sharp. She's a vindictive, manipulative woman who was going to destroy my family's legacy. Not only was she kicking my father out, but she was planning to get rid of me too."

"So much for not knowing her, huh." She threw his earlier lie in his face.

"I said I didn't know her *personally*."

"Whatever. You certainly put on an exceptional performance showing me that Broadway playbill, swooning about how the sale of the firm would allow you to do what you wanted with your life."

Sullivan had the nerve to smile at the compliment.

Amanda wished she had seen through him, but some people

were skilled liars. "I think there's even more to this than you just being against the sale though," she tiptoed, testing out her new theory.

"Oh, yeah? What do you think you know?" Sullivan asked her.

"Dominique had damaging intel against your father, involving you. She blackmailed him to sell to her at below-market value."

Sullivan's eyes hardened. "She wanted his firm or his license."

"So you decided killing Dominique was the only way to stop all of that from happening."

Sullivan shrugged.

"All right, but why rope Corey into this mess? Why not handle things yourself?"

"Corey loves me, Detective. He would do anything for me."

It was sickening how Sullivan had exploited Corey and his knowledge about computers and ability to access the dark web. "Well, now he's going to prison for life, just like you." Amanda listed the formal charges against him and left the room. A sour feeling came from talking with Sullivan, but at least there was going to be justice for Christine Lane, Joel Blackburn, and Trent.

After notifying a uniformed officer to take Sullivan to the cells, she returned to her desk. A few minutes after sitting down, she got a call from the front desk informing her that Dominique Sharp had arrived.

Amanda collected her and said, "If you'd come with me..."

"What's going on?"

"We just need to have a little chat." Amanda phrased it as if the proposal was harmless. But Dominique had to know after providing the code to her safe, it was only a matter of time before her dark secret would come to light. Amanda stopped outside of an interview room and gestured for her to go inside.

"Fine, but I hope the room has been thoroughly cleaned." Dominique swept ahead of Amanda into the room, pulled out a chair, and sat down. Her lips were curled in disgust, and one would think she'd never been in such a room to represent clients. Or it may have felt different being the one under suspicion.

Amanda closed the door behind them. She was armed with her discovery from the safe and ready to confront Dominique. "I'm just going to get right to the point. I think you knew who wanted you dead all along." That revelation was the more bittersweet aspect about all of this. Lives could have been saved. Trent may not have been stabbed.

"As I've told you many times, I wouldn't be doing my job if I didn't have enemies."

Amanda couldn't understand why Dominique was playing dumb. It must have been some ploy. "Fine, play it how you like, but I found all I needed in your safe. Howard Gabay took on a case ten months ago. Hackett. He was an unscrupulous businessman. Howard was supposed to represent him, but the file showed he did a poor job of it, and Hackett was sent to prison for fraud. Around that time, Howard was working with the district attorney's office to make DUI charges against Sullivan Gabay disappear. But along with some interesting reading, there was a recording on a USB stick. If you like, I can play it or read the transcript for you?"

Dominique narrowed her eyes.

"All right, I'll summarize. I'm sure you're very familiar with what was on there. A conversation between Howard and his son. Howard told him he had a deal worked out to sacrifice his client to the prosecution in return for his son's pardon."

Dominique shrugged. "What of it?"

Amanda was under no illusion that Dominique didn't get the implication. "Let's start with how you got this recording."

"I choose to exercise my Fifth Amendment right."

It was a constitutional law that allowed people to remain quiet if talking would incriminate them. "That says enough. You had no legal right to record this conversation, but you used it as leverage to get revenge on Howard Gabay."

"That's ludicrous. Why would I need to get revenge on Howard? I was buying his firm, for God's sake."

"We both know you wanted revenge, but we'll get to that. Backing up a bit, after you came into possession of this conversation, Hackett was sent to prison. That happened six months ago. Around the same time you approached Howard with plans to blackmail him. You threatened to expose him to the bar and have his license stripped if he didn't sell his firm to you for a bargain."

"The only proof you have is what Howard Gabay did. You can't prove I blackmailed him."

"One plus one equals two, Dominique. There's no other reason Howard would have been selling you his firm for so little."

"You can't know that."

"But I do. I spoke with Howard earlier this morning, telling him I found out everything you had against him."

Dominique crossed her arms. "Nah, I'm not buying it. Why would he confess to this? He'll lose his license to practice law."

"He was tired of having it weighing on his conscience. But you had to see how your blackmailing him would have painted a target on your back. You were forcing a man out of a company that had been in his family for generations. Yet you kept quiet, thereby interfering with a murder investigation."

"No, that's not true. How could I have known that Howard would order a hit on me?"

Amanda grimaced. Dominique's powerful reaction showed the thought had crossed her mind. She'd hold off disclosing who was behind the hit for now. "When you beckoned Howard for dinner on Saturday night, it was just to make sure he was still under your control." Her further chat with Howard also cleared up the true nature of their dinner conversation.

"None of that matters."

"You needed to assume the power that he took from you years ago," Amanda added.

"I don't know what you're..."

"He raped you back in college. You filed a police report, but charges were never laid against him." This wasn't something Amanda found in the safe. Howard had confessed this to her.

"The police did nothing to help me. *Nothing*. I suffered the embarrassment of a rape kit, and it was just stuffed into some cabinet. Howard's father had powerful people in his pocket with a reach into the MPD. But that humiliation... it never goes away."

Police failing her in the past might be another reason she resisted their help. "I feel for you, Dominique, I do, but that doesn't excuse blackmailing your attacker. It doesn't bring back an innocent woman who was murdered in your home. She was a mother and had people who loved and cared for her. Or your friend Joel Blackburn, who died because he got caught up in your mess. Yet, still, you said nothing."

A single tear dropped on Dominique's cheek that she was quick to swipe away. "I never thought Howard would have the balls to do this."

"Here's the thing. Howard Gabay didn't order the hit on you. His son, Sullivan, did."

"Sullivan? Why? I never did anything to him."

"From his standpoint, you came after his father." The bigger picture that Amanda didn't need to spell out was that a father had protected his son, and now the son was repaying the father. Even the rough edge that Sullivan projected against his father had been a performance. Amanda waited a few seconds, then said, "Silence has consequences just like actions do. You will be charged for blackmailing Howard Gabay. He has nothing left to lose, and I'm sure he'll testify against you."

"It will never hold up. You'll see."

"We will, but you better get accustomed to cramped quarters. I am also charging you with obstruction of justice for interfering in a murder investigation."

"No, please, you can't be serious."

Amanda stood. "I'm serious, Ms. Sharp. People lost their lives, others were hurt, some will be burying their loved ones. If I have any say in the matter, you will go away for a very long time." She'd also lose her license to practice law. But as Amanda left the room, she was saddened by the other repercussions of Dominique's choice to remain silent. Riley Lane was delayed closure, Joel Blackburn would still be alive, and Trent would be by her side and not in a hospital bed.

FIFTY

Amanda filled Malone in on her conversations from that morning and was now walking through the hallways of the hospital toward Trent's room. Her heart was hurting as she drew closer to his room, despite the nurse saying he was doing great "considering." It was the *considering* part that played on her mind.

She stopped outside his door, took a deep breath, and went inside.

Trent was lying in bed watching the television across the room. He smiled when he saw her and turned off the TV.

"How are you doing?" Her steps were leaden as she walked toward his bed.

"The doctor says I'll live." He laughed, making light of his ordeal.

"Well, that's good."

"I think so. And now I'll have a fresh scar to go with my previous ones."

"You realize it's not a competition, and those aren't things you should be collecting."

"It's not all that bad. They remind me not to take a single moment for granted."

His statement hit her in the heart. She loved him, yet he could never know just how much. He was with Kelsey. She with Carter. But how much of her life would slip by before she was brave enough to admit the truth? That she saw her future with Trent.

"But enough about me. Fill me in."

"Ah, right." His request pulled her out of her thoughts. *Saved* her from them. "Well, the entire case is wrapped up tight." She shared everything from that morning with him.

"So, Dominique had an idea who wanted her dead all this time and said nothing?"

"Yep."

"Even though it cost her friend's life, she wouldn't swallow her pride. Unbelievable. Have you questioned the Anaconda Killer yet? Do we know her real name?"

"No to the first, and yes to the second, we do. Her prints identified her as Jessica Reese, thirty-nine. She served ten years in prison for attacking a woman with a knife. The woman didn't die, but Jessica was charged with attempted murder. Apparently, Jessica thought she was sleeping with her boyfriend."

"Having a record could explain why she was so meticulous at her crime scenes."

"Except for she messed up at Blackburn's, remember? The blood she left on the glass. Well, the blood type has been confirmed as the same as Jessica's. We're still waiting on the DNA results to solidify that. Not that there's any doubt she was at Blackburn's that night. When Jessica's personal possessions were taken from her, there was a tarp, rope, and the same cleaner she'd used at Sharp's house in her backpack. Ballistics testing confirmed the gun she arrived with last night, a Glock 19 with a silencer, was a perfect match to the fragments and casings."

"We've got her."

"As I said, it's all wrapped up tight." She paused there, the terminology souring in her stomach. *Wrapped up, like the Anaconda did to her victims...* She went on. "Also the brown hair found in Sharp's robot vacuum was the same shade as Jessica's. More tests will be done to confirm if they are a match. I've already called Agent Hester and informed her we have the Anaconda Killer in custody."

"Worthy of celebration."

"Yes, and they are having Death at Your Door taken down. Now you said you were feeling good... I was just going to talk with Jessica Reese. Would you like to join me? She's just down the hall. If the doctor approves, I can wheel you to her room and back when we're finished."

"That sounds fantastic. It definitely beats sitting here watching endless television."

* * *

Jessica Reese scowled at Amanda the moment she walked into her hospital room. An officer was posted outside her door, and the woman was cuffed to the bedframe. The formidable Anaconda Killer didn't look so scary now. She passed a look at Trent in the wheelchair, and Amanda swore she saw a smirk on her lips. It made Amanda want to smack it off.

"Jessica Reese," Amanda said.

"So you know my name?" Jessica rolled her eyes. "Congratulations."

"This conversation is a formality." Though, there was one point Amanda wanted to raise. "You're being charged with seven murders and assault with a deadly weapon on an officer."

"Whatever." She glanced at Trent.

"Whatever?" Amanda boomeranged back. "Those were people with family and loved ones, with plans for the future, and you just wiped them out as if they didn't matter. Where do you get off?"

"We all have our God-given talents, Detective, and we work with what we're given."

"You're going to bring God into this?" Trent spat and wheeled himself closer to the bed.

"It's where we get life. Listen, I'm not going to apologize because I'm not sorry. People hired me to do a job, and I did it. You could say I was an excellent employee."

Amanda's chest flared hot. "We're going to need the names of your *employers*."

"You can *need* it all you want, princess, but that doesn't mean you're getting it. Surely by now you've figured out that I get hired through sites on the dark web. We don't meet and shake hands, make friends."

Her response was expected but it still stung. Unless something changed, the people who ordered the murders of her five other victims would remain free to go about their lives. "How many people have you killed? More than seven?"

Jessica smiled. "Wouldn't you like to know?"

That's why I asked! Amanda positioned herself behind Trent's wheelchair, having heard enough from this woman. The case was solid against her, and there was nothing left to say. Trent spoke, stalling her from pushing him out of the room.

"What turned you into this person?"

"Everything led me here. That slut, the one I tried to kill with a knife, who got me sent to prison. She did me a favor. It was there that I discovered my true value. What I do..." She was smiling and staring into space. "It's art."

"Whatever you say." Amanda wheeled Trent from the room then, unable to stomach another word out of that woman's mouth. Before coming here she'd considered showing her Christine Lane's photograph, humanizing her, but the effort would have been wasted. She hadn't benefited from her stint behind bars; she came out worse than before.

The only positive in all of this was she and Trent had done their part to set things right. Justice would prevail, the guilty would be sent to prison, and for that she would sleep soundly when her head hit the pillow tonight. But before she got there, she couldn't wait to go pick up Zoe. She was going to squeeze her until she complained. A week apart was far too long.

EPILOGUE

Saturday, one week later

Amanda and Zoe were at Libby and Penny's house, but the plan for today had changed a bit because the memorial service for Christine Lane was booked for that afternoon. Amanda had every intention of going and standing by Spencer's side. She hadn't spoken to him since she brought him in, and it was on her to make things right between them.

Libby came into the living room holding a tray of pink lemonade, which elicited a squeal from Zoe. Amanda smiled as she ran a hand over her daughter's blond hair. She'd gone on for hours last week after being picked up from her grandparents' house.

"They spoiled me, but I missed you, Mom! You're the best!"

Amanda chose to forget that Zoe was angling for a later bedtime.

"Here you go." Libby had set down the tray on the coffee table and was handing a glass to Zoe.

"Thank you."

Amanda's heart swelled at the girl's manners, and she sat

back while Libby settled next to her fiancée. She took Penny's hand.

Zoe slurped her lemonade. "Ahhh," she exclaimed and wiped her upper lip.

Everyone laughed.

"Zoe," Libby said, "there's something we'd like to ask you."

"What?" Short and clipped. Her beautiful eyes were on the pink lemonade in her glass.

"You know we're getting married. We'd love for you to be involved in the wedding."

"You want to marry me too?" Zoe scrunched up her face, and the adults laughed again.

"No. We'd like you to take part in the celebration. What would you say to walking down the aisle ahead of us, tossing out flower petals?"

"Whoa. That sounds amazing. Wait, would I be able to wear a puffy dress like a princess?"

"Absolutely, whatever you'd like," Penny said.

"Mom?" Zoe turned to Amanda. "Can I?"

"If you want to," Amanda told her.

"Then, yes, yes, yes, I'll throw those petals like a boss."

This girl! And wherever had she picked up that phrase?

* * *

Amanda walked across the graveyard toward the modest gathering under the white awning. It was calling for rain that afternoon, and they were ready if it did. She wasn't alone as she took brave steps across the grass. She had her five siblings with her. It had taken little effort to get them there to support their half-brother.

A white coffin was above the gravesite with flowers laid on top. Next to it was an A-frame sign with a large photograph of Christine Lane.

Amanda's throat constricted as the pain from losing Kevin, Lindsey, and her unborn son washed over her. Her sister Kristen put a hand on Amanda's shoulder as if she'd sensed her sadness. Amanda clamped hers over it.

"Amanda?" Emma Blair said, causing Amanda to turn around.

Kristen set off into the crowd.

"Emma, I—"

Emma threw her arms around Amanda and held her tight. After drawing back, she said, "I'm sorry for coming at you like I did. He's just my son, my only child, and I'm... well, I can be protective of him."

"As you should be."

"But I also owe you an apology for calling your father. I overstepped with that move too. I could justify it by saying I was feeling desperate, but there are no excuses."

"I get it." And as a mother herself, Amanda understood. If she perceived a threat against Zoe, she'd lose her grip on her sanity for a spell.

"And I never should have questioned whether I can trust you."

Amanda touched Emma's shoulder. "I'd love to put all of this behind us."

Emma nodded. "Me too. It's so nice you turned up today." Her gaze drifted past Amanda, causing her to turn. Emma was looking at Amanda's siblings, the *you* extending to all of them.

It was then that Amanda spotted Riley Lane. "Emma, could you excuse me?"

"Of course."

Amanda went over to Riley, and the teen hugged Amanda before she could say a word.

Afterward, Riley said, "Thank you for catching Mom's killer. I'm sorry that I didn't handle it well."

When Amanda had told the girl last week they had arrested

everyone involved in her mother's murder, Riley had cried and left the room. "There's no right or wrong way, Riley. We all deal with loss in our own way. I'm just sorry that you need to say goodbye to her."

"Yeah." Riley sniffled.

Amanda saw Spencer talking with Riley's father and headed over there after excusing herself from Riley. "Spencer?"

He turned to her. "Amanda? I never expected to see you here."

She'd set aside the fact that judgment hurt, as she could understand his side. "We all wanted to be here for you." She gestured toward her siblings. When Spencer didn't speak, she said, "I owe you an apology."

Spencer held up his hand. "You were doing your job, but that doesn't mean it didn't suck for me."

"I might have been a little hard on you, the overcompensating bit. If it helps, I never thought you killed Christine. Never. And I'm sorry that I haven't called you since your release."

"I respect you were focused on finding Christine's killer."

"I was, and thank you for seeing that. If you'd let me, let *us*" —she waved her siblings over—"we'd like a chance to get to know you better, have you become a part of our lives."

Spencer bit his bottom lip and nodded. "I'd like that." He hugged Amanda and made his way around to all of them.

Amanda caught sight of a man standing in the distance, tucked close to an oak tree. Her heart pinched as she recognized who he was. She left the group and went to him.

"Dad." She gave him a quick hug.

"I just had to show up, you know. Show my support. Your mother knows and is okay with it."

Seeing her father now reminded her of what she saw in him most of the time. He'd never hurt those he loved intentionally. She didn't know what was going on in his life or her parents' marriage during the time of his affair. Not that she excused the infidelity, but she pardoned the man. Amanda took her father's hand. "It's nice that you came. I'm sure Spencer would love to see you."

They walked toward the gathering hand in hand. Amanda squeezed her father's hand even tighter as she listened to the eulogy for a woman who was loved and would be deeply missed. As she watched the casket lower into the ground, tears fell for Christine Lane and for her own losses. Nothing could be done to change the past, but Amanda would do her best to make sure that everyone she loved knew just how much. She intended to make every moment count.

A LETTER FROM CAROLYN

Dear reader,

I want to say a huge thank you for choosing to read *Dead Woman Walking*. If you enjoyed it and would like to hear about new releases in the Amanda Steele series, just sign up at the following link. Your email address will never be shared, and you can unsubscribe at any time.

www.bookouture.com/carolyn-arnold

If you loved *Dead Woman Walking*, I would be incredibly grateful if you would write a brief, honest review. Writing this book was a lot of fun and a switch from child victims. I hope you enjoyed the bit of a twist in the middle. While you might have been expecting another murder to hit the page, I hope Blackburn's injuries had you rapidly flipping the pages wondering what was going to happen to him. In fact, I hope the entire story had you racing through the twists and turns to the end. If so, you'll be happy to know there will be more Detective Amanda Steele books.

Before the next book comes out in the series, though, you should know I also offer several other international bestselling series for you to savor—everything from crime fiction, to cozy mysteries, to thrillers and action adventures. One of these series features Detective Madison Knight, another kick-ass female detective, who will risk her life, her badge—whatever it takes—

to find justice for murder victims. Then there's my latest series, featuring Sandra Vos, a top negotiator with the FBI. These reads are fashioned to be pulse-pounding thrillers. And you already "met" Lakisha Hester, who had a spotlight in this book. She is a supporting character in the Vos series.

If you enjoyed being in the Prince William County, Virginia, area, you might want to dig into my Brandon Fisher FBI series. Brandon was mentioned in this book and is dating Amanda's best friend, Becky. You can be there when Brandon and Becky meet in *Silent Graves* (book two in this series). These books are perfect for readers who love heart-pounding thrillers and are fascinated with the psychology of serial killers. Each installment is a new case with a fresh bloody trail to follow. Hunt with the FBI's Behavioral Analysis Unit and profile some of the most devious and darkest minds on the planet.

For those familiar with Prince William County, or who have done some internet sleuthing, you'll recognize some differences between reality and my book. This also extends to the Prince William County Police Department. All of this is me taking creative liberties.

I'd like to thank everyone who helped me with this book. A shout of appreciation to Ed Adach, retired detective from the Forensics Identification Services with the Toronto Police Service, for sharing his knowledge about ballistics. George, my husband and best friend, and all the editors who worked on this book. And you, my beautiful reader, thank you so much for your support.

Before I sign off, please, don't underestimate the power and influence of word of mouth. Talk to your family and friends about my books, your local bookstores and librarians, your neighbors, the people at the checkout counter, your dentist, your... well, you get the point. Thank you!

And last but certainly not least, I would love to hear from you if you're so inclined to drop me a note! You can reach me via email at Carolyn@CarolynArnold.net. You can also follow and interact with me on Facebook and X at the links below. To investigate my full list of books, visit my website by following the link below.

Until the next time, I wish you thrilling reads and twists you never saw coming!

Carolyn Arnold

> Connect with CAROLYN ARNOLD Online:
> www.carolynarnold.net

- facebook.com/AuthorCarolynArnold
- x.com/Carolyn_Arnold
- goodreads.com/carolyn_arnold

PUBLISHING TEAM

Turning a manuscript into a book requires the efforts of many people. The publishing team at Bookouture would like to acknowledge everyone who contributed to this publication.

Audio
Alba Proko

Commercial
Lauren Morrissette
Hannah Richmond
Imogen Allport

Cover design
Head Design Ltd

Data and analysis
Mark Alder
Mohamed Bussuri

Editorial
Laura Deacon
Kathy Callesen

Copyeditor
Ian Hodder

Proofreader
Becca Allen

Marketing
Alex Crow
Melanie Price
Occy Carr
Cíara Rosney
Martyna Młynarska

Operations and distribution
Marina Valles
Joe Morris

Production
Hannah Snetsinger
Mandy Kullar
Nadia Michael
Charlotte Hegley

Publicity
Kim Nash
Noelle Holten
Jess Readett
Sarah Hardy

Rights and contracts
Peta Nightingale
Richard King
Saidah Graham

RAISING READERS
Books Build Bright Futures

Dear Reader,

We'd love your attention for one more page to tell you about the crisis in children's reading, and what we can all do.

Studies have shown that reading for fun is the **single biggest predictor of a child's future life chances** – more than family circumstance, parents' educational background or income. It improves academic results, mental health, wealth, communication skills, ambition and happiness.

The number of children reading for fun is in rapid decline. Young people have a lot of competition for their time, and a worryingly high number do not have a single book at home.

Hachette works extensively with schools, libraries and literacy charities, but here are some ways we can all raise more readers:

- Reading to children for just 10 minutes a day makes a difference
- Don't give up if children aren't regular readers – there will be books for them!

- Visit bookshops and libraries to get recommendations
- Encourage them to listen to audiobooks
- Support school libraries
- Give books as gifts

There's a lot more information about how to encourage children to read on our websites: **www.RaisingReaders.co.uk** and **www.JoinRaisingReaders.com**.

Thank you for reading.

www.ingramcontent.com/pod-product-compliance
Lightning Source LLC
LaVergne TN
LVHW040000250226
832502LV00014B/844